When Hearts Attach

LEAH OMAR

PEMBERLEY PRESS

When Hearts Attach

©2024 Leah Omar

All rights reserved. This is a work of fiction. All characters, organizations, and events are either a part of the author's imagination or used fictitiously.

No part of this publication may be reproduced, distributed, or transmitted in any form or by any means, including photocopying, recording, or other electronic or mechanical methods, without prior written permission of the publisher, except in the case of brief quotations embodied in critical reviews and certain other noncommercial uses permitted by copyright law.

Published by: Pemberley Press

Edited by: Cindy Hale Editing Services

Paperback ISBN: 979-889298538-3

eBook ISBN: 979-889298537-6

Book Cover Design and Interior Formatting by 100Covers.

Table of Contents

Dedication V
Prologue VII
Chapter One 1
Chapter Two 12
Chapter Three 22
Chapter Four 35
Chapter Five 51
Chapter Six 61
Chapter Seven 69
Chapter Eight 80
Chapter Nine 86
Chapter Ten 104
Chapter Eleven 112
Chapter Twelve 126
Chapter Thirteen 135
Chapter Fourteen 146
Chapter Fifteen 157
Chapter Sixteen 164

Chapter Seventeen	*176*
Chapter Eighteen	*186*
Chapter Nineteen	*195*
Chapter Twenty	*200*
Chapter Twenty-One	*211*
Chapter Twenty-Two	*220*
Chapter Twenty-Three	*237*
Chapter Twenty-Four	*247*
Chapter Twenty-Five	*258*
Chapter Twenty-Six	*268*
Chapter Twenty-Seven	*284*
Chapter Twenty-Eight	*294*
Chapter Twenty-Nine	*306*
Chapter Thirty	*317*
Chapter Thirty-One	*328*
Chapter Thirty-Two	*339*
Chapter Thirty-Three	*347*
Chapter Thirty-Four	*362*
Chapter Thirty-Five	*371*
Epilogue	*376*
About the Author	*385*

To all the girls out there who once thought that being bad at math meant we'd amount to nothing.

Look at us now.

Prologue

I've always felt like an imposter.

I'm about to graduate from a sought-after medical school with Alpha Omega honors. It's match day, and I discovered earlier this week that I've gotten in somewhere. At tonight's ceremony, I'll find out exactly where that is. But the imposter syndrome I constantly feel, well, it's because I'm also very terrible at math. And being bad at math and getting through medical school rarely go hand in hand. Sometimes, I feel like the only future doctor who struggles with this subject.

Being a surgeon is all I've ever wanted to do, ever since I was in middle school and went out to the garage where my older brother Forest, and his best friend Keegan, were experimenting on a frog that they'd found dead in the afternoon sun. I was fascinated. All Forest and Keegan ever talked about was someday leaving Cherry behind to become doctors in a big city. If that was their dream, why couldn't it be mine too?

Oh yes, the being bad at math thing. When I told all of my teachers what I wanted to do when I grew up, they reminded me that I struggle with the basic concepts of algebra and that I'd need to get my math grades up to make it a reality. Others told me to find a new dream.

I'm nothing if not tenacious. And resourceful. I studied harder than anyone. I met my teachers before and after school. During undergrad, I hired a tutor, worked in the labs, stayed connected to my professors, and received excellent grades. But then I took the MCAT, the required test to get into medical school, and I bombed it.

I'll never forget the day I called my brother Forest sobbing.

"My grades are great, but no school will ever accept me with that score." I sobbed into the phone, wiping my tears away with the sleeve of my shirt.

My effort was better than anyone's, but my math aptitude was abysmal.

"You can retake them, Luna. It's not the end of the world," Forest said. He never seemed to worry about anything.

It felt like the end of the world. I reached out to a respected MCAT coach and waited for her reply. For months, she helped me study and organize my thoughts. I'll never forget the email I received from Keegan the night before my test.

The only thing standing between you being the best surgeon in the world isn't the MCAT, Luna. It's your confidence. You've wanted this for as long as I can remember. The medical profession needs you. Not mathematicians. So go into the test tomorrow with your head held high because this world needs nothing more than it needs you as a doctor.

That email was by far the nicest thing anyone had ever said to me. And it was said by Keegan of all people. He was about to start a fellowship in Cardiothoracic Surgery, and all of this doctor stuff seemed to come easy to him. He left high school early to take college credits at a local community college and then graduated from Harvard at twenty. He was also one of only thirty-five people who got a perfect score on the MCAT the year he took it. If my brother's dorky but brilliant best friend believed in me, I could believe in myself.

I walked into my MCAT retake with my head held high and got a score that would eventually gain me entrance into many of my top-choice medical schools. And all because someone said the words that switched the chemistry in my brain enough to believe in myself.

My medical director walks to the front of the room, and we all applaud as names and residencies are called out. My stomach moves to my throat when I hear my name.

"Luna Oliver," he says, and I push off my seat and stand. "New York Presbyterian, Weill Cornell Medical Center. General Surgery."

My parents rise, and both take turns hugging me. I walk to the front of the room, my knees wobbly beneath me. My life plays in my head like a film. All the hours I spent in the garage conducting experiments with Forest and Keegan. The anatomy books I studied for hours in my bed, and all the time I spent after school in the biology lab. It all led to this moment. I only let myself dream that I'd get into my first-choice residency. But here I am, finally going to be a doctor. And moving to the city where my brother Forest and his best friend Keegan live.

New York, here I come.

Chapter One

Three Months Later

The millions of people in the city occupy the space in my body where fear used to live. I am home. The apartment building looks exactly like it did in the pictures. I grab my phone from the middle console of the truck I rented and bring up an image. This is definitely the apartment I chose, sight unseen, with two other surgical residents I haven't met. Half of the building are rooms that the hospital subsidizes for employees. It was the cheapest option for living in New York.

I throw on my hazards and wave to Forest who stands on the sidewalk, watching me park. Cars honk all around me, but this is where the building manager instructed me to park.

"Hey, kiddo." Forest comes to the driver's side door. I step down onto the pavement, and he pulls me out of the truck, wrapping his arms around me. He holds me, straight-armed, to take a look at me. "You're here. You're actually here."

"Longest drive of my life." I hug Forest and cup his face to get a good look at him. His blue eyes that mirror mine stare back at me. I haven't seen him in person since he came home for a few days over the holidays, which was nearly six months ago. His hair is a shade lighter than my brown locks, and his face is cleanly shaven.

I open the back of the truck, where a few pieces of furniture and a bunch of boxes are. I'm finally in Manhattan. The sun finds openings through the tall skyscrapers and beats down at me. It's a brutally hot late spring day in the city, and the concrete beneath me attempts to burn my feet through my flimsy sandals.

"This is all of it." I nod toward the stuff, and Forest grabs his first box.

"Keegan's on his way too," Forest says, balancing the box on his hip. "He would have been here already, but he's coming straight from the hospital."

It's not surprising that Forest and Keegan both ended up as doctors in the same city, at the same hospital. It was always their plan. I was their little shadow and tried to absorb everything they'd talk about.

"I barely remember what the guy looks like." I grab a box too, and lead Forest inside, where the office manager said she'll be waiting to give me my keys. "It's been at least eight years since I've seen him in person."

"How is that even possible?" Forest shakes his head. "I know he can't wait to see you."

After getting my key, we take the elevator to the eighth floor. The heavy wooden door sticks, but then I push it open and get my first view—and smell—of my new place. Forest sets his box down, and I put mine on top of his.

The apartment somehow feels smaller than it looked in the photos. The kitchen is a narrow galley and has a counter open to the living room. The windows are large, but the view is nothing more than building after building. Whoever lived here before must have burned Nag Champa incense like it was going out of style, because that's all I can smell, and the smoke blows around from the draft of the old windows.

Forest walks down the hallway. "Three bedrooms. Nice." He peeks into one room and then moves onto the next.

"Yeah," I say. "Raven and Myles both arrive at some point tomorrow, which means I get the first pick. That's only fair, right?"

Forest opens the door at the end of the hallway. "This is the biggest."

His phone buzzes, and Forest pulls it out of his pocket. "Keegan's out front. Let's meet him downstairs so he can help with the furniture."

We step into the old elevator, and a suffocating wave of humidity washes over us. I graze my forehead, feeling the beads of sweat forming there. The air hangs heavy and stagnant as if time itself has settled upon these halls, leaving behind the scent of aging wood and dust. I glance at the elevator's cramped interior, realizing that there is no way that the couch I bought will fit inside this thing.

And honestly, I feel horrible about it. Not for Forest. He's my brother. He owes me. But I do feel bad for Keegan, who I'm sure Forest roped into helping. I helped Keegan pack up his old apartment when he left medical school in Boston to move to New York. But none of that involved carrying a couch up eight floors.

Forest and Keegan are six years older than me, and both moved out of our house when I was twelve. All Keegan did was sit around reading medical journals. His clothes were always about two inches too short, and his thick-rimmed glasses were crooked and held together with duct tape. But I've never met a more intelligent person in my entire life than Keegan Baldwin.

I wanted so badly to be included in their activities, and most of the time, they'd let me follow them around. But time together was hard to find. Between Mathletics, Robotics, and Future Scientists of America, the men had remarkably busy schedules.

The last time I saw Keegan was when he graduated from medical school when he would have been around twenty-four. My parents made me come with them because

Keegan was their bonus child. Or at least that's what they called him. That was the last time I saw him in person. I still remember so much about the night of his graduation, when Forest and I helped pack boxes all night in his cramped Boston apartment.

For the past eight years, I've been in Minnesota studying to be a doctor, and he's been in New York, actually being one. When he would come home with Forest to see my family, I was hours away at Medical School. When I'd be home visiting my parents around the holidays, he was on call at work and couldn't come.

We reach the ground level, and not a moment too soon because the elevator now feels like a sauna. We step into the sun, and all I can see is a tall man illuminated by the rays of sunshine, peeking through the steel skyscrapers.

"Hey, man." Forest approaches Keegan and gives him a fist bump. He then turns to me. "Look who's finally in the city."

"Keegan."

I know I shouldn't, but I start laughing and then move my hand to my mouth to cover the sound. Keegan has changed so much. He left Cherry twelve years ago as a boy. But this person in front of me is a man. I don't know why this little fact shocks me so much.

"You look…" I begin to say but am unable to finish the sentence.

"Luna. Hi." His lips press into a straight line, and his dark eyebrows knit together with curiosity. I'd forgotten the intense gaze that he's perfected.

Neither of us looks away, but I do manage to stop laughing. Keegan was always tall, but now the rest of his body has caught up with his height. His hair is a deep chestnut, and the sun makes it shimmer as if it's laden with crystals. His glasses have been replaced with contacts. His shirt hugs his arm muscles. His joggers are tight around his thighs, and I shake my head when I realize I'm staring at him. And those forearms. Where did those come from? And is that a tattoo on the inside of his upper arm, peeking out of his shirt?

It's the Keegan I've known my entire life, I know that. He still has the same square jaw, blue eyes, and full lips. He no longer looks like a caricature because everything else has caught up. When we see a person every day, the changes are so gradual. But when they are physically out of our lives, the differences are palpable. I'm somehow looking at the Keegan I've always known, and someone I'm meeting for the first time.

"Ahh." My mouth hangs open, but I don't know what to say. "It's really you."

Keegan steps in my direction, and bends down to hug me. It's quick, awkward, and over before I can blink.

"What can I do first?" Keegan looks at Forest, then me.

"There's a few pieces of furniture." Forest's voice brings me back to reality. "And not all of it will fit in the elevator. I'd say we start there."

"I'm so sorry," I say, shaking my head, and forcing myself to look away from Keegan. "I'll owe you both forever."

"It's not a big deal," Keegan says. He grabs one end of the couch and starts sliding it out of the back of the truck. I stare at how his arms flex with the weight of it as if it's not hundreds of pounds. Forest grabs the other end, and I fan myself because the outside air temperature seems to have increased by about ten degrees in the past minute.

The men end up having to take a few furniture items up the stairs, while I load boxes into the elevator. Once the truck is empty, we've gone up and down at least ten times. Keegan turns on the faucet and pats water onto his face. I force myself to look away as water soaks the top of his shirt.

"This is your place?" Keegan looks around, raising an eyebrow. "Are your roommates also residents?"

"Yeah." I open a box that says dishes and fish out a couple of glasses for Forest and Keegan to drink from. "I met them on Presby's social page. They're also first-year gen surg residents."

"It's so dusty in here," Forest says, and Keegan nods.

"After I open some windows and air this place out, it won't be so bad," I say, putting my hands on my hips as I look around.

Keegan walks to the bedroom I claimed, and I follow him. He points to the unassembled bed on the floor. "I can put this together."

"No, no," I put my hand on his upper arm, and my face flushes when I feel the hardness of the muscles beneath his thin shirt. He glances at me over his shoulder, and I immediately let go.

"That is really unnecessary. You've already done so much. Go, be with your people. Do what people do in New York City. Or doctor things. Or the gym, you know, to work on all those muscles."

Keegan doesn't pay attention to my babbling, which I always tend to do when I'm nervous. I always manage to put my foot directly into my mouth. Instead, he gets down on his knee, starts fiddling with the parts, and then grabs the bag of screws.

"It won't take me long," he says.

"My kid sister. A surgical resident." Forest stands in the doorway smiling. "I'm happy you took my advice and came to New York. It's the best program. You're going to love it."

"What if I can't cut it?" I say, glancing at Forest, and then Keegan. "Is it normal to be this nervous going into a residency?"

"Cut it. Get it?" Forest laughs, and I roll my eyes.

"You've got this," Keegan says, looking only at me. "And I'm here if you need help with anything as you get adjusted."

He studies me with so much intensity that it causes my entire body to blush. Forest plops on the floor next to us.

"I'm just happy we all found a way out of Cherry," Forest says, and Keegan and I nod.

Keegan finishes assembling my bed, and I'm grateful I'll have a soft place to collapse into tonight. After driving all day to get here, I'm going to want to crash so hard. And in two days, my new life of hell will begin.

"Do you need any more help, Luna?" Forest says as we find ourselves back in the living room.

"No. Thanks for everything, you guys. The last thing I have to do is bring the truck to a return location. Where do I need to go?" I scroll through my phone for the details and see an address in Brooklyn.

Keegan grabs my phone in one swoop before I have time to react. He presses on the screen and then hands it back to me. "I texted myself the address."

"No, no." I shake my head. "You don't have to do that."

"I know." Keegan stands in front of me, his arms folded over his chest.

"Let the man help you," Forest says.

"Fine." I blow out a breath as I hand Keegan the keys. "I really appreciate it."

Forest pulls me into a hug. "Now that the three of us are living in the same city, finally, we have to make sure we connect. I'm thinking we need to try for a weekly family dinner. I can host the first one. Just let me know what your first month's schedule is, Luna."

"Sure," I say, and Keegan continues to study me as if I'm a problem that he can't quite solve.

In all the years since I've seen him, I'd forgotten his level of intensity or the number of thoughts that always seem to be in his head, even though his face gives none of them away. Being in his presence can quickly remind a person of their mediocrity. His every word is measured and purposely chosen. And every look holds meaning. He's the opposite of me. I speak without thinking and gravitate toward spontaneity.

"Well," Forest says, putting his hand on Keegan's shoulder. "I'll let you get settled. I know your roommates arrive tomorrow, and Monday will begin your five years of absolute hell."

Forest smiles, then adds, "You're going to love it."

Forest walks out first, and then Keegan follows him but then turns to me. His eyes trail down my body before he quickly adjusts them. "Welcome to New York, Dr. Oliver."

My lips creep into a smile, because I'm finally a doctor, and in a couple of days, I'm going to start work after spending the past eight years studying. I may be beginning my journey as a lowly first-year resident. But I'm finally a doctor.

Keegan's mouth twitches at the corners as if he's reading my thoughts and realizations.

I smile. "I'm happy to be here."

He nods his head and shuts the door on his way out.

Chapter Two

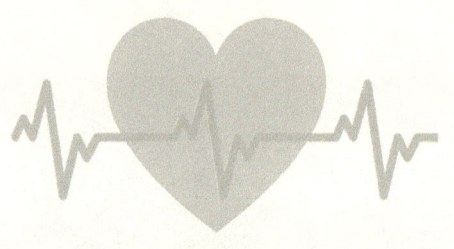

The following day, Myles is the first roommate to arrive. He looks just like his online profile from the residency lodging finder. Short stature. Thinning brown hair. Wire-rimmed glasses. Doctorish-level smart. He rolls in two large suitcases, and a backpack hangs low on him.

"You must be Luna." He slings the pack off of him, and it hits the wood floors with a thump.

He puts his hand out to shake mine, but instead, I wrap my arms around his shoulders. He, our other roommate Raven, and I have been speaking for three months after finding each other on the resident finder. It feels like we've known each other for ages.

"Myles." I release him and grab one of the rolling bags to show him the remaining bedroom options. "It's so great to finally meet you in person."

He chooses the first room and looks around the place. "My moving truck should arrive by tonight. At least I hope it does, or I'll be sleeping on the floor." He pushes his glasses up his nose.

"What's up, roomies?" A loud voice bellows out, and Myles and I both go to see who it is. Raven stands with an older gentleman and runs to hug me first, and then Myles. "We are not in Charleston anymore." She looks at the man with her. "This is my dad, Curtis. Dad, this is Luna. She's from Minnesota. And Myles, from Texas."

Raven is exactly like I imagined she would be—larger than life. She's about my height and wears her long hair in braids, which are currently tied on top of her head.

"It's nice to meet you both." Raven's father stands at the door. "I'm going to grab a few things from the truck."

"I didn't bring anything from home except my clothes," Raven says when her dad walks out. "I ordered a bed and some furniture from the city, which will be delivered later. It seemed so much easier that way."

Presbyterian has an impressive resident lodging database. You look through people's profiles and hit the match button if you want to consider them as a roommate. On paper, the three of us are compatible, and I hope that translates to how we actually live together. We'll rarely be in the apartment at all anyway.

"We'll just walk to the hospital, right?" Raven says as she lays on her stomach on the living room floor several hours later, an almost empty pizza box in front of her.

Myles pulls out his phone and starts studying a map. "It looks like we're only about six blocks away, so yeah."

"Even in the winter?" Raven says. "I'll need to buy myself a coat because this girl doesn't have one."

"Are we going to be able to sleep tonight?" I reach to the floor and grab another slice of pizza. My stomach has been tied in knots all day thinking about tomorrow, yet the food is going down nicely.

Raven sits up and shakes her head. "I've been having a recurring nightmare ever since my white coat ceremony where I forget everything I've learned the last four years. I mean everything."

Myles removes his glasses and blows on them. "My nightmare is that I show up on day one, and my name isn't on the list of expected residents, and it turns out, I didn't get in."

I stand up. "I just need tomorrow to come and go so I can start sleeping again. The anxiety is going to be the death of me. In one scenario, I show up to the hospital naked. In another, I end up having to treat a patient without supervision, and I miss all the signs of a heart attack and my patient dies."

Raven tilts her head back and sighs loudly. "My hands can't unpack another box, so that will have to wait until another day." She stands and brings the now empty pizza box to the kitchen.

"I'm going to give my girlfriend a call, and then I'm going to hit the hay too," Myles says.

I look around the apartment, and boxes are stacked against the walls. When three people take their lives and combine it into a thousand square feet, it's probably going to take a while before we feel settled.

"Here goes the rest of our lives," I say, stretching my arms and yawning.

I head to my bedroom where the majority of my clothes still lie in a pile on the floor. I think about working through the mounds of it and finding my box of hangers, but instead, I get into bed, pop a melatonin gummy in my mouth, and stare at the squares on the ceiling above me.

*****

Myles, Raven, and I were so nervous about being late, that we got to the hospital almost an hour early. We're shown to the changing rooms, and I put on a pair of scrubs and leave my street clothes in the locker. I pull on my white coat and glance at myself in the full-length mirror. My brown hair starts to curl from the humidity, so I tie it on top of my head.

All eight of the new general surgery residents file out of the changing room and meet in a conference room to get our first assignments. For the next four or more years, these will be our people. A doctor approaches us and lays a few stethoscopes and pagers on the desk, even though most of us already have one around our necks. The doctor is a tall man, not much older than me, and probably a fourth or fifth-year resident.

"Good morning, fellow doctors." He looks at us spread out over three small, round tables. "I am Dr. Parse. Your Chief Resident. Welcome to year one. I have your rotation assignments. There are no good or bad rotations. You'll all have an opportunity to see all the different surgical areas of the hospital."

"Rotations will be two to six weeks long," Dr. Parse continues. "It will include general surgery, surgical oncology, trauma surgery, vascular surgery, cardiothoracic, and care of the burned patient."

He puts papers on the tables, and I wait until one gets passed my way. I see my name immediately. Dr. Luna Oliver. Trauma surgery. Emergency room. Myles and Raven have the same first rotation.

Dr. Parse quiets us. "Your stethoscope should be an extension of your body. There is no reason to go anywhere without it. The same goes for your pager. When you are on call, you must be reachable at all hours of the day and night."

Dr. Parse leans against the back wall of the conference room. "I'll start with the trauma surgery rotation, and today is all about airway management, charting, and sutures. You will not practice medicine unless you are under the direction of me or one of the attending physicians."

Raven elbows me in the arm and raises her eyebrow. I glance to my left and then right, and all the residents take in every word. She leans closer and whispers into my ear. "Shit just got real."

Dr. Parse continues by paraphrasing the Hippocratic oath. He tells us to imagine the patients are our loved ones and treat everyone we see how we'd want our favorite people to be treated.

"My group, let's go." Dr. Parse opens the door to the conference room, and those assigned to him start following. "We're going to start our day doing rounds." He takes the chart and hands it to me. I look through the papers and then hand them to Raven.

We enter an exam room, and me and my fellow residents stay in the background. A nurse has already started an IV. Dr. Parse glances at us. "Fifty-one-year-old female. Loss of appetite. Vomiting. Sudden pain on the right side of the abdomen. Flushed face. High temperature. Any ideas?"

"It sounds like an appendicitis." Myles steps forward confidently like he belongs, and Dr. Parse nods.

"Here are the labs." Another nurse walks in and hands Dr. Parse the paperwork.

"The white counts are elevated." He studies the paper and then turns to me. "What should we do next?"

I look around, aware of everyone's stares. I try to push my self-doubt far down. "We could do a urine test to rule out a urinary tract infection or kidney stones. Or we could bring her right to imaging and get an abdominal x-ray."

Dr. Parse turns to the nurse. "Let's get our patient to imaging."

My first patient as a resident was a softball throw, but I know cases will get more complicated. I'm able to scrub in for the appendectomy, and after that, we move on to more rounds.

The day flies by. We follow Dr. Parse around and see a multitude of things, from broken bones to a heart attack, to a staple gun mishap. As we walk to the next exam room, Dr. Parse looks at me.

"You're Dr. Oliver?"

"Yes." It takes a moment for me to form the words as he hasn't spoken directly to me yet. "Luna Oliver."

He nods. "There's a Dr. Oliver in Cardiology. A relative of yours?"

"My brother."

Dr. Parse nods, and we turn down another hallway. I'm already learning we don't walk anywhere. Instead, I practically jog to keep up.

"A family of physicians." We turn into our next room. "I did an internal medicine residency with Forest before I decided to go the surgical route," Dr Parse says.

Medicine isn't actually in my family at all. Forest and I are the first. My dad is an elementary gym teacher and basketball coach, and my mom works at the school library. Forest was the first to be interested in it, and I followed shortly after. My favorite place in school was the biology lab.

Dr. Parse asks me to check in with the patient and get his symptoms.

"The patient is experiencing severe pain in his abdomen," I say as the man holds his gut and moans as I examine him.

A younger woman holds the man's hand and looks at me. "Dean never complains of pain. He's been acting off for a couple of weeks, and then today, he dropped to the ground, grabbing his stomach."

"I'd like to order an abdominal CT," I say, and the patient once again moans.

"Do you think that's necessary?" Dr. Parse places his hands on his hips and waits for me to respond.

The caretaker with the patient watches me, her eyes pleading with mine. "Yes, I think it's necessary."

Dr. Parse nods, and we call down to get Dean into CT.

We see a few more patients, and as we're walking by the exam room Dean is in, I step in and check on him.

"How are you feeling, Dean?" I ask, and he sits up a little straighter.

"Like someone put their first into my stomach and pulled out my guts."

"Dean, we didn't need that visual." The woman lets go of his hand and shakes mine. "I'm Sally. Dean's daughter-in-law. Thank you for ordering the abdominal CT. I'd been asking for it for an hour, but apparently, none of these doctors seem to think it's necessary."

"Hopefully it gives us some answers." I rub Dean's shoulder and check his vitals.

"I turned eighty yesterday," he says. "And this weekend, all of my grandkids are coming to the city to see me. I haven't seen them in almost a year."

"Take a deep breath." When he fully exhales, I ask, "How many grandkids do you have?"

"Six." He tries to smile but grimaces instead. "And we get together every summer. They call it Grandpa Camp."

"Dr. Oliver. A word please." Dr. Parse sticks his head in the room and then walks out into the hallway. I smile at Dean and Sally and walk out.

"Did the results come back yet from radiology," I ask him, and Dr. Parse hands them to me. I study the film and know what it is immediately.

"A perforated bowel. Good thing I ordered a CT. We'll have to get him to surgery." I hand Dr. Parse back the results.

He hangs his head. "Dean isn't a surgical candidate, Dr. Oliver. I pulled his medical records, and he has so many co-morbidities. I just got off the phone with Gastrointestinal, who said there is no way he'd survive the surgery."

"So, what can we do?" I grab the paperwork back from him like it will hold the answers to save our patient.

"We'll get him admitted," Dr. Parse says. "And make sure he's as comfortable as possible."

Dr. Parse asks me to speak to the family, and I return to the room. Dean and his daughter-in-law don't see me come in, so I stand at the door and press my body against the cold wall. She holds his hands, and they say a prayer together. When they look in my direction, I step forward and tell them the hardest thing I've ever had to tell anyone. Something I'll need to repeat so many times in my career.

This isn't survivable. Who should we call? I'm so sorry. Questions come my way, but then it's only stunned silence. I feel like an intruder watching the reality of mortality wash over both of their faces and somehow, they hold each other tighter. Tears spill out of Dean's eyes, and in this moment, he's not just a stranger I'm meeting for the first time. But he's everyone I've ever lost. The face of anyone who's felt pain. And I can't help but feel it too.

There is hope in not knowing when the end will come, but also inevitably in the fact that it will arrive for all of us. A tear drips out of one eye, and I brush it away before they notice. I'm going to need thicker skin, but there is something about Dean that reminds me of my grandpa, and I can't help but feel sad.

"Thanks for being honest with me," he says. "I guess it's my last call."

I stand, the emotion so close to the surface. "Take care of each other. I'll send a nurse to discuss pain management."

Dean nods, and I walk out of the room.

Chapter Three

From: Keegan Baldwin <Keegan.Baldwin@med.cornell.edu
To: Luna Oliver <Luna.Oliver@umn.edu

Date: September 20

Are you okay??? I just got off the phone with your mom. Then Forest. Luna, you aren't in Cherry anymore. If you study late at the library, ask a security guard to walk you home. Or study with someone. Please let me know if you're fine, as I've been worried sick. It's all I can think about.

From: Luna Oliver <Luna.Oliver@umn.edu
To: Keegan Baldwin <Keegan.Baldwin@med.cornell.edu

Date: September 20

I'm fine.

When I walk into the hospital the next day, it's like I didn't even leave. I change into my scrubs, pull my hair into a top bun, and wait for orders from Dr. Parse. Raven stands to my left, and Myles to my right. I already know the winding hallways of the emergency room and adjacent operating rooms. It feels like I've worked here for years, instead of this only being my second day.

"Dr. Oliver." Dr. Parse points and summons me over to the nurse's station of the emergency room. "Today you will be with one of our attendings, Dr. Ian Lanson."

As if on cue, a physician walks toward me. He adjusts the pager on the waistband of his scrubs, and he scratches his chin, which has about a day-old shadow. Dark hair escapes the deep V-neck of his top. He narrows his eyes, studying my face.

"Let's go," he says.

He walks quickly down the hallway, and I jog to keep up with his long legs, while the other seven residents wait to get their assignments for the day. "Dispatch called. A father and daughter are about to arrive. He lost control in the tunnel. The daughter is stable, but his injuries are critical."

We stand at the ambulance entrance, and when it arrives, we rush to the gurney of the man, and another team goes to the next ambulance to assist the child. Everything happens fast, and I feel like I'm floating above my body. Dr.

Lanson tries to ask the patient questions, but he's unable to speak.

"Dr. Oliver. Intubate our patient."

My eyes shoot to my forehead like the release of a slingshot. "Me?"

"Now, Dr. Oliver." He looks on impatiently.

I rush to the patient's side, and don't bother to tell Dr. Lanson that I've only ever intubated a cadaver and a pig. He talks me through it though. I open the patient's mouth and insert the blade to the right of his tongue. Don't hit his teeth, I remind myself. I see the tip of the epiglottis, then the larynx. I can feel it when I arrive at the trachea, and I gently pull out the stylet.

"Good work, Dr. Oliver." Dr. Lanson looks at the screen with the patient's vitals. "And now what should we do?"

Presbyterian Cornell is one of the best teaching hospitals in the country, yet in the two days I've been here, I'm still caught off guard that these trained surgeons ask my opinion. Everything is trial by fire, and I'm still transitioning from medical student to actual doctor, and I'm nowhere near having the instincts that it takes with this level of trauma.

He raises an eyebrow. "I'm waiting."

"Umm. . ." I pause, looking around the room, but then find my voice. "He has a weak pulse in one arm, and the EMT said he was complaining of chest pain before he lost consciousness. Let's start with a CT. Rule out internal bleeding or damage to his aorta."

There are always so many things happening at once. Two nurses are in the room, and Dr. Lanson continues his physical examination of the patient.

"Okay." Dr. Lanson nods. "Call down to CT. Tell them our patient will be there, stat."

We go with our patient, and a nurse is instructed to contact his next of kin. I ask after the daughter, who I'm told is doing well.

Dr. Lanson flies by me. "Luna, it's an aortic dissection. I just paged the on-call cardiothoracic. If he's going to survive, he needs to get into surgery. Now."

Our medical team, led by Dr. Lanson, takes the patient to the operating room where he's prepped for surgery. Keegan rushes around the corner and stops when he sees me. He looks surprised as his mouth hangs open. Dark hair peeks out from his black surgical cap, full of red hearts, with the words the heart matters etched on the front.

My mom made his cap for him. I'll never forget her hands sewing all the hearts. She gifted it to him, as well as a couple of others she sewed when he got accepted into a six-year integrated residency program. I shake away these thoughts because it's not the time.

"Ah, hi." Keegan's mouth opens to say more, but he stops himself and concentrates on scrubbing up to his elbows.

Dr. Lanson glances at me, and then Keegan, and starts giving him the details. "Dr. Baldwin. Our patient is a thirty-seven-year-old male who lost control of his car in the tunnel. He has a partial tear in the ascending aorta."

We hand our patient's care over, and I watch through the window as Keegan preps for surgery in the scrub room and then pushes through the double doors. Dr. Lanson grips my arm at my elbow.

"Do you want to watch the surgery from the viewing area?"

"Yeah." I tuck my thumbs into the waistband of my scrubs. "That'd be great."

He nods. "Let's go."

We aren't the only doctors in the viewing room. Other surgical residents also fill the space. I lean forward, looking at the big screen display, watching the precision of Keegan's first cut. And then the aorta comes into view.

"Do we always page the specialist surgeon when we know the issue?" I turn to face Dr. Lanson.

"The advantages of a large institution like Presby." He folds his hands behind his head and then looks at me. "I could fumble my way around the aorta, but why risk it when I don't have to?"

"Do you know Dr. Baldwin?" Dr. Lanson's elbow brushes against me. "When he saw you, I thought I saw recognition on his face."

Thoughts flood my mind. There are so many reasons, nepotism included, that I don't want to share that I know

Keegan or let it be widely known that my brother is a cardiologist here at Presbyterian. Luckily, I don't have to answer, because Dr. Lanson turns back to the screen where the dissection is being fixed.

"Dr. Baldwin is the surgeon you want on call when anything cardiac comes to the ER that can't be handled by general or trauma surgeons. He's the best in the field." Dr. Lanson leans back and crosses a leg over another.

My eyes dart to Dr. Lanson, and I try to keep a neutral face. Keegan was always in such a hurry to grow up and get out of Cherry. We watch the surgery for about thirty minutes before Dr. Lanson's pager goes off. "We'll check on our patient later."

The rest of the day is less dramatic as the cases that come in aren't as emergent. At the end of my shift, Dr. Lanson asks if I want to go to the ICU to check on our patient. We get to his room, and Keegan is in there, monitoring the patient's vitals and graft effectiveness.

"There was a lot of damage," Keegan says, first looking at me, and then Dr. Lanson. "I was hoping to be able to do this endovascularly, but because of the location of the dissection, a sternotomy was required."

Our eyes meet, but then I move mine lower, taking him in. My brain continues to be misaligned. There's a huge disconnect between the boy I grew up with, and the man standing in front of me. He's authoritative and confident. The coat hides his arms, but I can still see the outline of them. He catches me staring at his surgical cap.

Dr. Lanson coughs. "I'm sorry. Dr. Oliver, this is Dr. Baldwin. Dr. Oliver is a general surgery intern."

Keegan opens his mouth to say something, but before he has a chance, I extend my hand. "It's nice to meet you, Dr. Baldwin."

"Call me Keegan. Please." He clears his throat and then swallows, causing his Adam's apple to bob up and down. His massive hand envelops mine. "Welcome to Presbyterian."

"Thank you." I pull away and tuck my hands into my white coat, stretching out my fingers that were just touching his. "And call me Luna."

Dr. Lanson's pager goes off, and he holds a finger up. "Wait here. I'm going to see what this is." He walks out of the room and heads down the hallway, his heavy feet noisy against the hospital floor.

Keegan turns his back to the patient but then holds my gaze. Back home, he never went anywhere without glasses, but now he must opt for contacts, and I can't believe how light his bluish-gray eyes are. He then looks at the chart.

"Our patient is lucky to be alive. It was almost a full dissection."

"I'm sorry—" I begin, but then a nurse walks in. She shoots me a look like not only does she know me, but that she disapproves of me too. She narrows her eyes and then shakes her head.

"Dr. Baldwin. I was hoping you'd be on call today." The nurse pats his back and then adjusts the patient's IV. "You are a breath of fresh air."

"Thank you, Lex." Keegan smiles. A real, actual smile. And I can see his white teeth. He rarely smiles. "You know you're one of my favorites, too."

The awkward man that I knew all those years ago disappears in front of my eyes, and this handsome, talented, easy-to-converse with doctor appears in his place. I don't know why it takes him talking to a nurse and not the lifesaving surgery he just performed for me to further recognize the transformation.

"Okay, Dr. Oliver. Let's get back to the ER." Dr. Lanson waves me over, and I once again follow him. Keegan looks away from Lex the nurse and nods at me as I walk out of the room.

When Dr. Lanson finally releases me for the day, I've been at the hospital for more than fourteen hours, which means I'm already trending toward being over the allowable eighty hours a week a resident is permitted to work. I change into my street clothes, stand at the hospital exit, and look at the dark summer night outside. As strong as I try to be, the darkness at night still scares me. I hesitate. Maybe I should call a car service to bring me the short distance home.

"Hey." The words are low, and I know it's Keegan's voice before I even turn around.

"Hey." I glance back as he emerges from the hospital doors. His hair is dripping wet, and he's now out of his scrubs and back in pants and a button-down shirt.

"Please tell me that you weren't contemplating walking home alone." Keegan stands next to me, and a backpack hangs off him. "I don't care if this is the Upper East Side."

"It took me less than fifteen minutes to walk from my apartment to the scrub room this morning." I tuck a strand of hair behind my ear. "I'm sure I can get home by myself too."

But Keegan grips my elbow and nudges me forward. "Come on. I'll walk you."

"You don't have to," I say, but find myself walking beside him and breathing a little easier. "Do you even live in this direction?"

Keegan glances back. "I live five minutes from the hospital. In the other direction."

We walk in silence for the next minute. He's always been a man of few words, except when he emails. Keegan was a perfect fit in my family because most of us never stop talking. But the quietness between us doesn't bother me. Maybe I'll get to know him better through the silence.

Keegan tucks his hands into his pockets. I glance at him at the same time he turns to me. "Your brother would kill me if I let you walk home alone in the dark."

I go to take a right, and at the same time, Keegan tries to go left. We brush up against each other, and I almost lose my balance. He squeezes my upper arms to steady me.

"I find Forest's need to control everything very antiquated." I turn away from Keegan and we start down the sidewalk again. "I'm going to have to walk home alone sometimes."

Keegan raises an eyebrow. "He's not controlling. He just cares."

"Yeah," I say. "I know Forest pretty well too, thank you very much. Why would he care if I walked home alone?"

A car honks at someone running through the street, and the pedestrian starts yelling obscenities at the person in the car. The smell of ice cream reaches us as we walk by what's become my favorite shop which has over a hundred flavors of ice cream called Icy New Yorkers.

"Because of what happened to you in college." Keegan's voice is soft as he peers down at me.

I stop walking, so Keegan does too. He stands so close to me that I need to strain my head to look into his eyes. "I forgot that you knew about that."

"He—"

"I can't have a chaperone every night here, so I may need to invest in some pepper spray and stay on well-lit roads."

"He was really shaken up when he found out." Keegan's body stiffens. "Whether you realize it or not, he's always felt protective over you."

I raise my hand to stop him. "I know."

It's not something I think about much anymore. Yet the trauma lives in me, and hearing the words come out of Keegan's mouth brings me back to that night. That's the hold that PTSD has on me.

Nothing happened. Not really. But it could have. It almost did. I was on campus, studying at the library until it closed at eleven like I had done so many times in the past. As I was walking back to my dorm room, someone hit me from behind and then got on top of me. I screamed and fought like my life depended on it, and campus security arrived before it progressed—before anything was taken from me. I escaped the entire ordeal with bruises and a bad headache. And a very real and paralyzing fear of the dark.

"Just promise me you'll be safe, Luna."

My building comes into view, and Keegan runs his hand across his face in one large, downward motion. I study his blue eyes, a contrast against the darkness of his hair and olive complexion. I squint, trying to figure out the answer to the most ridiculous question I've ever asked myself. Has Keegan always been kind of hot, or is this a new thing? I shake away my thoughts.

"I'm sorry about earlier," I blurt out, coming back to the present. "About pretending to not know you. I just, well, I don't want people to know about our connection because they may think I'm trying to gain favors or something."

Keegan presses his lips together and begins rubbing the back of his neck. "If you want to be strangers at the hospital, we'll be strangers."

"Well, we're not strangers anymore," I say. "Because I got introduced to you today. So now I know you. But you'll have to act like you don't know how I got the scar on my chin when I was seven. Or that I broke my arm in sixth grade during math class, or that you and Forest scared away my first crush when he came over with cookies he'd baked, and that I secretly still harbor resentment toward both of you because of it."

Keegan grips my chin lifts it toward him, and runs his thumb along the three-inch scar. The touch causes my heart to hitch in my chest. "Got it."

He squares his body to mine, and I point at the building behind me. "Well, this is me. But you know that already because you were fortunate enough to get to help move me into the shithole that is my apartment." I glance at the door, and Keegan scrunches up his face, confirming that he doesn't think too highly of it either.

"Luna." He opens the door for me, and I walk through it. "Don't walk home alone at night. Please promise me that."

I press my finger against my bottom lip and tap it. "I'll consider it."

"Luna." Keegan stares at me. "Why are you always so stubborn?"

"Fine," I give in. "I promise."

Chapter Four

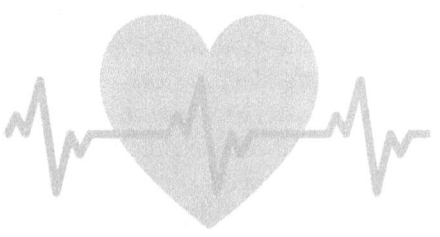

From: Keegan Baldwin <Keegan.Baldwin@med.cornell.edu
To: Luna Oliver <Luna.Oliver@umn.edu

Date: October 17

Hey Luna. Is it starting to cool off in MN? It is still really hot in NYC, and part of me is missing fall back home. My apartment is small, especially with five guys living here. There is no AC, and it's too hot to sleep. But in better news, my roommates and I booked a trip to Amsterdam over Thanksgiving. We somehow managed to get the same few days off. We're researching hostel options now. Anyway, I hope your first semester is going well. How's your Bio Chem course going?

From: Luna Oliver <Luna.Oliver@umn.edu
To: Keegan Baldwin <Keegan.Baldwin@med.cornell.edu

Date: October 18

I would pay good money to be a fly on the wall, watching Keegan Baldwin in Amsterdam. and in a hostel. I read that they only wash the sheets in those places about once a month. Imagine all the bodily fluids that you'll be sleeping on. Also, a friend of mine stayed at a hostel in Amsterdam, and the room had twenty beds, and people openly had sex in front of others, and the showers were co-ed. I can't think of a place less Keegan Baldwin than a hostel in Amsterdam. But good for you branching out.

From: Keegan Baldwin <Keegan.Baldwin@med.cornell.edu
To: Luna Oliver <Luna.Oliver@umn.edu

Date: October 18

Change of plans. We are splurging on a hotel.

It feels good to wear clothes that aren't scrubs or sweatpants, even if it is only because I'm going to Forest's place for our family dinner. During my first two weeks in New York, I've barely seen anything outside of my apartment and the hospital. Every day is the same, and I've never had to use my brain like I am now. It literally hurts by the time I get home after my shifts. I keep reminding myself that life won't always be like this, but right now, being a first-year resident is my entire life.

"You look nice." Myles glances up from his bowl of cereal as I walk into the kitchen. "Like someone definitely not heading to the hospital."

"And it feels so good."

I look down at my sundress. My roommates and I joke that the moment we come home from the hospital, we put on our apartment uniform. Myles can always be found in a ratty red Stanford shirt, the white letters falling off, and a pair of sweatpants. Raven wears an Emory University shirt with scrub bottoms, and I can usually be found in a bright gold University of Minnesota shirt and scrub pants. We are poster children for the places where we studied medicine.

Myles stands and rinses his bowl in the sink. "Any fun plans on your night off?"

"I'm going to my brother's place for dinner. So the word fun is debatable."

Raven walks out of her bedroom, arms stretched in the air, her hair on top of her head, with pillow marks on her cheek. "Is it just you and your brother?" She pulls out a stool and sits. "And when do I get to meet this brother of yours?"

"Soon I hope." I lean against the counter, facing them. "My brother's best friend who we grew up with will be there too."

I've gotten to know Myles and Raven quite a bit in the past couple of weeks of living together. They couldn't be easier roommates, although my bar is low. When a dish is used, it's washed. When the bathroom floor gets wet from the shower, it's mopped up. When it gets late, the lights are out. And so far, they put up with my messiness, even though I am trying my best not to bring that part of me into this apartment. But we're all still getting to know each other, so I haven't talked much about my brother, and not at all about Keegan.

Raven rests her head in her hands. "And your hometown friend lives in New York? Small world."

"Is he a doctor too?" Myles leans against the sink and dries his hands.

Myles and Raven look at me expectantly, and I nod.

A mischievous grin takes over Raven's face. "I'm so curious. Tell us everything."

"There's nothing to tell," I say. "Dr. Baldwin is a cardiothoracic surgeon. Keegan. He works at Presby too."

Raven slaps her hand down on the counter. "The Dr. Baldwin who was on call this week in the ER." Raven's tongue flicks out to wet her lips. "He's a childhood friend of yours?"

"I guess." I fold my arms over my chest. "I mean, he's really my brother's friend more than mine."

Myles's lips turn up, and Raven leans toward me even farther and says, "You do know that pretty much every female at the hospital calls him beautiful Baldwin."

An intense warmth spreads across my face, causing it to flush. I'm starting to understand the nickname. I wish I didn't. "I wasn't aware."

"I've even heard the nurses gathered around the station talking about him," Myles says. "How do I meet this guy? Cardiothoracic has been the only route I've been interested in from day one."

I grab a bottle of water from the fridge and then smooth out my dress. "To me, he's just Keegan. My brother's best friend. And by some twist of fate, we all ended up in the same city."

Raven puts her face in her palm and pouts while looking at Myles. "I guess it's just you and me tonight, kid."

But Myles shakes his head and points to our group calendar that hangs by the door. "Sorry Raven. My overnight shift starts in about two hours, and I'm on for twenty-four hours."

"Well, okay," Raven says, getting up from the stool. "I guess I'm on my own tonight."

"I really need to go." I throw a few things into my bag. "But the next time we have a night off at the same time, we're going out. It makes no sense that we live in this amazing city but don't see more of it."

"I'm holding you to that," Raven says. "And say hi to beautiful Baldwin for me."

"Not if you keep calling him that." I hold the door open and give them a wave. "See you later."

The subway station holds all the heat of this hot summer day, like a furnace, making the atmosphere almost unbearable. But I'm adamant that I will learn my way around it because it is the most economical option. I purchase my ticket, my clothes already sticking to my skin with perspiration, and I board the train that will take me from my apartment on the Upper East side to Forest's in the Chelsea neighborhood. Unless I get on the wrong train. Then I'm headed downtown.

Heels are a thing of the past because living in New York requires so much walking. I get off at the closest stop and find my way to Forest's low-rise apartment. His building is a lot fancier than mine, and when I arrive, a doorman rings Forest to come down and let me up.

"Hey, kiddo." Forest walks across the expansive lobby of his building and hugs me, pulling out the name he used to call me. "Fashionably late once again."

"Yeah, well." I look down at my outfit. "I'm trying to figure out this public transportation thing."

Forest hits the button to his floor. "I remember feeling like that when I first got here." He holds the door for me when we reach his floor. "It gets easier."

I clasp my arm around his. "Are you cooking anything good?"

"Takeout, Luna." Forest raises his eyebrows and then laughs. "It's like you don't know me at all."

Forest swings his door open, the hinges creaking slightly, and ushers me inside. As I enter the apartment, I see Keegan, who leans against the window, book in hand. He glances at me, pushing his glasses up his nose. They're back, but no longer the broken, taped-together ones he used to wear. No. These somehow only magnify his eyes.

For a moment, his gaze lingers on me, his eyes intense and unwavering, making me feel momentarily off-balance. Keegan swiftly closes his book and strides across the room, his footsteps echoing against the wooden floorboards. The space between us rapidly shrinks.

"Luna." He reaches me, and I take him in too. Beautiful Baldwin. I laugh inside thinking of a bunch of nurses sitting around fawning over him. He smells good—nothing strong, but like he only recently showered.

"You look—" he begins to say, but I cut him off.

"Like I need a drink to cool off from this heat." My hair sticks to the back of my neck, and although I had the best intentions of wearing it down for once, I grab the elastic band around my wrist and tie my hair up.

Forest opens his fridge and hands me a cold beer, and then he grabs a few menus that are on the counter. "What are we craving? Indian? Thai? Chinese? Vietnamese?"

"I'd like something lighter in this heat." Keegan takes the menus out of Forest's hands. "There's a great new sandwich place I've been wanting to try around the corner."

"Sandwiches?" Forest scrunches up his face. "I've been craving Indian."

"That's so heavy." Keegan shrugs and looks at me. "But if that's what you want."

"Indian it is." Forest claps his hands together before anyone waits for me to weigh in.

After I open my beer, I hold the bottle against my neck and then take a long and slow drink.

"Oh, hey man," Forest says, grabbing a beer, and handing one to Keegan. "How'd my patient fare that came in for a routine physical and then ended up getting the quadruple bypass the same day?"

When Keegan hears the mention of the exciting surgical case, a sparkle illuminates his eyes, and he leans forward, joining in the conversation. Meanwhile, I take my beer and make my way over to the couch, inwardly groaning at the predictability of their behavior as I once again fall into third-wheel territory.

"Is this what you guys do when you get together?" I take a seat on the couch, away from them at the table. "Talk about work the entire time?"

Instead of fading into the background, I find my opening. "Because if that's what we're going to do, let me tell you about the patient that came in after her bachelorette party that had an unidentified foreign object up her vagina."

Keegan and Forest's eyes shoot to me like they're remembering that I'm here for the first time. "She had no recollection of putting anything up there. It was quite the extraction process and ended up being the head of a Barbie."

Keegan raises his eyebrows so sharply that they could cut into layers of skin better than a scalpel.

Forest starts laughing and says, "Okay. We can discuss other things too. How are you? How are your roommates? Are you picking up after yourself, or are you still Lazy Luna?"

I roll my eyes at the nickname. He's called me that ever since I was little. "So, I'm a tad messy. I own it."

"A tad?" Forest shakes his head. "Girl, you're a disaster. Your bedroom door back at home wouldn't even open because of all the crap you had on the floor."

"Yeah," Keegan nods his head. "I remember that too. And I swear you've never made a bed in your life."

I grab a couch cushion and throw it in their general direction, but it falls short and lands on the floor.

"See. My point exactly," Forest says. "Already making a mess in my apartment."

A pager vibrates against the table, and Forest grabs it. "Ugh. I was told there would be almost a zero percent chance I'd get paged tonight."

He grabs his phone and goes to the other room, while Keegan and I stare at each other in silence. I open my mouth to fill the space, but then Forest comes back.

"I have to go in." Forest gathers his things. "I'm so sorry. Make yourselves at home. Order food. Drink my beer. Catch up. Do whatever. I'll reschedule this."

Keegan and I look at each other uncomfortably after Forest rushes out of the apartment.

"Umm," he says, tucking his hands into the front pockets of his shorts as he stands. "Are you hungry?"

I glance down at my phone as if that will save me. "Yes. But it's Saturday night. I'm sure you have places to be. I'll head home and order food, and now you can try that new sandwich place. Food without Forest bossing you around like he always does."

"Forest doesn't boss me around," Keegan says. "And I don't have plans tonight."

A jolt of surprise courses through, and I freeze in place. I slowly turn my head to face him, my eyes wide. Keegan calmly reaches behind his body and pulls out his phone from his back pocket, his fingers deftly navigating the screen before he tucks it away again.

"Do you want to go out and grab a bite?" Keegan studies me, his face tilted, his thick but manicured eyebrows doing all the asking. "Or do you want to eat here?"

"No," I say. "I mean, I don't want to eat here. Let's get out. I've barely seen the city."

"Yeah?" Keegan holds the door open, and I start getting nervous at the thought of having to spend one-on-one time with him. "If you're sure."

I slip past him and walk out into the hallway. "I'm sure."

We ride the elevator down in complete silence. The only sound is the soft humming of the air conditioning. I am acutely aware of the sound of my heartbeat, which seems to be racing so fast that it feels like it could burst out of my chest at any moment.

I can't shake off the feeling of being hyper-aware of Keegan's presence, and the fact that we are alone in this confined space only intensifies my unease. We've never had a relationship where we hung out outside of Forest or my parents. Not having Forest with us throws off the balance.

When the elevator opens, he holds the door and lets me get out first. We walk into the late afternoon sun and pause. We have no idea where we're going. I regret saying I could eat, as I'm oddly nervous.

"What are you hungry for?" Keegan stares down at me. And because I am wearing flats, he towers over my frame.

"Well." I hold my hands up to my mouth and tap my finger against my lips. It's a nervous habit like all the answers in this world live in that bottom lip of mine. "I've been dying to try street food."

"Street food?" Keegan's lips fall into a straight line.

"You asked." I tuck loose strands of hair behind my ears. "And isn't New York kind of famous for that?"

"Street food?" He stares at my hand still fiddling with my hair. "I could take you to a nice restaurant and we could enjoy something good, but you want street food?"

"Yes." I nod, ignoring the way he's watching me. "We're in Chelsea. Why don't we try Chelsea Eats? I heard they have a lot of great vendors. I saw a flier for it at the hospital."

Keegan shrugs and starts walking down the street, and I follow. I glance up at him, admiring the dark-rimmed glasses that he wears. When my skin warms, I force myself to look away.

We walk a couple of blocks in silence as I take in this new neighborhood. The streets are lined with mature trees, and we stroll past beautiful brownstones, protected by dark, iron rod fences. When we reach a subway stop, people pool onto the street from underground, and I move out of the way as they walk between Keegan and me.

And then Chelsea Eats comes into view. There are a few food trucks parked along the streets, as well as some white tents with vendors. The overwhelming aroma smacks me in the face. I smell spices, meat, and hot oil. I stop at the first tent I see that is selling street tacos.

"Yes." I point decisively. "This is what I want. They smell so good."

Keegan rolls his eyes at me. "The first vendor? You don't want to look around?"

I lick my lips, and Keegan's eyes move to them. "A girl knows what she wants. This is it." I start fumbling through my bag for money.

Keegan puts his hands over mine, and the touch sends a jolt of electricity through my spine. I'm a doctor. There's only one explanation. It's probably nothing more than nerve branches entering the dermis from the subcutaneous fat forming both a superficial and deep nerve plexus. Because the only chemistry I believe in is the kind I learned in medical school.

"Let me pay." Keegan reaches for his wallet. "Residents don't make shit."

"That was a bit patriarchal." I shake my head. "I can afford to buy myself food."

Keegan reaches into his back pocket. "I'm sure you can. But please. I'd like to buy you dinner. Even if it is shitty street food."

I notice the subtle movement of his lips as they twitch at the corners in a way that seems almost involuntarily like he's trying to suppress a smile.

Keegan and I sit on a nearby bench with our food. He ordered the same thing I did. I take a bite of my first taco, and it's delicious and everything that street food should be. I close my eyes and listen to all the people around me in this great big city and let out a moan.

When I open my eyes, Keegan is staring at me. He then scrunches up his face. "Do you know how much bacteria are in street food? I hope you don't end up in the ER tonight with a case of E. coli or Salmonella."

"Look at you." I take another bite as he watches me, and I wipe the hot sauce off the corner of my lip with my thumb, and then stick it in my mouth. "Talking all dirty to me."

A flush of color peeks out underneath Keegan's shirt, and spreads up his neck, and then face. I make him nervous. For some reason, the thought both thrills and calms me. I grab his hand that holds a taco and bring it to his mouth.

"Do it, Keegan. Take a bite. You know you want to."

He looks at me, and for the first time, he smiles—opened mouthed, full teeth, and happy eyes. And then he bites into his taco, closes his eyes, and savors the bite.

"Okay, Luna." He covers his mouth as he chews his food, and I pull my hand back and watch him. "It's not bad." He grabs a napkin and wipes the corners of his mouth.

I press my shoulder into his. "You've lived in New York for years, but have you even lived?"

He takes another bite, but his eyes watch me from above his taco. "I can say with certainty that I haven't."

After eating, we take the subway back to our neighborhood. A busker sits on the concrete playing a saxophone, and a small crowd gathers to listen. I buy a funnel cake from a pop-up food truck.

"How can you eat like that and look like—" Keegan's eyes flick to my body, and he shakes his head, but he doesn't continue.

Keegan then points at my paper plate, as I wipe powdered sugar off my face. "As a heart surgeon, I feel obligated to tell you how bad these things are for you."

"You are a buzzkill." I tear off a small piece of the warm, sugary funnel cake, and hold it out towards Keegan, offering it to him with a small smile. Any unease I felt earlier has dissipated. For a moment, he hesitates, his gaze locked onto mine as if weighing some unspoken decision. Then without warning, he reaches out and takes my hand, bringing it up to his mouth in one fluid movement. He eats the funnel cake, his lips brushing gently against my fingers in the process.

Words escape me at first, as we stand, watching each other. But then I laugh. "Wow, Keegan. Who even are you? I'm kind of impressed."

"For clogging up my arteries?" He takes his thumb and rubs the corner of his mouth. "You are going to be a bad influence on me, aren't you?

"I call it spontaneous."

We reach my building, and Keegan squeezes the back of his neck and says, "I guess that's a word for it."

His lips twitch at the corners, and I shrug. "I'd rather be spontaneous than be boring."

Keegan drops his hand from his neck and tilts his head to the side. "You think I'm boring?"

I ponder that thought for a moment. I don't know him well enough to have an opinion. "Maybe not boring but definitely safe."

"You're right." He nods. He studies me so intently, that the city disappears around us. I run my hand over my face, sure that I must have something stuck to it.

"It's never too late to start taking some risks." I smile and reach my arm out to his but then pull back. I lean against the door frame and something in his expression changes.

"Maybe I will." Keegan's chest expands as he takes a deep breath. "Speaking of safe. I should get to bed. I have a long day tomorrow."

And then Keegan walks away. My mind races, filling me up until I'm consumed. Keegan has always been Forest's, but surprisingly, I had fun tonight. These new feelings confuse me because we're not just friends or acquaintances. We are family, and that's the only way we've ever seen each other. But tonight, I felt seen by him. In ways I don't when Forest is around.

Chapter Five

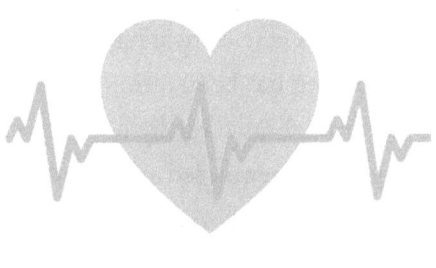

As I step through the hospital doors the next day, the familiar scent greets me—a distinct blend of antiseptic and artificial cleaners laced with a hint of both hope and despair. I notice the sounds even more than the smells. People, rushing in all directions, being helpful, saving lives, and solving medical mysteries. Most days at the hospital are dark and challenging, but I wouldn't want to be doing anything else. Presbyterian Cornell accepts eight general surgery residents a year, and I'm one of them.

"Hey, girl," Raven says as she rushes in the other direction. "George's tonight? A bunch of the residents are going."

"Pretty sure I'll be there," I say, heading in the opposite direction, and I grab her arm. "Who are you with today?"

"Rounds with Parse. You?"

"Lanson." As if on cue, Dr. Lanson catches up to me, and I match his pace. "See you later."

George's is a dive bar that doesn't fit into the vibe of the neighborhood. Everyone tells me it's a huge hangout for the Presby staff, and Raven has been trying to get me and Myles to try it out. And tonight, we finally have the same evening off. And as Raven has reminded me, I promised that the next time that happened, I'd go out.

"Dr. Oliver." Dr. Lanson's voice brings me back to the present. "Keep up."

We reach the exam room, and my eyes immediately fall on the man lying on the table, writhing in obvious distress. His face is contorted in pain, and beads of sweat drip down his forehead. My heart races as I watch him lose consciousness, his body goes limp, and his breathing becomes shallow until it stops completely.

"He's coding," Dr. Lanson calls out to no one in particular. "Dr. Oliver, grab the paddles."

I rush to the defibrillator and set the amount of energy. When the paddles become fully charged, I place them over him and shock his heart. Nothing. I turn the energy amount up, and everyone stands back as I once again shock the patient, and this time, I'm able to restore sinus rhythm to him.

A nurse brings in an ultrasound machine, and Dr. Lanson further examines the patient. "He's bleeding out. It looks like an abdominal aortic aneurysm," Dr. Lanson says with more urgency. "Prep operating room two. Now."

We wheel our patient to the operating room, and upon arrival, Keegan is already scrubbing in. Everything happens so quickly, from the point of diagnosis to getting the patient in the operating room where our surgery team awaits. Dr. Lanson also scrubs in and leaves me out in the hallway. I head upstairs to the observation room but can only stay for some of the surgery because I get paged to the emergency room to help with sutures.

There is rarely down time because another patient is usually waiting for us. There is always a new emergency—a new person having the worst day of their life. So much of my job is embracing the empathy I feel for these people while dissociating so I can wake up and do this all over again the next day. It's a balance, and some days I do it better than others.

What hasn't been surprising is how little math I've needed on the job. Yes, all the calculus I took is important to better understand the unknown variables in relation to a system over time. But the reality is, the only math I've remotely needed so far is basic arithmetic. If the patient weighs this much, then let's give this dose. Sometimes I wonder how many people, women especially, are steered away from a career in medicine because they aren't good at math. I can't believe I was almost one of them.

After my shift, I meet Raven in the changing room, and she reminds me that everyone is going to George's for a drink. I look down at my scrubs and let out a deep breath. It would feel so good to go home, put some pajamas on, watch a show, and go to bed.

"Come on." Raven senses my hesitation. "Myles is going to meet us there too. It'll be fun."

"Okay." I pull my jeans on and then slam the locker door shut. "But I can't stay for long. This entire week is kicking my ass."

"Not for long is better than not at all." Raven hooks her arm in mine, and we leave the hospital and head across the street to George's.

We walk in, and a bell attached to the door announces our arrival. It takes a moment for my eyes to adjust to the dimly lit bar. There's a wall full of booths, and then a few high-top tables throughout the small space. In the back is a jukebox. Raven and I see Myles at a table by himself and head in his direction.

"It's about time you guys got cut." Myles moves his chair to make room for us. "I've been here an hour already."

Raven raises her hand when a server goes by. "It was so busy today. I can't tell you how many rectal exams I did on the step-down unit. It was all ass, all day."

"I mostly focused on airways in the simulation lab," I add. "Well, after seeing a triple-A and then doing sutures for about two hours straight in the ER."

We must not be the only people who recently finished our shifts, because groups start to file into the bar, and the bell on the door rings constantly. Raven grabs my arm and says into my ear. "Look who's here. It's beautiful Baldwin."

My eyes dart up, and I spot Keegan walking in with a man and a woman. He doesn't see me, but I watch as he sits at one of the booths by a window. He lets the woman slide in, and then he takes the end. He looks uncomfortable as his knees graze the table.

"You do see it, right?" Raven presses on. "I mean if you like that tall, dark, and handsome thing. But who likes that, right?"

"No. Nope." If I say no enough, perhaps I'll convince myself that I don't see it. I take a sip of the drink the server just put on the table. "When I say I grew up with him, I literally grew up with him. Plus, I've sworn off men until at least my third year."

Raven laughs and dramatically flicks her hair back, the beads in her braid hitting the back of the chair. "Why would you swear off men?"

"Let's just say I over dated the past few years." I shake my head thinking of all the duds I went through.

The past few years have taught me that it's not only women who tend to fall fast—men do it too. I haven't wanted a serious relationship because I've had plans for my life, and I didn't want anyone getting in the way of those plans. Every guy I dated wanted something more serious than I was willing to give. The last guy I dated wanted me to forget about New York and try to match in the Midwest to be nearer to him. That's where it all starts. We women compromise on something, and before we know it, the life we're living is unrecognizable from the life we hoped for.

"Myles is so lucky that he's already found his person." Raven rests her head in her hands. "I'm getting sick of this dating thing."

"I'll be right back," Myles says. "I'm going to play a song on the jukebox."

"I can barely keep up with my schedule now." I fiddle with the napkin on the table, nearly ripping it to shreds. "How can you even think about dating?"

"Maybe what I need is sexy time." Raven's eyes cut to her forehead, and then she puts her hand on mine and leans into me. "Don't look now, but beautiful Baldwin is coming this way."

I swivel in my chair as Keegan walks toward me, slowly closing the space between us. He arrives and presses his palms onto the table.

"Hey." Keegan looks at where he was sitting in the corner, and everyone at the table glances our way. "I'm here with two of my fellows."

"Hi." I then look at Raven. "Dr. Baldwin. This is my friend, Dr. Raven Craik."

Keegan puts his hand out to shake hers. "Please call me Keegan. It's nice to meet you."

"And call me Raven." She gives him her best, toothy grin. "Luna has told me so much about you, Keegan."

He glances at me, and I'm thankful George's is so dimly lit because heat floods my face.

"Umm, Keegan." I swivel my chair, face him, and turn my back from Raven. "I wanted to ask you. How'd our patient fare? You know, the one with the Triple-A?"

"He didn't make it." Keegan presses his lips into a thin line. "He got to us too late, and there was too much blood loss."

"Oh." I take a long blink, and when I open my eyes, Keegan continues to watch me. "That," I begin to say, pressing my finger against my lips. "Well, that's too bad."

"You gave him a fighting chance, Luna," Keegan grips the edge of the table, and his knuckles go white. "But sometimes our best isn't good enough."

It doesn't feel right that I'm in a bar, listening to Myles' jukebox choice of Texas country music while talking about a patient who didn't make it. I know this is life, but I never want to get to a place where I can separate so much that hearing these things doesn't affect me.

"I'm sorry." I stare down at Keegan's hands. He catches me looking at them. "But it's hard for me to reconcile that I saw someone alive, and now, poof. They're gone."

"Oh, hi." Myles comes back to the table and sees Keegan, who was just about to respond to me. "Dr. Baldwin. I met you yesterday when I was shadowing Dr. Parse. I'm Dr. Myles Worth."

"Keegan." He extends his hand, and with his other, points to Myles' faded shirt. "So, you're a Stanford guy?"

Myles smiles, looking down. "Only for medical school. I went to Texas for undergrad."

Keegan moves closer to me to make room for Myles to sit. His arm presses against my body as he stands over me. Myles puts his hand in the air to get the server's attention, and then Keegan asks, "How do you all know each other?"

"We're roommates," Raven says quickly. "We're in one of the hospital-subsidized apartment buildings a few blocks away."

"Ah." Keegan nods his head. "I helped Luna move in, but you two hadn't arrived yet. So, you're the roommates."

"And Keegan and I grew up together. We're from the same hometown, and he and my brother are best friends," I say.

"Speaking of your brother," Raven says. "When do we get to meet him? I'm starting to think he doesn't exist."

Keegan and I glance at each other, and then I turn to Raven. "Soon, I'm sure. He's been on call constantly, it seems."

Raven smiles as she looks at Keegan, me, and back at him. "Three people from Cherry, Minnesota, all at the same hospital. What are the chances?"

"Yes." I hold my hand up. "Besides the two of you, I haven't told anyone I know Keegan personally. I don't need Chief Resident Parse or anyone else for that matter thinking I only got my general surgery residency because of my connections."

"If anyone says that, I'd tell them that you got the residency because you finished near the top of your class in medical school and are going to make a helluva surgeon." Keegan only looks at me when he speaks the words.

My mouth hangs open, but before I can say anything, Raven grabs my arm. "What a sweet thing to say about Luna, Keegan."

"Plus," Keegan says. "Being here makes so much sense due to all the work you've done on disparities in healthcare."

Weill Presbyterian Cornell was the general surgical residency program I wanted above all the others. For one year, they send their residents to Jamaica Hospital in Queens. I'll also get to be on call at Jamaica Hospital. The injuries I'll be able to treat are grossly different from Presby's, and I'll get to handle more impact wounds. The patient population is also more diverse, and that's where my true passion lies.

"Anyway." Keegan glances at the table he was previously at. "I should go join my colleagues."

"Before you go." Myles shoots up and walks to our side of the table and looks at Keegan. "I know I'm only a first year and should be contemplating all areas of surgery, but all I've ever wanted to do is cardiothoracic. Could I take you to coffee sometime? Pick your brain?"

My stomach churns because this is the exact scenario I've wanted to avoid. I don't want Keegan to be put in a position where my friends are asking him for favors. But then he reaches into his back pocket, pulls out a wallet, and hands Myles a card.

"That would be great," Keegan says, and his smile tells me he's being honest. "My email address and cell are listed. Reach out anytime."

"Thank you so much." Myles shakes Keegan's hand voraciously and then walks back to his side of the table.

"Thank you, Keegan." I lean forward, and he dips his head to hear me over the music. I can smell the soap and aftershave that is part of his orbit. "Seriously."

"Your roommates seem great." Keegan bends even lower and his warm breath is against my skin when he speaks next. "And Luna. Don't walk home alone."

I turn to face Raven and Myles and face him and smile. "Me? Never."

His lips turn up, ever so slightly, the closest thing I'll get to a smile directed at me tonight, and he walks away.

Chapter Six

From: Keegan Baldwin <Keegan.Baldwin@med.cornell.edu

To: Luna Oliver <Luna.Oliver@umn.edu

Date: November 22

Hi from Amsterdam. How is Thanksgiving in Cherry?

From: Luna Oliver <Luna.Oliver@umn.edu
To: Keegan Baldwin <Keegan.Baldwin@med.cornell.edu

Date: November 22

You must not have talked to Forest yet. Thanksgiving has been horrible. I brought my roommate home with me because she's from Ohio and didn't want to go all the way home for such a short time. And guess what happened? Forest hooked up with her!!! I'm pissed at both of them. Forest and I had a long talk, and I had to tell him that siblings DO NOT hook up with each other's friends. I was so upset that we ended up leaving Friday to come back to campus, and I've reached out to housing to get a new roommate. Forest and I aren't talking. And Kelsie and I aren't talking. So yeah. I'm great.

From: Keegan Baldwin <Keegan.Baldwin@med.cornell.edu
To: Luna Oliver <Luna.Oliver@umn.edu

Date: November 23

Sorry for the late email. The time difference and all. I haven't talked to Forest, but I'm sorry you are upset about this. We can't always help who we develop feelings for. But I'm sorry you're hurt.

From: Luna Oliver <Luna.Oliver@umn.edu
To: Keegan Baldwin <Keegan.Baldwin@med.cornell.edu

Date: November 23

Feelings? He knew her for a few hours. The man needs to stop thinking with his dick. Also, I know you're an only child, so I'll say it louder this time. SIBLINGS DO NOT DATE EACH OTHER'S FRIENDS.

Forest and I have always been close, despite our age difference. He was six years old when I was born. My mom had two miscarriages in the years between us, which accounts for our age gap. By the time I started kindergarten, Forest was in middle school, and when I reached middle school, he was already in high school. When he turned eighteen, graduated from high school, and moved out of the house, I was only twelve. There was never much overlap, but as little sisters usually do, I adored everything about my big brother. We were far enough apart in age that there was never any actual conflict. But close enough in age that I looked up to him.

He's always been my person. We're a lot alike. We're both spontaneous and laid back. We both rely on humor to lighten the mood. We're different in a few ways too. He's confident, while I tend to be self-deprecating. He is a total neat freak, and I'm messy. He's good at math. I am not.

Forest and I jog down the concrete sidewalk in Central Park, side by side. He tries to pull ahead of me, but then I kick it into my next gear to catch up with him. We're on our fourth mile, and he's not letting up.

"I talked to Mom this morning." Forest glances at me and says the word so effortlessly, not like we've been running for miles.

"Yeah?" I breathe heavily, the jog finally catching up with me. "How's Mom? We've been playing phone tag for the past two days."

Forest slows, and I follow. When he comes to a full stop, I bend down, rest my hands on my knees, and take slow, deep breaths. I stand fully and pull my legs behind me to stretch my quadriceps, and then Forest and I walk toward an outside kiosk that sells coffee.

"She went on and on about how excited she is that you and I are in the same city. Not only together, but with Keegan." Forest reaches the counter first and orders two coffees.

"They're arriving here next week, you know?" Forest hands me a coffee, and I moan when I take my first sip. I've never drank as much coffee as I have since becoming a resident. I'm considering getting a PICC line that feeds me constant dark roast, all the time.

"Yes. I'm aware." I remove the lid and blow on it after nearly burning my tongue with my first drink. "They'll stay at a hotel, right? I don't think Mom and Dad, or my roommates, would appreciate them staying with me. And you only have one bedroom."

"Or at Keegan's." Forest shrugs. "His place is massive. I mean, by New York standards."

Forest and I walk in the direction of Tavern on the Green in Central Park. When we see a bench, I head toward it. My legs are noodles and are barely holding up the weight of my body. I sit, and Forest follows.

"She also mentioned she ran into Rain at the grocery store." Forest leans back on the wooden bench and crosses one leg over the other. "I guess she was not in good shape. High off something."

"Rain?" I raise an eyebrow. "Keegan's mom, right? Wow. I haven't heard her name in ages."

Forest looks at me over his coffee cup. "The one and only."

The coffee warms my belly. I never was privy to what the situation was with Rain, but I always knew there was some reason that Keegan spent every moment at our house. I don't know when it started, because I can't recall a time when it wasn't Forest and Keegan together. I was too young to understand.

As I got older, my mom shared a little bit, but it usually didn't involve any more details except that she struggled, and Keegan felt safer spending his time with us as he was growing up.

"What's Rain's deal?" I ask. "I mean, what kind of mom lets their kid spend every second at another family's house? Seems so odd."

"Well." Forest squirms and then shakes his head. "I feel like that's Keegan's story to tell. But let's just say it was messy."

Most nights during the week, Keegan was at our house. Forest had two twin beds in his room, and one was Keegan's. He was there at dinnertime, and almost every day, he took the bus home from school with Forest. When the basement at my parents' house was finished, Keegan moved to a room down there.

Forest stands up, starts stretching his muscles, and pulls his leg up behind him. "How's the hospital treating you? How are you getting on?"

He stares at me, and I stand up too. We start walking in the direction of his place. "I work constantly. And when I'm not working, I study, sleep, and dream of work. This being a doctor thing is life-consuming."

Forest nods, and his lips turn up in a smile. "I remember that. And I know it may not seem like it, but it does get better. Honestly, Luna, get through your first year. Are you still swearing off men?"

Forest grabs the empty cup out of my hands and throws it in the garbage. We walk a bit more in silence, before I finally say, "That's the plan."

"One must have really done a number on you." Forest continues to press on.

"Not really," I say. "But my last two boyfriends wanted me to upend my life to follow their dreams. Seb wanted me to move to a developing country and delay my residency while he did charity work. And then TJ asked me to give up my dreams of doing a residency at Presby and follow him home to Alabama. No thank you."

"You know you don't have to put your life on hold until you're out of a residency," Forest says. "That sounds like a miserable next five years."

"True," I say. "But I also have no plans on following a man and his dreams. If someone wants to be with me, they can follow my dreams. Let's not forget about my five-step plan."

Forest laughs. "I get it. The best thing I did during my first year was not let women distract me. And trust me, they tried."

"Yes." I shove Forest in the arm. "I'm sure they were lined up trying to date you."

He laughs. "Believe it or not, they were. And Presby isn't unlike any other workplace. It's a cesspool of interoffice romances."

"It can't be that bad." I glance at Forest, wide-eyed.

"Worse," he says, without hesitation. "Every doctor in the place once dated another resident, attending, or nurse. You name it."

"And what about you?" I stare at Forest, as he continues to look forward. "Who have you dated?"

"A few, unfortunately." He puts his face in his hands. "Have you worked with Lex, the emergency room nurse?"

"Actually, yes." I put my hands on my hips. "I met her recently."

"Well, she's the last person I dated. And it didn't work out, and she's made my life miserable ever since."

"Forest." I hit him on the arm. "No wonder she's always so cold toward me."

"Yeah, well." Forest playfully rubs his upper arm where I hit him. "She's pretty much told all of her nurse friends to stay away from me and has since become obsessed with Keegan. Like, she may keep a photo of him in her locker."

"This is all really good to know." I raise an eyebrow. "But people at the hospital are the only people we ever see."

True." Forest starts laughing. "And as long as we always talk before we date each other's friends, I promise your resident friends are safe with me."

"Yeah," I shake my head at him. "Let's use Kelsie as a cautionary tale."

Forest laughs. "Or we could use my medical school friend Joe. Your pick."

"Oh, I'd forgotten about him," I say. "Although it was hardly the same."

"I will never cross you again, Luna. I learned my lesson." Forest runs a hand through his sweaty hair and chuckles. "But honestly, I hope you'll take time to get acclimated before you date too seriously. I remember how hard the first year of residency is."

"I've sworn off men." I wrap my arm in his. "I find your entire gender clingy and a bit on the selfish side."

Forest winks at me. "That's my girl."

Chapter Seven

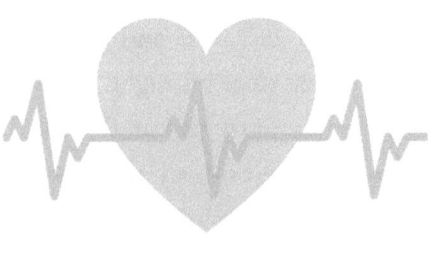

The Emergency Department seems to have two scenes. The first is the storm, and the second is the calm before the storm. When it's slow, we all stand around, trying to keep ourselves busy. I find myself constantly looking at the doors, waiting for the next person needing our help. It's an anticipatory anxiety that doesn't go away. And then there is the storm. And somehow, even after the waiting, no one ever seems to be fully prepared for it. Today has been one of the slower days.

Lately, I've been assigned to Dr. Lanson, and today, Raven is as well. We follow him down the long hallway, his two students, eager to learn everything he's willing to teach us. Myles walks toward us, holding several charts in his hand, his remaining hair standing up in all directions.

"What hour are you on?" Myles slows when he reaches us.

Raven and I look at each other, and I hold back a yawn. "Fourteen. You?"

He scrunches up his face and then rubs his eyes. "Sixteen. And I barely slept all night. There was a steady flow of people. I'm about to get cut, though."

"Please sleep for the both of us." Raven grips Myles' arm. "If I'm here much longer, I will turn back into a pumpkin, and no one wants to see that."

"Will do. It's been a day." Myles turns back one more time to look at us before walking off in the opposite direction.

"Okay, Dr. Oliver. Dr. Craik." Dr. Lanson stands with his arms folded over his chest, waiting for Raven and me. "There's been a shooting. The patient's stable but will need a bullet extraction."

We enter the space where an emergency room physician and team are assessing the male patient's vital signs. He's in distress with a gunshot wound, and the care team quickly works on him. The bullet entered through the back without an exit wound.

"Let's get him to CT," Dr. Lanson says as a nurse inserts an IV. "We need to see what we're dealing with."

Dr. Lanson has me contact the radiology department to schedule a CT, and the care team prepares the patient for surgery.

Dr. Lanson glances at us. "Who wants to scrub in?"

Our hands both shoot up at the same time, and he points to me. "Okay, Oliver. You're in. Craik, see if Dr. Parse can use you."

Raven lets out a defeated sigh and then leans into me. "He always chooses you."

"Not true," I whisper back. "My hand was a tenth faster than yours. That's it."

"Yeah. Keep telling yourself that." Raven rolls her eyes in my direction and then leaves the room.

Once in the operating room, I assist Dr. Lanson with inserting the chest tube, and we study the CT film. In medical school, when I did a surgery rotation, my time in the OR was usually spent looking at the back of the surgeon's head. I smile beneath my mask, happy that I'm finally at the table.

"A million-dollar wound," Dr Lanson says. "Look, Dr. Oliver. The bullet entered his lower back, traveled north, and got lodged in his rib, while somehow missing every major organ."

He opens up the patient and navigates to the bullet using fluoroscopy. I study the monitor, which is a map of the patient's insides, and when Dr. Lanson reaches the bullet, a surgical assistant hands him forceps for the extraction, and with precision, Dr. Lanson removes it. The intact bullet clanks against the metal bowl when Dr. Lanson places it in there. I can smell burning skin as he cauterizes around the wound, as the patient has some bleeding from where the bullet tunneled through his body. Dr. Lanson closes the patient up, and then the care team watches him in recovery.

Following the gunshot wound victim, a woman presents with a severed thumb from a cooking injury. We promptly treat her and stabilize the wound, and then the care team preps her for the vascular surgeon. Raven hasn't reappeared, so I end up getting some unexpected one-on-one training with Dr. Lanson. Before I have a chance to take a breath, I accompany him as he advises a patient on the general surgical floor about their hernia surgery that will occur later in the day.

By hour nineteen of my twenty-hour shift, I'm running on pure adrenaline and coffee. There's a lull in the action, and I go into an empty exam room and sit on the edge of the bed. I put my head in my hands, and rub my eyes, willing them to stay open.

"Hey." I look up to see Dr. Lanson, and he closes the curtain behind him. He massages his temples and then brushes his hair back. "Another long day."

I unclasp my hair, shake it out, and then run my fingers through it. At the end of my shifts, my head hurts from the tension of my ponytail. "It gets easier, right?"

Dr. Lanson barks a laugh. "I haven't figured out if it gets easier, or if we just fall so deeply in love with it that it feels like it does."

"So, there's hope?" I try to smile, but even my facial muscles are tired.

I sit up straighter, and my legs dangle off the edge of the exam bed. Dr. Lanson walks toward me. I take a long blink, and when I open my eyes again, he's even closer. I study him, in his scrubs, curly, dark chest hair peeking out, and his hair slicked back on his head.

"Please don't call me Dr. Lanson when it's only the two of us. That's my dad."

He moves between my dangling legs, and my breath catches in my chest. He puts his hand on my knee as if I'm a woman who consents to the touch. He opens the top drawer of the bed, pulls out gloves, and stuffs them in the front pocket of his scrubs. My body stiffens under the touch.

"It's Ian."

I glance at his hand, still touching me. I want to tell him to remove his hand, but instead, my mind flashes to the night I was attacked. I freeze, unable to articulate how uncomfortable I am.

"Luna." Ian's hand stays on my knee, and he's close enough to me that I can smell the coffee on his breath. "With a patient as large as our gunshot victim, don't be scared to go a little deeper with the chest tube."

"Yeah, okay." I nod, repeatedly.

"But I liked your confidence," he says.

"Yeah."

That's all I can say. My eyes move up to his, and I wonder if he's even aware of the placement of his hand. My brain starts to hurt as I think through all the options to put space between us.

"Dr. Lanson." I know the voice as soon as I hear it, and the curtain is thrown open. Dr. Lanson backs away from me as Keegan walks into the room.

Keegan's gaze meets mine first, and then he briefly glances at Ian before returning his attention to me. A sudden surge of adrenaline courses through my veins, and I hastily jump off the exam bed. Keegan scrutinizes me with his eyes before he clears his throat.

"I was paged. You have films you wanted me to look at?" Keegan folds his arms over his chest.

"Yes. Of course." Ian looks down at his pager. "Blunt force trauma to the chest."

Keegan nods and walks out of the room with Ian. I rush to the changing room, feeling like I need to shower. Tonight, the storms brewed from all directions. My mind spins with all the patients I saw and touched today, but I also can't stop thinking about Ian, as I process what just happened. I second-guess myself and wonder if I'm overreacting. I open my locker to grab my stuff and slam it closed, and then I sit on the bench, head between my legs, and take deep breaths.

The adrenaline I feel coming off a shift always takes me by surprise. It reminds me of my dad who coaches high school boys' basketball back home. After games, whether his team wins or loses, he paces the hallway of our home, studying stats, and waiting for his mind to shut off. That's how I feel after a shift at the hospital.

After several minutes, I change into my street clothes and force myself to stand. I've been at the hospital for twenty hours, and I need to get home, shower, and sleep. I glance at my phone, and Raven texted me over an hour ago letting me know that she was cut and heading home.

When I get outside into the evening darkness, my shoulders stiffen when I see Keegan standing there, watching the door, waiting for me. He stuffs a hand into the front pocket of his pants, while his other scrapes the sharp corners of his jaw.

"I figured you were finishing up, so I waited."

I pause but then walk forward. "I thought you had films to look at."

Keegan slowly blinks, never removing his gaze from me. He looks as tired as I feel. "I looked."

His voice is low, like he's trying to keep something between the two of us. I catch up with him, and we walk in the direction of my place. When he finds his stride, I have to take quick steps to keep up.

Even the sound of the ambulances headed toward the hospital, the horns honking at a car double-parked in front of a restaurant, or the line of people outside of the ice cream shop don't drown out the noise of my breaths, slowly going in and out.

I glance at Keegan who continues to look forward. "Are you going to say anything, or do you plan on walking me home in silence?"

Keegan's head slowly turns in my direction. "You don't like the silence?"

"I don't always mind it," I slow my pace and point at him. "But not when you're over there with those judgy eyes."

"I'm not judging you, Luna." Keegan stops walking and squares his body to mine. "I wanted to see if you're okay."

Someone behind me curses as they almost run into us as we block the sidewalk, and I can't find the words.

Keegan turns his head slightly to the side and says, "I was thinking about women in medicine. And how hard it must be for you, especially as a surgeon, because the field is so male-dominated."

Emotions of the day start to catch up with me. I cross my arms over my chest. "I'm so sick of men. You're everywhere. Almost every leadership position in this hospital is held by a man. I'm so tired of the entitlement of some of you."

"I agree." Keegan pulls his lips into a thin line and his chest expands. His blue eyes pierce into mine, but I refuse to get lost in them. "I'd avoid Dr. Lanson. As much as possible."

"There it is," I chuckle. "The judgment. You don't know what you saw. I did nothing wrong."

Keegan's hands abruptly leave his pockets, and he clenches them tightly into fists. Without a word, he begins to stride purposefully toward my apartment, and I follow, swallowing the surge of frustration that continues to bubble to the surface. I try to regulate my breathing, knowing that I need nothing more than to get inside my little apartment, where I can close my eyes, maybe have a good cry in the shower, and start fresh in the morning.

"You know how my dad died when I was ten?" Keegan's words surprise me so much that my head jerks in his direction.

"Vaguely," I say. "I was really young."

I look at him, but he continues to face forward. "He had picked me up early from school because we were planning to drive to the Twin Cities and go to a baseball game. We stopped home to pack our overnight bag, and he was taking forever, so I went into my parents' room to check on him, and he had collapsed. I called 911, and in the minutes it took them to arrive, I'd never felt more alone in my life."

The details are new to me, but not that his dad died. That was something I grew up knowing. But I've never heard Keegan speak about it.

"It seemed like it took forever for the ambulance to arrive, and I tried my best to give him CPR. I was so young. I didn't know what I was doing."

My eyes widen, and part of me has this overwhelming need to pull Keegan into a hug, but I don't. Keegan continues, "My dad was rushed to the hospital, but there was nothing they could do for him. My mom arrived shortly after the ambulance, but he was already gone. He had an aortic dissection. The best CPR in the world wouldn't have saved him."

We reach the door to my apartment building, and I lean back on the hard, brick surface, and it's cool against my flaming skin.

"Very few believed in me when I said I wanted to be a doctor. I was a small-town boy. But my dad was my why. Anytime I felt like giving up, I thought of him." Keegan takes a long blink, and a glow from a streetlamp catches between each one of his long, dark lashes.

"I'm sorry," I say, shaking my head. "I am. But I don't understand why you are telling me this. I've known you—"

"Luna." He says my name slowly, elongating every syllable. "We all have an answer to why we chose medicine. Remember yours."

"What?" I rub my eyes, and Keegan comes into greater focus. "You don't think I know why I'm here?"

"That's not what I'm saying." Keegan reaches toward me, and with two fingers, clasps them around my wrist. His hands are cool and comforting. "There are assholes like Ian Lanson everywhere. Insecure, entitled assholes. I've seen men like him step so far over the line, that they can no longer see the line."

Keegan stops talking and unclasps his fingers from my wrist. He looks down for a long beat and then glances back at me.

"I know you did nothing wrong. But don't let men like Ian Lanson ever make you question the fact that you deserve to be here. You belong. You are here because you earned it. Don't let anyone make you feel inferior."

"Okay, Eleanor Roosevelt," I say under my breath, and a boisterous laugh escapes Keegan, and he covers his mouth with a hand. I continue to look down at the pavement, because hot, wet, and tired tears start rolling down my cheeks without my consent, and I refuse to let Keegan see them. I wipe them away before looking up at him again.

"Kiddo." Keegan uses Forest's moniker for me. He lowers his face and speaks into my ear. His breath smells like mints, and it's so reassuring after smelling the horrid coffee on Ian's. I feel safe. "Everything always feels better after some sleep."

I squeeze my eyes, making sure no more tears are a threat to spill out. "You're right. I'm exhausted. I've been up for too many hours and am about to lose all of my shit, and if you stay for a minute longer, I'm going to use your sleeve as my snot rag. I'd suggest you leave immediately."

The corners of Keegan's mouth turn up. "You've earned your right to be here. Never forget that." Keegan kisses the top of my head, pausing a moment. His warm lips against my skin. He pushes me through the door and then walks in the direction of his apartment.

Chapter Eight

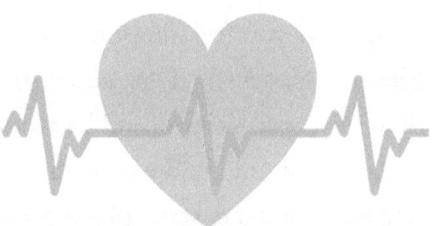

"How long have you been with your girlfriend?" Raven asks, sprawled out on the floor, a carton of Chinese food propped on her chest.

The three of us work such different hours these days, so when we are all home on the same night, we've been making it a habit to spend it together.

"Since high school." Myles stretches his legs across the couch, and forks noodles into his mouth. "And most of that time, it's been long distance."

Raven hands me a carton of noodles, and I spoon some onto my plate and study Myles. It's hard to know someone by their looks only, but one glance at Myles, and you know immediately that he's a kind person. Everything about him is unassuming. It's not surprising to either Raven or me when he shares that he has three sisters. He's disarming and has quickly become someone I trust.

"Since high school? That's a long time," I say. "Will she move to New York?"

Myles smiles as he starts scrolling through his phone. He shows me a picture of a ring, and I clap my hands together and then give Raven the phone, and she squeals.

"We've been together nearly a decade, and I know it seems weird that I'm only about to propose now, but Jules and I have talked about it, and she knew how important it was for me to get out of medical school and established in a residency program before we got engaged. She plans to move to New York in early June, once her teaching year is complete."

Myles moves to a sitting position. "And Jules isn't big on surprises. Neither am I. So, she knows it's coming. She told me some of the ring styles she likes. The only thing she doesn't know is exactly when I'll do it."

"And Jules is okay with the fact that you live with two women?" Raven raises her eyebrows and hands the phone back to Myles. "Attractive women, I may add."

"Raven." I kick my foot out. "Seriously."

Myles laughs. "It was definitely a discussion. But well, she trusts me, and financially, this place made the most sense, and we're trying to save money. Y'all will love her. She's great."

I put my plate down and rub my very full stomach. "When will we get to meet her?"

"We have a rule that we don't go more than two months without seeing each other. We're thinking the Fourth of July weekend."

"Oh, I love, love," Raven says, standing up. She grabs our plates and brings them to the kitchen. "I need to start putting myself out there more."

Raven continues. "And there are so many options. We need to start hanging out at George's more after our shifts to get to know the Presby staff."

"Yeah, just what you need." I stand and start helping Raven with the dishes. "Some complicated entanglement with a colleague."

"Oh, Luna." Raven lets out a sigh. "How are you not tempted at all by all the men in uniform?"

Myles comes into the kitchen and joins us. "Did I tell y'all I had coffee with Dr. Baldwin this morning? He is amazing. We set up a monthly coffee. Great connection, Luna. Thanks."

"That's awesome," Raven says. "Did he ask about me? Did I come up at all?"

My phone starts vibrating on the counter, and I dry my sudsy hands before picking it up.

"Hey, Forest. What's up?" I put the phone on speaker so I can continue to help with the dishes.

"Are you working Saturday evening?" Forest says the words quickly and then waits for my response."

"It depends. Why?"

"Luna." His voice is insistent. "You're either working, or you aren't."

"No. But I'm back on the clock early Sunday."

Forest sighs audibly into the phone. Raven turns off the faucet and then leans against the counter, listening to us. "I've got this thing, and my date bailed, and I have no time to find a new date."

"What's this thing?" I finish drying the last dish and hold the phone in front of me.

"It's a gala. The American Heart Association of New York is hosting, and Keegan bought a table, and I need a seat filler."

"You want me to be a seat filler?" Raven laughs in the background, and I quiet her. "I'm so flattered, Forest."

"Yes, Luna," he says. "The table wasn't cheap. And I thought you might enjoy it. It would be a great networking opportunity. What do you say?"

"A gala?" I lean back against the kitchen counter. "How fancy is this thing?"

"It's a black-tie event."

I laugh into the phone as I think about the clothes I moved from Minnesota to New York. Nothing is even close to black tie appropriate.

"Forest, I don't have an evening gown. Or anything resembling one."

"I figured," he says, "Which is why a new dress is on me. Pick out anything you want. Within reason."

Raven starts clapping her hands together and mouths the word makeover in my direction.

"What was that?" Forest asks.

"Nothing." I hold my finger up to my lips to quiet Raven, who looks more excited that I'm going to a gala than I am.

"And it's Saturday? As in, two days away?"

"Yep. It starts at 7:30. I'll pick you up."

"Fine," I finally say. "I'll let you know how much money you owe me after I go dress shopping."

"You're the best, Luna."

I go to respond, but Forest hangs up before I can.

"Obviously, you'll let me go shopping with you." Raven's entire body shakes in delight. "And also, your brother's voice is sexy. I need to see a photo of him."

I walk to my room but scroll through my phone until a picture of Forest comes up. It's from when he visited Minnesota during the holiday season. I hand the phone to Raven.

"You've got to be kidding me." Raven looks at me, then back at my phone, her eyes wide. "How have you been keeping your gorgeous brother away from me? If you don't want to go to the gala with him, I will gladly go in your place."

"I kind of feel like I should never introduce you to him." I grab a pillow from my bed and toss it at Raven.

She catches the pillow and laughs. "Wise decision. But seriously, I'm going to make sure you look fabulous for Saturday."

Chapter Nine

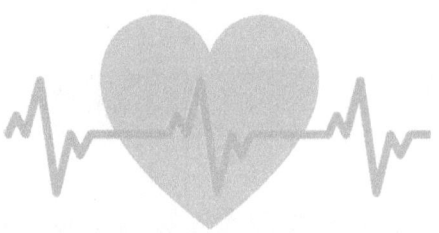

From: Keegan Baldwin <Keegan.Baldwin@med.cornell.edu
To: Luna Oliver <Luna.Oliver@umn.edu

Date: December 27

I was surprised when I met your parents at JFK, and you weren't with them. I was looking forward to showing you the city. Maybe next time.

From: Luna Oliver <Luna.Oliver@umn.edu
To: Keegan Baldwin <Keegan.Baldwin@med.cornell.edu

Date: December 30

My boyfriend invited me to go to Big Sky because his family rented a house there. Give my parents a hug for me.

From: Keegan Baldwin <Keegan.Baldwin@med.cornell.edu
To: Luna Oliver <Luna.Oliver@umn.edu

Date: January 1

Happy New Year, Luna.

On Saturday, Raven and I hit up several stores and finally found the perfect dress. Everything took so long and Forest will be here at 7:15, so I have less than an hour to shower and do my hair and makeup.

I decide to wear my hair down, because every day at work, all I do is put it in a messy bun. I blow dry it, then sit on the barstool in the kitchen and have Raven do my makeup.

"I'm going to give you a smokey eye." She pulls out different shades of eyeshadow from a makeup bag. "Make the blue pop against your brown hair. Also, I never noticed all your little freckles on your face."

"I hate them," I say, grabbing the shade of eye shadow she's chosen for me. "Remember, less is more. I'm not a big makeup person."

"The sign of good makeup is to make sure it looks like you aren't wearing a ton. I've got you, Luna."

I check my phone and have a message from Forest that he'll be here in twenty minutes—and he sent it ten minutes ago.

"I've chosen a golden rose for your lips. Your pouty lips are fabulous." Raven stands back. "You're so lucky. You're going to a fancy gala, and I'll be sitting here doing nothing."

"I should have offered you up for the gala." I smack my lips together. "I'm in the mood to put on jammies and watch mindless reels."

Raven claps her hands together as she stares at me. "You are my masterpiece, Luna."

I don't even bother looking at myself in the mirror. Instead, I run to my bedroom where my kelly-green dress hangs in the closet. The fabric is so silky against my skin, and Forest is going to have sticker shock when he knows how much it cost, but the moment I tried this dress on, I knew it was the one.

The slender straps of the dress delicately trace the curves of my shoulders, while the length flows down my body, culminating in a dramatic slit up one leg, revealing the perfect amount of skin. The luxurious fabric clings to my body like a second skin, its silky texture caresses every inch of my frame. The delicate material and form-fitting design make me feel confident and beautiful.

As I hurry to the bathroom, my curling iron beckons me with a warm glow. My reflection in the mirror takes my breath away as I admire the masterpiece that Raven created.

Subtle curls frame my face and perfectly complement the dress, adding a touch of playfulness and whimsy to the overall look. I can't help but smile at the sight of myself. Well done, Raven.

My phone dings, and it's Forest, letting me know he's here.

"Don't forget your clutch," Raven says as I exit the bathroom and head for the door. "Luna, you look gorgeous."

"Thank you for everything, Raven. Don't wait up." I wink at her before I leave.

When I get outside, Forest is standing against the car, and he even does a double take. "Well, shit, Luna. You look. . ." His voice trails off, and he clears his throat. "Like an actual woman. I don't like it."

"Umm, thanks." I slug him on the shoulder and look down at my outfit. "I hope you like the dress, Forest, 'cause this one cost you a pretty penny."

The car takes us to a high-rise building downtown. We arrive and a stream of people get here at the same time and we all work our way inside. We reach the elevator and go with the group to the thirty-third floor. When we get up there, we walk into a large ballroom, decked out in American Heart Association signage. Forest checks in and hands me a name tag. What woman would wear this hideous thing over an evening gown? I decide to slip it into my clutch.

"We're table nine," he says and then waves to someone in the distance. "I need to go to say hi to someone I see from medical school. Will you go to the bar and grab us a couple of drinks? I'll only be a minute."

Forest rushes off before I can say anything. I know I'm nothing more than a seat filler for the expensive table, but I don't want to stand alone all night either. I go to the bar, order two drinks, and put one of them on table nine. I look around the room and decide to walk over and look at the silent auction items.

Tables are lined up, and as I move to the right, the auction items become higher stakes. Someone approaches from behind, and I turn to look. Keegan. He rapidly blinks when he registers that it's me.

"Luna." Keegan stares at me. His gaze starts on my face, and my skin pebbles when his eyes rake down my entire body. He lifts his hand, then drags it down his face.

But my eyes are drawn to him also, and I can feel myself succumbing to the magnetic pull of his presence. Keegan Baldwin looks hypnotic in his impeccably tailored tuxedo, which accentuates every contour of his sculpted physique. His broad shoulders and muscular thighs are emphasized by the form-fitting garment, and I can't help but feel a rush of something I can't quite articulate course through my veins. Tuxedos were made for men like Keegan. I try to avert my gaze, but I'm drawn back to him like an atom to an electron.

"Keegan." I force my stare from his body to his eyes. I rapidly blink, and then start fanning myself with my clutch because it suddenly feels like it's one million degrees in here.

"Forest dragged me here. I guess his date bailed, or at least that's his story. So, he told me he'd buy me a dress, and I hate dressing up, and I have so much makeup on, and my hair, and yeah, anyway." The words vomit out of my mouth.

He stares at me, mouth open, and then shakes his head back and forth quickly.

"You look…" But he doesn't finish his sentence. He pulls his gaze off me and glances at the table with the auction items and points. "Well, I'm happy you were able to come. Will you bid on anything?"

I turn my attention from Keegan and stare at the picture of a beautiful, large home on a beach in Montauk.

"You know residents don't make any money." Half of Keegan's mouth goes up in a smile. "I'm living on coffee and ramen noodles currently."

"Yes. More healthy choices you are making." I don't think I imagine his eyes moving to my lips. "But if you were going to bid on something, does anything catch your eye?"

"This house in Montauk doesn't look so bad," I say. "I've never been, and now that I'm in New York, I'm so close, but so far away. But that house, Keegan. Look at that house. The thought that a short drive could get me out of this concrete jungle, if only for a couple of days."

Keegan pushes the paper toward me, his hand brushing against mine, sending a jolt of electricity coursing through me. I need to quit lying to myself. Keegan is gorgeous. Perhaps he was always too big for Cherry, so he kept himself invisible. But he's blossomed in every way. He's done everything he said he was going to do, and now he glows and is magnetic.

I liked him better when I wasn't imagining him roaming his large hands up my legs, bringing my dress up, lifting me onto this table, and pressing.

"You should bid on it." Keegan leans down so he can speak closer to my ear, and his breath pebbles my skin with goosebumps. I look up at him and he winks, and for a moment, I forget how to breathe.

My eyes fixate on the glossy photo in front of me, my mind already drifting away to the far-off world of sun-kissed beaches and endless blue skies. The image captures the essence of luxury and relaxation, with a sprawling beachfront home nestled in the heart of Montauk, overlooking the pristine ocean.

But it's the promise of the weekend ahead that truly makes me continue to stare at the photo and dream. The thought of escaping the city and spending lazy days lounging on the sand, sipping cocktails, and immersing myself in a world of beauty and relaxation. But I'm a resident. There will be no winning a weekend in Montauk for me.

"And," Keegan continues, "the money goes to charity, after all."

"True," I say slowly. And to Keegan's point, only the highest bid gets the house and is on the hook for the payment. I can come in low and make sure I don't win. It doesn't hurt to bid, right?

"I'll bid if you do." I hold the slip of paper against my chest like I'm guarding something precious.

Keegan steps closer to me, his presence enveloping me like a warm embrace. He reaches down for a piece of paper, and I'm hit with an intoxicating scent that sends my senses reeling. It's a heady mix of camphoraceous with a soft soap.

"Deal, Luna Oliver." He grabs a pen and turns his back from me just slightly so I can't see the numbers he jots down. "If you win, you need to host a Fourth of July weekend and invite me. And if I win, I'll do the same."

I turn my back to him too, but we're so close that I can feel the heat of his body up against my backside. I write my name on the paper and think about how much to bid. I wasn't joking when I said residents don't make much, and it is expensive living in New York, even if the rent is reasonable due to the building being hospital subsidized. But this is also a high-ticket item, and realistically, no amount I put down will get me this house for the weekend.

After some thought, I write down my number. Three thousand, five hundred dollars. High enough to be respectable, but low enough that it won't have any shot of winning. Because I don't actually have that much money lying around. I peek my head over my shoulder to look at Keegan, just as he's turning to face me.

He slowly takes his piece of paper and folds it, and I do the same with mine. I dramatically put my paper in the bowl, and Keegan's lips turn up in a smile.

"Good luck." Keegan reaches his hand out to shake mine. It envelops mine, and my breath hitches in my chest. "And to you," I say. He looks down at our clasped hands, and realization seems to spread across his face before he drops it.

"There you are." A voice rings out behind me, and I turn to look, as a woman walks up to us and stands at Keegan's side.

She eyes me and puts her arm around Keegan's waist and squeezes him.

"Hi." She continues to study me like she would a painting. "I'm Dr. Elise Smith."

Keegan clears his throat. "Elise is a Congenital Heart Pediatric Surgeon at Presby. Elise, this is Dr. Luna Oliver. She's a general surgery resident at Presby. She's also Forest's sister."

"You're Forest's sister?" Elise's eyes light up and a look of amusement spreads across her face. She holds her hand out to shake mine. "It's great to finally meet you. He said you'd be coming tonight. He and I have been friends for ages."

I smile but can't focus. Instead, I study Elise's proximity to Keegan, but his eyes never leave me.

Someone on stage with a microphone asks us all to take our seats, as the presentation and dinner portion of the evening is about to start. Keegan and Elise also walk to table nine. Forest is already there, and I take a seat next to him. Keegan and Elise sit near each other on the other side of the round table. Forest introduces me to the other people. A married couple, both cardiologists. Graham and Layla. And then directly next to me, another couple, Ford, also a cardiologist, and his wife, Hadeel, a trauma surgeon.

Food is served during the program. And a patient tells their story, which is a great reminder of why we became doctors in the first place. When I glance across the table, Keegan stares back at me. As he tilts his head, a lock of his chestnut brown hair falls over his forehead. I used to find his intensity annoying, but now, it makes me curious and draws me in. His gaze is like a laser beam, cutting through all the distractions and noise of the world around us. And when he looks at me, I feel like I'm the only person in the room, even if he is seated next to his date for the evening.

When dessert is served, someone comes back on stage. "We've been busy tallying our silent auction totals all night, and we're finally ready to announce tonight's winners."

She goes through all of the items, starting from lowest to highest. A signed baseball from a Yankees player I've never heard of. Tickets to the Met, a Broadway show, and the list goes on. I sip my white wine and let it warm my body.

"A weekend in Montauk," The lady says into the microphone, and I sit taller in my chair. "A gorgeous home on the ocean, with the most picturesque views you've ever seen."

She looks down at the clipboard she holds. "And the winner at twenty-three thousand dollars is Dr. Keegan Baldwin."

When I hear his name, I raise my brow, and my mouth hangs open. He looks at me, but only briefly, and then Elise pulls him into a hug. He won. He actually won. Not only that, but he donated twenty-three thousand dollars for a weekend. Two nights in a house—for all that money.

"Wow," Forest says, bringing me back to reality. "I better be invited out this weekend. I'll request it off now." Forest laughs, and I can only shake my head.

Yes, it's a good cause, but twenty-three thousand dollars is not something I could just donate. The woman goes to the next auction item, but Keegan glances at me. Finally, I give him a smile and shrug.

We all work our way to the door when the event wraps up. Men and women in their most elegant clothes are herded into the elevators because no one cares where we go, but we can't stay here.

"I can't believe you have that house for a weekend in Montauk." Elise loops her arm in Keegan's, and he stiffens. "How do I get on the short list of people you'll invite?"

"Seriously, Keegan," Forest says. "How does one get on this list?"

I don't say anything, but I secretly wonder if he meant it when he said I would be part of the group. He probably wasn't serious because of all the people he could invite, I don't think I'd make any list.

Keegan, Elise, Forest, and I stand outside on the warm summer night, and Forest looks at me and yawns. "I'm headed to Chelsea. Are you fine getting home without me?"

My mouth opens to answer, but before I can, Keegan jumps in. "I'm headed to the Upper East Side. I can share a car with Luna."

"I'm headed to the Upper East side too, between seventy-seventh and seventy-eight. Is that close to you?" Elise asks.

"We're both going around fifty-ninth," Keegan says before I can respond and let her know we can all share a cab.

"Okay, it's settled then," Forest says. He hugs me and pulls his phone out to get a car. "Tonight was really fun. Thanks for having us, Keegan."

"Goodnight, Keegan." Elise lifts onto her toes and hugs him. She then turns to me. "It was nice meeting you, Luna."

"Yes. You as well." Elise then heads off in a different direction, right as Forest's car arrives.

Keegan and I are left standing on the sidewalk, as people continue to file out of the building who were all at the gala, talking loudly, and deciding if they'll call it a night or head somewhere else in the city.

He shows me his phone, and it says it will take at least twenty minutes for a car to arrive. "Let's walk a few blocks. We'll have a better chance to catch a car. There are too many people here."

I nod in agreement, and Keegan and I walk in silence. The farther away we get, the quieter the street becomes. My feet ache from the uneven sidewalks, and I start regretting my fashionable, but impractical, heels.

Keegan stops in front of an ice cream shop and looks at me. "I could go for some ice cream. You?"

My stomach growls. Our dinner was good, but the serving sizes were on the pretentiously small side.

"I can always go for ice cream." I stop in front of the bright light of the ice cream shop, happy to not be walking more than anything else. "Have you been to the Icy New Yorker by me? It is literally the best."

We order through the outside window. Keegan gets cherry, and I go with mint chocolate chip. We then walk to a bench, and my feet thank me. I slip out of my heels, pull a foot onto my lap, and start rubbing it.

Keegan turns to me on the bench. "Since when do you wear heels?"

"I tried on my Chucks with this dress, but they didn't look right." I squeeze my foot and dig a thumb into my heel.

"You're hilarious." Keegan leans back against the bench, his gaze on me. The corners of his lips twitch like he's trying hard not to smile. "You just look so grown up."

"Well." I push his arm. "I'd like to think I am grown up."

The air is thick with the sounds of the city, the rumble of the traffic, and the chatter of the pedestrians providing a constant backdrop to our silence. Keegan hands me his cone and loosens his bow tie. It's like watching a butterfly emerge from its cocoon, each movement slow and deliberate. His fingers deftly work at the knot until it finally gives way.

He reaches up and unbuttons the top of his shirt, revealing a hint of his chest. He breathes out heavily, and it's like the tension melts away from his shoulders. He stands up and removes his tuxedo coat, revealing a crisp white shirt. I find myself holding my breath as I watch him, transfixed by the way his muscles ripple under his skin. These new intrusive thoughts about Keegan overwhelm me.

Then he sits, and I hand him his ice cream cone, which is close to dripping. He takes a long lick, and then rests his arm on the back of the bench. "I meant it."

Confusion spreads across my face. "Meant what?"

"A weekend in Montauk." Keegan's tongue darts out of his mouth as he wets his lips. "I mean if that isn't too boring for you. Because the last thing I'd want to do is bore you, Luna."

"Keegan," I say, covering my face with my hand. "You are never going to let me forget saying that, are you?"

"Not likely." Keegan finishes his cone and turns his body toward me. "I need to find a way to prove to you that I can be fun."

I wrinkle my nose. "Do you think you'll have time between all your doctoring and Mathletics practice?"

Keegan's head rolls back, and he belly laughs. "You do realize I've changed in the past twelve years since leaving Cherry, right?"

"No more Mathletics, you're saying?" I smile, lean my elbow against the bench, and prop my head up. "Because you'll need a lot of time to change my mind about you. I've got a lot of years of bias working against you."

"Wow." Keegan nods, but smiles, and with every word, we've managed to inch closer together on this bench and now, our knees are almost touching. "You've always been my toughest critic, Luna Oliver."

"Well." I bite my bottom lip to suppress my smile. "This new Keegan who wears fancy clothes, grew all these muscles, and has perfected mysterious and intense looks from across the room may fool a lot of people, but you aren't fooling me."

Keegan's mouth falls open with amusement.

"And just so we're clear." I tap my bottom lip, aware that I should have quit talking about eight sentences ago. "I have not noticed your muscles. At all. But when you were young, you were so tall and gangly, and. . ." I bite my lip, forcing myself to stop talking.

Keegan puts his hand on my arm and smiles. I don't think I imagine that somehow, we've managed to move so close together, that I can practically feel his breath on me. His hand is so warm against my upper arm.

"Luna," Keegan says, tilting his head slightly. I'm torn between needing to know what he wants to say and being too scared to hear whatever is going through his mind, so I don't let him continue.

"Elise seems really nice." When I say the words, Keegan's hand drops from my arm. "We could have all shared a cab. We were going in the same general direction. And wow. A congenital pediatric heart surgeon. She must be brilliant too."

Keegan backs away from me. "Elise is nice. She went to medical school with Forest."

I slip my shoes on and stand. "Are you two, you know?"

"Friends." Keegan stands up too. He releases a deep breath, and I can't help but feel like I've said something wrong. "We should probably get a car."

We wait at a street corner, and a car arrives. Keegan opens the door for me and then slides in the backseat beside me. He gives the driver my address.

I look down at my gown, the long slit to my thigh, and Keegan's leg pressing against mine. When I glance at him, he's staring but then quickly shakes his head and looks away.

The car stops, and we're here. Keegan gets out and holds the door open for me, and I slide through his side. He walks me to the door of my building and tucks his hands into the pockets of his tuxedo pants.

"Thanks for making sure I got home." My heart thumps in my chest. "And for the ice cream. Oh, and a weekend in Montauk."

One of my dress straps escapes my shoulder, and before I can adjust it, Keegan reaches his hand up, puts it in place, and squeezes my shoulder.

"Hopefully the ride back to your place didn't utterly bore you." Half of Keegan's mouth goes up in a smile.

"It wasn't the worst," I say, holding my clutch close to me.

Keegan nods. "Let me know if I need to pull some strings to make sure you get off the Fourth of July weekend. I know Thomas Parse well."

"I'll do what I can." I take a deep breath. "Who else will you ask to come? Forest of course. And I assume Elise."

Keegan narrows his eyes and adjusts the tuxedo coat that's draped around his shoulder. "Why would I do that?"

"I know you said you're just friends," I say. "But it's obvious she's into you."

"No," Keegan says. "It's not like that. Not with her."

Relief builds in me for no good reason, because even though he isn't with Elise, that little fact changes nothing for me. I decide I don't care that I'm on a dirty New York sidewalk, and I lean down, and take my shoes off, losing several inches of height.

He looks down at my bare feet and then shakes his head. "Did you know that in a recent study, there were over thirty-thousand different types of fecal bacteria found on New York sidewalks?"

The moment he says it, I start laughing. "There he is. The boy from Cherry I remember so well."

My laugh seems to surprise him, as he jumps at the sound. I put my hand on his arm and smile. "Goodnight, Keegan. Thanks again for getting me home."

He watches me go into my building, and I get into the elevator, with my dirty, bare feet.

Chapter Ten

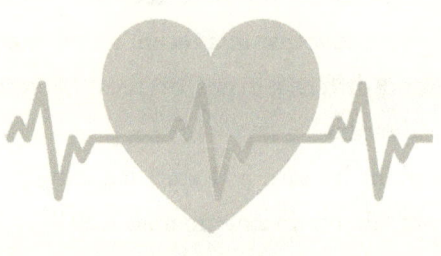

Everyone in the city seems to be in the emergency room today. There's hardly a bed available, and I've been on my feet for six hours already without a break. A code blue is called through the speakers, and Dr. Parse turns to me. I haven't seen Dr. Lanson since the knee-touching incident. When I came to work the next day, I was informed that he'd been reassigned to other residents, and I've been mostly with Dr. Parse ever since.

"Dr. Oliver, follow me."

A man lies on the table with no pulse, and the machines buzz out in all directions. Dr. Parse rushes to his side, as medical staff try to stabilize the patient.

"He's in V-Fib," Dr. Parse calls out. "Dr. Oliver, grab the paddles."

Upon administering a single shock, the patient achieves a normal sinus rhythm. A woman, who looks to be about my mom's age, cries in the corner, and her sobs reverberate through the room until a nurse removes her. Dr. Parse gets his stethoscope out and studies the EKG.

"Do you hear that, Dr. Oliver?" His eyes meet mine, and I step closer.

"Yes," I say through a deep exhale. "I hear a fourth sound."

"Okay," he says. "What do you suggest we do?"

"Let's run some labs and get the patient in for an echo."

"You heard the doctor," Dr. Parse says, and everyone sprints into action.

I follow the patient into the ultrasound room. He's stable but heavily sedated. The tech puts gel on the transducer, and when the heart comes up on the monitor, the sound of it beating echoes out.

A tech comes into the room and hands us the labs. Dr. Parse pages the on-call cardiologist to look at the films, and then Forest walks into the room.

He studies the screen and points. "It looks like hypertrophic cardiomyopathy, and there is no outflow from the left ventricle."

Forest looks at me and Dr. Parse. "Dr. Oliver, go talk to his mom and make sure his records are sent our way. I need to examine the tests further, but it looks like he's in advanced heart failure."

I locate the patient's mom, still sitting in the corner of the room we have recently transferred her son from. She sits in a chair, her head tucked into her hands, and her chest visibly quivering.

"Hi," I say, and she looks up at me. Her face is blotchy, and her eyes are red-rimmed and swollen. "Are you Noah Anderson's mom?"

"This can't be happening. Not again." Her face is pale, with black drips of mascara in vertical lines down her face. "He was playing soccer with a friend in our backyard and just went down. Like a ton of bricks."

"We're going to need his medical records. Do you have a history of any heart disease in the family? Sudden cardiac death?"

She stands up. "His dad died at thirty-five. Cardiac arrest."

I nod. "We're doing everything we can to keep your son comfortable and to get some answers. We sent him for a Cardiac MRI and then will review his films. I'm going to come find you as soon as we have a clearer picture."

Mrs. Anderson lets out a desperate sob, and I rush out of the room and head down to where he's getting the MRI. When I walk into the imaging room, Keegan, Forest, and Dr. Parse study the films.

"You were unfortunately right, Dr. Oliver." Keegan glances at Forest. "His left ventricle is barely pumping blood."

Dr. Parse looks at me. "Did you talk to his mom?"

"Yes," I say. "His charts are being sent over, but he hasn't been diagnosed with any heart disease up until this point. The only other significant history is that his dad died of cardiac arrest at the age of thirty-five."

"That's a sick heart. We need to get him on the transplant list immediately," Keegan says as he once again looks at the films. "His heart isn't going to last until there's a match though."

Dr. Parse turns to Keegan. "Can we put him on ECMO?"

Keegan shakes his head. "He'll never get off of it. He needs a heart."

I look between Keegan, Forest, and Dr. Parse. "Is medication an option?" I ask.

"If this was caught earlier, maybe. His heart is too sick for a septal myectomy too." Keegan shakes his head.

Keegan glances at me. "Have the operating room prepped and page the VAD rep."

Keegan and Forest rush out of the room, and I get into action by calling down to the OR to get it prepped. Dr. Parse and I get the team ready and have them page the rep and ask someone to update his mom.

We arrive at the operating room at the same time as Keegan. He looks at me. "Do you want to scrub in?"

"Really?" I nod vigorously. "If there's room. Sure."

He then looks at Dr. Parse. "Dr. Parse, you in?"

We go to the prep room to wash up. I watch Keegan as his dark hair vanishes under his surgical cap, and his face disappears under his mask. I put mine on too. A tech wraps us in our surgical gowns and then slides our gloves on.

When we get into the room, anesthesia has already been started, and the patient is intubated. Keegan makes about a three-inch incision on the left side of the patient's body. He looks up at me, and all I can see are his big blue eyes.

"I'm going to do a thoracotomy. The left ventricular assist device is only a bridge to transplant. Our patient is going to need a new heart, and it's challenging to do a sternotomy when one has already been done, so I want to leave him with a virgin chest for whoever puts in his new heart someday."

His voice is low and calm as he teaches. The room is silent as everyone listens to the brilliant Dr. Baldwin as he takes time to walk us through each step of the surgery. The surgical light he wears on his head points in the direction of the incision, and he starts putting a lead through and watches the patient's heart on the screen.

"The VAD," he continues, "Is going to help his ventricles until we can get him a heart. It will assist the heart to pump oxygenated blood to the body."

Keegan holds up the device for me to see. "The impeller within the pump spins thousands of times a minute, resulting in continuous blood flow. Not all surgeons like to use VADs, but it can buy someone time in situations like this and will get our patient out of the hospital while he waits for a heart."

He gets the device in the right location and continues to look at the screen. He screws it in place, and the left ventricle of our patient's heart starts beating normally.

"When he gets a new heart, they'll do a sternotomy, and the device will be removed along with the sick heart."

Keegan's voice is soothing. It has a gentle and reassuring quality to it, and I immediately feel at ease. Even as he performs the delicate task of placing a device on a man's heart, his voice remains calm and composed, radiating a sense of confidence and professionalism.

As I watch him work, I am struck by the precision and skill of his hands. Every movement is deliberate and measured, as he dexterously threads the lead to the device with the utmost care and attention to detail. His hands seem almost weightless as they move effortlessly.

After checking the settings on the VAD, Keegan observes as I help close the patient up. When I'm done, Keegan checks my work and then walks out of the room. Dr. Parse follows, so I do too.

We remove our surgery gear and throw everything in the hamper. Keegan looks over Dr. Parse's head and toward me. "Would you like to speak to the patient's mom with me?"

"Yeah." I nod. "Of course."

"Good work today, Dr. Oliver," Dr. Parse says, patting Keegan's back, then mine, before he walks out.

The elevator doors glide open, and we step inside, standing side by side. Warmth emanates from his body. In this confined space, the air around us seems to vibrate with a quiet intensity.

My eyes stay glued onto Keegan, and he turns to me, and a faint smile flickers across his lips. His eyes soften, and for a moment, it's like there is no one else in the world but the two of us.

"Thanks for letting me scrub in for that." I finally break the silence from my thoughts.

"You did great in there, Luna. I always knew you'd make an excellent surgeon. Maybe you shouldn't discount cardiothoracic."

The elevator door opens, and I follow him to the waiting room.

"I don't think so," I say quietly. "But it was fascinating getting to observe your work. But I think I'm going to avoid the heart at all costs. That was intense."

When we reach the patient's mom, Keegan does all of the talking and I observe. Mrs. Anderson looks both relieved and distraught. Her son's life was saved, but she also hears the difficult news that he needs a new heart. Keegan's voice is soft when he delivers the message and I think of how many times he needs to talk to the loved ones of the patients he both saves and those who die. This is where I want to shine too. As surgeons, we can't always control the outcome, but we can control the compassion we give.

"Your son is in the ICU, but you should be able to visit him soon." Mrs. Anderson reaches her hand out and squeezes Keegan's, and we walk away.

We both see Dr. Lanson standing down the hallway, and Keegan says to me. "Good work today, Dr. Oliver." He then heads in a different direction.

Dr. Lanson raises an eyebrow when our eyes connect, and I glance at my watch. I'm now on my eleventh hour of this shift.

"Not all first years get to scrub into a VAD surgery with a cardiothoracic surgeon." He narrows his eyes. "Dr. Baldwin must like you a lot."

I shrug. "I'm not going the cardiac route, but it was so educational to get to witness."

We turn down another hallway. "Interesting, the attention he's paying you."

Luckily, I don't have to respond, because the emergency room door swings open with our next life to save. And instead of feeling panic about the latest trauma coming our way, I'm relieved that I won't have to answer Dr. Lanson's questions.

Chapter Eleven

From: Luna Oliver <Luna.Oliver@umn.edu
To: Keegan Baldwin <Keegan.Baldwin@med.cornell.edu

Date: February 11

Hey, Keegan. Just checking in. I haven't heard from you in so long. Everything good?

From: Keegan Baldwin <Keegan.Baldwin@med.cornell.edu
To: Luna Oliver <Luna.Oliver@umn.edu

Date: February 12

Hey, Luna. All is good here. But really busy.

My parents arrive in New York today, and after my long shift at the hospital, I don't have time to go home and change, so instead, I throw on my workout clothes that I wore to the hospital and head to Forest's apartment where we're all having dinner.

The doorman buzzes up to Forest's apartment, and then I wait in the narrow but bright entryway. A few minutes later, Keegan comes out of the elevator.

"Keegan." I raise my eyebrow.

He scratches his face and then holds the elevator door open for me. "Forest wasn't convinced your parents would be able to find their way to his place, so he went to the airport to meet them."

I glance at my watch. "Why did he tell me to be here at seven then? I could have gone home and showered or changed into something presentable."

Keegan looks at me and then shrugs. "Why did Forest tell me to be here at six, and then leave five minutes after I arrived to head to the airport?"

"Forest." I shake my head. "How do we put up with him?"

We get into Forest's apartment, and it's spotless like always, thanks to his cleaners, and not because of anything he does. I understand why he wanted to move to Chelsea, even if it is farther from the hospital. The apartment is light and airy, and the neighborhood is cute with shops underneath his building.

"He invited us all here for dinner. Is he going to cook when he gets here?" I look through the fridge, and there isn't much. The options seem to be yogurt, moldy cheese, or green olives.

Keegan drags the palm of his hand down his face. "I was thinking that. And knowing Forest, he'll order takeout, after we spend thirty minutes agreeing on a place. And then it will take at least an hour for the food to get here, which means your poor parents aren't going to eat until at least nine."

"Can we admit that I'm the better Oliver?" I put my hands on my hips. "You're too good to be his friend. Get out while you can. Save yourself. You're better than this."

"There was never any question that you're the better Oliver," Keegan says, no hint of sarcasm in his expression. "But who would keep Forest alive and well if I didn't stick around?"

He then pulls his phone out of his back pocket and glances at it. "We could go to the store and get something to cook. We have time."

Keegan and I end up at the corner market. He rolls the cart down the narrow aisles and stops and grabs steaks. When Keegan passes by people, I notice the way women check him out. He's taller than almost everyone and his body is perfectly proportionate. His big, blue eyes are a contrast against his olive complexion.

"I make a pretty decent salad," I say, tearing my eyes off of him, as I throw ingredients in the cart.

"We could do loaded baked potatoes." Keegan tosses a bag into the cart. "And your mom will want a gin and tonic for sure."

"And your dad will want Bud Light." Keegan puts a six-pack into the cart, then puts it back and grabs a twelve-pack.

"Forest owes us," I say.

We check out, and while Keegan bags the food, I slip my card into the reader before he has a chance to. Keegan puts his hand on mine and tries to force his card in, but I check him with my body. He lets out a sigh when he realizes there is nothing he can do, as I've already paid.

When we get back to Forest's apartment, they still aren't there. I clean the potatoes and put them in the oven, I crack open a beer, my first Bud Light since I was a senior in high school stealing my dad's to drink at the quarry. I start making my salad. Keegan gets out a large platter and seasons the steaks. He must have known Forest wouldn't have anything at his place, so he grabbed that too.

"Have you been to the rooftop?" Keegan turns to me as we work side by side in the small kitchen. "It's where the shared grills are."

"No." I grab a beer for Keegan and follow him to the elevators where we go to the roof.

As I step out onto the rooftop, I am struck by the expansive surface that stretches out before me. It's a wide-open space, with multiple eating areas and several grills scattered throughout. The silence is deafening, and we have the rooftop all to ourselves. The beauty of Central Park is spread out before us like a lush, green carpet, its towering trees starkly contrasting the surrounding concrete below.

Keegan heads over to one of the grills, and I make my way to the railing. Leaning against it, I gaze out at the stunning views of the city, and a sense of awe and gratitude wash over me. It's hard to believe that I get to live in such an amazing city, with all of this beauty and excitement at my fingertips.

With a deep breath, I close my eyes, allowing the warmth of the sun to caress my face. The sounds of the city fade away, and I am lost in the moment, completely and utterly content. Breathing in through my nose, I take in the scent of the late summer flowers, savoring the purity of the moment. Then, with a long exhale, I let go of all my worries and doubts, feeling lighter and freer than I have in a long time.

The railing shifts under my arms, and when I look to my side, Keegan leans on it. He looks at me. "Breathtaking."

"It is." I hold his gaze, and he's looking at me and not the scenery around us.

"Did you notice all the women checking you out at the grocery store?" I say as Keegan tilts his head, studying me. "It's like they'd never seen a man pushing a shopping cart before."

"I don't notice things like that." Keegan blinks and then grabs the railing.

"You should," I say. "You've apparently become quite the catch since the last time I saw you."

Dark crimson spreads up Keegan's neck until it reaches his face. "I don't know about that."

"You're a cardiothoracic surgeon. You cook. You have muscles." I grab his arm playfully, then pull away. "Sorry, I can't help but sputter off embarrassing things at all times."

"Don't change," Keegan says. "You saying embarrassing things is one of my favorite things about you."

He flips the steaks and cuts into one of them, and it's the perfect medium pink. Keegan takes a drink from the beer I brought for him.

When the steaks are finished, we go back down to Forest's apartment, and I set the table. We're only there for a few minutes, when the door swings open, and my mom, dad, and Forest walk in.

When my dad sees me, he hurries toward my direction and pulls me into a hug. "Luna. Look at you."

Then my mom finds me, squeezes my shoulder, and cups my face. "My Luna. My moon child. My beautiful girl." She pulls me into an embrace.

She then sees Keegan. My mom is not a tall woman, and she has to stand on her toes to put her hands on his face. She wipes away a tear, and they wrap each other in a hug. "My beautiful Keegan."

Forest looks around, and his eyes register on the food. "You guys cooked?"

"I wasn't in the mood for moldy cheese and green olives." I swat his shoulder. "It was Keegan's idea."

Forest plops down on a chair. "I was planning on takeout."

"Well, isn't this a good option too?" My dad looks at the food, and I hand him a beer.

My mom starts looking in the drawers. "It is so wonderful to all be together."

"We had a long drive to the Twin Cities," my dad says, in his Minnesota accent thick, with every syllable emphasized. "And then the plane ride. A beer has never tasted so good."

Keegan hands my mom her drink. "Oh, Keegan. Bless your heart. This drink has my name written all over it."

"Are you three getting together regularly?" My mom asks. "And Keegan. Forest. Are you guys taking good care of Luna?"

"We get together for meals," Forest says, and then puts me in a headlock, messing up my hair, until I swat him away. "And I'm making sure Luna stays out of trouble."

"That's so great." My mom takes her palms and pats her eyes. "I can't tell you how I feel seeing you three together. My three babies."

We dish up and sit at the table. My dad grabs another beer and looks out the window. "I don't know how you kids can live somewhere this noisy and with this many people. You couldn't pay me enough money to call New York home."

"I love it so far." I cut into my steak. "I can disappear in the sea of people. The anonymity is freeing."

All eyes are on me, and then my mom drops her fork. "Luna. You are too thin. You're probably not eating enough. And you look so tired."

"Luna scrubbed into one of my surgeries this week." Keegan's eyes meet mine, cutting in to save me.

Forest looks at him and then at me. "The VAD patient we saw? You guys didn't tell me that." He pats my back so hard that I almost spit out my drink.

"She did great, too." Keegan's lips turn up, and he looks at my parents. "I let her close the patient up. She's a great surgeon."

"I told you that being bad at math wouldn't get in the way." My dad shakes his head and puts his fork and knife down. "But don't you all get too important to come visit your old parents back in Cherry."

My mom takes one hand and puts it on Forest's, and her other hand clamps down on Keegan's. There seems to be no distinction between who is biologically theirs and who isn't.

"Will we get to see the hospital while we're here?" My mom sips her drink. "I'd love to say hi to your colleagues. Especially that nice nurse of yours."

"For sure," Forest says. "I was thinking tomorrow afternoon would be best."

"And, Forest, thanks for finding us a hotel room so close," my dad says, leaving the table, and turning on the TV. "It's nice for us to have space, and for us not to take up too much of yours. It's a win, win."

After dinner, we all clear our plates, load the dishwasher, and then sit in Forest's living room. I find the corner of the couch and pull my feet underneath me. Keegan pushes me to the side as he takes a seat next to me.

"What else is going on here?" My mom asks. "Are any of you dating? You have to be dating, right?"

"I have many contenders," Forest says first. "But nothing too serious."

"It wouldn't kill you to settle down. You're not getting any younger, and I wouldn't mind a grandbaby." My mom looks in Keegan's direction, and then mine. "Are you two dating?"

"Mom. No. That's gross. It's Keegan." Before I can think, the words come out of my mouth. Words I would do anything to put back.

All eyes are on me, and my mom's mouth hangs open, and one of Keegan's eyes looks in my direction. He looks partly amused.

"I just threw up in my mouth a little," Forest says, feigning puking gestures.

My mom clears her throat. "I meant are you two dating anyone right now?"

My face flushes with volcanic-level heat, and Keegan saves me by answering. "I'm not at the moment."

Now all eyes are back on me, and I put my face in my hands and shake my head. "No. Not dating anyone."

"You're actually single?" Keegan turns his face to me. "Every time we emailed, you'd just broken one man's heart or another."

"He isn't wrong." My dad mutes the TV and glances at me. "I couldn't keep up with the names half the time."

"Very funny," I say. "I date a lot. I thought that's what people are supposed to do at my age."

"Well." My mom throws a couch pillow at Forest and then pinches Keegan's arm. "You two better be looking out for our Luna. Ever since that campus incident, I have worried so much. You better be protecting her."

"Mom," I say with embarrassment. "I'm fine."

"We are." Keegan's low voice speaks over mine

My mom nods her head in approval. "Maybe you two could make sure she eats more."

Forest rolls his eyes, but Keegan says, "Yes, ma'am."

"Mom," I say under my breath. "Please."

"A colleague of mine did ask about you, Luna." Forest smiles as he takes a sip of his drink. "Saw you around the hospital. He's a nice guy. I'm still debating whether I introduce you to him though. You seem to break the hearts of everyone you date."

"I thought you guys didn't date each other's friends?" Keegan says.

"Forest. Luna." My mom gives me a look. "Are you both still mad at each other because of Kelsie and Joe?"

"Nope. I never think of it," I say, my voice oozing with sarcasm.

"Yeah, me neither," Forest says kicking his foot in my direction. "I'm over that stupid pact."

"Yeah, okay," I say, not fully believing him.

I look at my watch, and it's almost ten, and I work early in the morning. I let out an exaggerated yawn. "I really need to go. I have a long shift tomorrow."

"Saved by work, once again." Forest laughs, and I punch his arm.

"Of course," my dad says, looking away from the baseball game he found on TV. "How are you getting home?"

"I'll hail a cab." I stand up and start gathering my things.

"All by yourself? A female, alone in a taxi. Oh, honey, that can't be safe." My mom's voice is overly concerned as if I don't do this all the time.

"I'll make sure she gets home safely." Keegan stands and shakes my dad's hand, but he pulls my mom into a hug. "I need to get going anyway. And we only live a few blocks from each other."

"You are such a blessing, child." My mom hugs him, and then me.

"I'd take Luna home too, but I'm already home," Forest says, leaning against his kitchen island.

My mom laughs. "I'm lucky to have all three of you."

We step out into the hallway of Forest's building and reach the elevator. I glance at Keegan. "You don't have to get me home. I will get picked up at this door and dropped off at my door."

He raises an eyebrow. "And lie? To your mother's face? Never." Keegan pushes the button to get us to the main floor.

We stand on the sidewalk and wait for the car Keegan ordered. I shake my head. "My parents are so embarrassing."

"Luna." Keegan looks at me. "Your parents are the best people I've ever met."

"They are great people. And embarrassing." I say.

Keegan's chest rises, and then he blows out a breath. He turns his body to face me. "I don't know what I would have done without them after my dad died."

I narrow my eyes and nod.

"My mom was such a mess."

Keegan shuts his eyes and takes a deep breath of air through his nose. "After my dad died, it got worse. Only me, my mom, and your parents knew how bad it was. And then the substance abuse started, and then it became…"

His voice fades, and I take a step closer to him. I put my hand on his arm. It's hard, and warm under my touch. "I didn't realize how bad things were."

"It's fine," he says. I continue to grip Keegan's arms, and he looks at my hand, and he seems very aware of the touch. "And my mom was sick. And once in a while, she'd almost get better, and try to parent. But I always ended up with you guys. Your parents saved my life. I can say with certainty that I would not have become a doctor without their support."

"Keegan," I say his name, blowing out one long breath. "I know my parents are amazing. I didn't mean to imply—"

"Oh, I know, I'm not saying that," he says. "It's just that seeing them makes me so fucking grateful."

As I look back on my childhood, everything suddenly falls into place, and the truth comes to light. He stayed with us out of necessity.

Car lights approach us, and I'm brought back to the present and drop my hand from Keegan's arms. We slide into the car and are quiet for several minutes, and then Keegan leans over and speaks into my ear.

"I have a serious question for you." Keegan sits back and slings his arm on the back of my seat. "Not only do you think I'm boring, but you think I'm gross too?"

"Keegan." I shift my body to face him and playfully hit him in the chest. "To be clear. I said dating you would be gross. Not that you were gross."

"Fully noted." His arm once again stretches behind my back. "If I ever start to get too full of myself, I'm going to come and find you. You'll bring me down a notch or two."

"I'll never be able to unsee Forest's face when I made that comment," I say. "I'm not going to live that down, am I?"

"Probably not." The cab comes to a stop.

"Thanks for getting me home." I reach for the door handle.

Keegan nods as I get out. "Thanks for always providing levity to any situation."

I've never subscribed to the ideology that boys and girls treat those they have a crush on badly. But everything that seems to come out of my mouth lately, is the opposite of how I am feeling toward Keegan.

"Feel free to ignore me for the rest of your life," I say. "I'd understand."

Keegan smiles at me as the cab drives off into the night.

Chapter Twelve

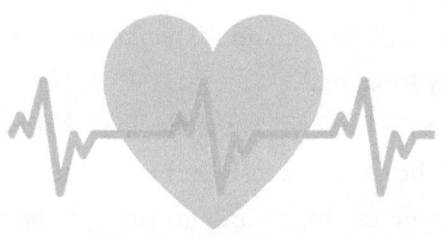

From: Keegan Baldwin <Keegan.Baldwin@med.cornell.edu
To: Luna Oliver <Luna.Oliver@umn.edu

Date: March 20

So…

From: Luna Oliver <Luna.Oliver@umn.edu
To: Keegan Baldwin <Keegan.Baldwin@med.cornell.edu

Date: March 22

So… Forest told you about my trip to Boston, I see.

From: Keegan Baldwin <Keegan.Baldwin@med.cornell.edu
To: Luna Oliver <Luna.Oliver@umn.edu

Date: March 22

Let me get this straight. Forest hooked up with your college roommate, and that was bad. You hook up with his best friend from Medical School and that is…

From: Luna Oliver <Luna.Oliver@umn.edu
To: Keegan Baldwin <Keegan.Baldwin@med.cornell.edu

Date: March 22

Different. Trust me on this one.

My life has become small. In medical school, sure, studying took up a lot of my time, but it's nothing like being a resident. Most weeks, I spend eighty hours at the hospital. I try to spend at least fifty hours a week sleeping so I don't entirely lose my mind, and that leaves only thirty to forty hours a week to do everything else. And everything else revolves around studying cases, doing laundry, and trying to nurture relationships with those in my life. It's not enough hours.

Today I'm on hour twenty-two of a thirty-hour shift, and even though I try to take every opportunity to sleep between patients, we're short-staffed and my pager goes off constantly. It's more painful to fall asleep and be woken up than trying to stay awake.

There is also nervous energy in the hospital today. On my walk here, the air was still, and the temperature was stiflingly hot. The sky was an eerie orangish pink color, and it feels like a storm is on the horizon. I've felt anxiety all day, but I can't pinpoint the source of it.

And when I finally start to come down, we're alerted that several ambulances are on their way because of a school shooting. All trauma one centers are asked to prepare for several gunshot victims. Raven rushes to a room, Myles follows Dr. Lanson, and I follow Dr. Parse into an exam room where the attending physician is already with a patient.

"Female, sixteen. Gunshot entered through her upper abdomen. No exit wound."

I help take her vitals. "Patient's in tachy. Blood pressure is low."

"I think she has internal bleeding. We need to get her to CT now and see where the damage is," the attending says with urgency.

I rush the patient down with Dr. Parse. She turns and looks at me. "It's my birthday." The words are gurgled. "My friends. I think they're all dead."

"We're going to do everything we can to fix you up." I squeeze her hand, and then she is rushed into CT.

Once the attending reads the CT results, our patient is rushed into surgery. She's bleeding out. I scrub in.

"We need blood," the surgeon yells. "O negative. Stat."

The surgeon opens the patient, and blood shoots out in every direction and fills the chest cavity. Dr. Parse and I suction. My surgical gown is covered.

"Damn it," the surgeon says. "Her aorta is almost completely dissected. She's not going to make it."

He works to repair it, while we simultaneously transfuse blood. I watch the trauma surgeon, fascinated by how many different procedures he needs to know in his line of work. The patient's blood pressure drops, and then she flatlines. We all work to do what we can, but the chest trauma is too great and she lost too much blood.

"Time of death, sixteen, thirty-two."

I stare at our patient and glance at her chart. Ella. Long, beautiful, blond hair. Her sixteenth birthday. I pinch my nose on the outside of my surgical mask. There are so many people from the shooting that still need attention.

I go back to the emergency room to check on a new patient. A man, or is he just a boy? Dr. Parse attends to him.

"Dr. Oliver." He looks at me. "Wrap the entry point, and let's move to the next patient. He's not emergent."

The patient looks at me, tears streaming down his face. "Is Ella okay? My girlfriend. I think she was brought here."

His chart says Ethan. "You were at the school too?"

"Yeah." He grimaces when I wrap his shoulder. "Some fucker. I don't even know his name. Have only seen him around. Had an AR15 and several magazines. He shot up the entire World Studies class. There were thirty students in there. How's Ella?"

I check his vitals and rush out of the room. But before I leave, I turn to him. "I don't know how she is," I lie. "I'll send someone in to update you."

"Thank you." He nods.

I join Dr. Parse, just as he calls the time of death for another teenage girl who took a shot directly to her neck.

Then I enter a room surrounded by police officers and am told that it's the shooter, and he's being wheeled up from CT. I glance at the film. The bullet entered and exited, and appeared to have not caused any serious damage. It's a handgun wound and must have been shot by one of the officers.

The killer gets to live today, but all the people that he pointed a semi-automatic rifle at weren't so lucky. It hardly feels fair, and now we do everything we can to ensure he lives and to keep him comfortable. A murderer. But we're doctors, and we try to help everyone. We don't choose who lives or dies. But the urge runs strongly through me to let him die. To rot.

In all, we received nine patients from the mass shooting, and other victims went to other hospitals. Of the nine people that came through our door, we were able to save three, one being the shooter, another looks like she'll be a quadriplegic, and the third, a man, who faced so much carnage today, may wish he didn't survive. Security is everywhere in the hospital, trying their best to keep the new's crews outside.

After my thirty-hour shift, I sit in the changing room, with my head in my hands. Why did I choose this life? My mind flashes back to all the people I saw die today. How does one see this and then show up for work the next day? How can I witness what I did, then smile, laugh, and act like my entire life and perspective didn't just change? At first, I'm numb, but then reality hits me like a lightning bolt to the chest.

I need Forest. I change into my clothes, leave the emergency room, and head to the cardiology building. I take the staff elevator to the fourth floor where his office is. I peek in, but he's not there. I'm about two seconds from breaking down, and I rush down a narrow hallway to the exit. It's hard to breathe and feels like I'm suffocating.

"Luna." The low, gravelly voice of Keegan rings out. He takes one look at me and asks, "Hey. What is it?"

I close my eyes, willing the tears to stay at bay, and shake my head. I can't even look at him, or all the emotions of the day will pool over.

"Come with me." He takes my hand.

Keegan pulls me into a room, with his name on the outside of the door. Keegan Baldwin, MD. Cardiothoracic surgeon. It's a nice office, with a window and a desk directly in front of it. To my left is a small sitting area. A loveseat and a chair, with a round table anchoring the space. Keegan leans back against the edge of his desk and lays his palms flat on the dark wood surface.

"Luna," he says again. "What's going on?"

"I was looking for Forest." I bite my bottom lip which has started to quiver. Then I start tapping my finger against it.

"I'm sure he's with a patient. Should I page him?" Keegan's blue eyes pierce into mine.

"No. No." I shake my head. "I don't want to bother him."

The intense emotions inside me reach their peak, and my control is slipping away. Suddenly, I can't hold back any longer, and a sob erupts from deep within me, causing both of my hands to shoot up to my mouth to contain the sound. But it's already too late, and tears start to flow down my face, like a torrent of water being unleashed.

Grief envelopes me like a prickly, wool blanket, and I need to escape these intense feelings. My eyes land on Keegan, who stands frozen in shock, watching me. Without hesitation, I rush toward him and throw my arms around his neck, seeking refuge in his embrace.

He pulls me into his chest, with his one hand on my lower back and his other on the back of my head, brushing my hair off my face and away from my tears. I soak his blue dress shirt, and his hand strokes my head and then my upper back. He holds me close to his body. The pounding of his heart against my ear.

"It's going to be okay, Luna," Keegan says quietly. His fingers spread across my back, keeping me pressed against him. I breathe in the clean, freshly laundered, scent of his shirt.

"I can't do this," I say the words into his chest. "I hate this world. They were just kids."

My voice trails off. Keegan rubs his hands up and down my arms rhythmically. "I didn't realize you were in the ER today."

"Why do we do this?" I ask, and his hands tighten around me. "I'm not cut out for this."

Keegan takes his hand, and with his thumb, brushes away new tears that begin to fall. His eyes narrow in on me. He reaches for a box of tissues on his desk and hands me one. I dab my eyes.

"I'm sorry you had to see that." Keegan cups my face, keeping my hair out of the way of my tears.

Keegan's mouth turns up slightly, and his big eyes are kind, accepting, and nonjudgmental. I've been so wrapped up in my breakdown, that I didn't realize all of my weight is pressed on him as he leans against his desk.

I feel relief from my grief being in Keegan's presence. I take my hand and push back a strand of hair that always ends up in front of his eye. It's this pesky piece of darkness that always tries to hide the lightness in his eyes.

"Hey." Keegan grasps my wrist, and I drop my arm to my side. "You're not alone. Ever." With two fingers, he makes circular patterns on the inside of my arm.

I make the mistake of looking at his lips. They are full, and a pale shade of pink. It feels good to be comforted by Keegan. I want to be transported somewhere else and have the ability to think of anything but the past few hours. I'm tired. Emotional. I need the pit in my stomach reminding me of the carnage I witnessed to disappear.

For all of those reasons, I inch forward, and place my hand on his face. Keegan is unwavering, pressed against his desk, and frozen. Our faces are inches apart. I squeeze his shoulder with my other hand, then slowly remove the gap between us until my lips are pressed against his. Keegan's mouth opens slightly, and his hands drop to his side. His lips are soft and taste like peppermint ChapStick.

His hands squeeze my shoulders. "Luna," he says against my mouth. "Not like this."

"I don't know…" My hands shoot to my mouth. "That—"

"Luna." Keegan takes a step toward me, but I move toward the door. "It's okay. It's just that—"

"I have to get out of here." I shake my head, cutting him off.

"Please. Can we talk?" Keegan says, reaching for me.

I grab the doorknob and bolt out.

"Luna," he calls after me, but I'm already halfway down the hallway.

Chapter Thirteen

Forest: "You're really not coming to dinner tonight?"
Luna: "I'm really not coming. I told you I have plans."

Sure, I didn't have plans when Forest picked today as our get-together with the two of us and Keegan, but once he suggested tonight, and after I realized that for the first time in forever, Myles, Raven, and I have the same night off, I made other plans.

Another text comes through from him.

Forest: "Fine, Luna. But it's important to Mom and Dad that we try to have a semblance of family out here. You better not cancel for the Fourth of July weekend."

I sigh into the phone and throw it onto my bed.

"Are you almost ready?" Raven stands in my open doorway, and peers in.

"Look at you, pretty lady," I say, and she spins, and her tangerine-colored skirt twirls around her.

We're embracing our night off and decided to get fancier than usual for a night out on the town.

"Are you ladies ready?" Now Myles stands in my bedroom doorway. "Because I've been ready for the past hour."

"Yes." I take a final sip of wine and follow them out the door.

"Love your outfit," Raven says when we step inside the elevator. She takes in my body suit tucked into a flowy, short skirt. "You have a great sense of style. Natural. Effortless. Girl-next-door vibes."

"I wish I had an ounce of your style," I say as Raven checks herself out in the elevator mirror. "I stole this entire look from a magazine."

Myles shakes his head. "No one is going to know we're doctors who work more than we sleep. Our disguises are amazing."

"Agreed," Raven says and takes my hand when we reach the ground floor. I smile, happy that after some convincing, Myles agreed to come out with us.

We start our night at a club on the Lower East Side that we heard about. Well, Raven heard about it from one of her emergency room patients. The music is loud, and the beat thumps so deeply, that I feel like it's controlling the rhythm of my heart. I've never been a drinker. I like to have one or two drinks at the most here and there, but I hate the feeling of being out of control. Tonight though, the alcohol is flowing.

It's the perfect escape from the pressures of the hospital and most importantly, Keegan. That awkward one-way kiss happened only two days ago, and I want to put so much more time and distance between it. He's the reason I absolutely could not go to Forest's for dinner.

Raven talks to someone at the bar, and I grab Myles's hand and pull him onto the dance floor. He hesitates, then follows me.

"When is Jules arriving in New York?" I yell over loud music.

"Right before the Fourth weekend," he yells back. "She can't wait to go to Montauk."

I'm not sure who is going to Montauk to stay in the mansion that Keegan bid on, but Myles, Raven, and I requested two and a half days off as soon as we could, so the three of us will be there. It also coincided with when Jules will be visiting from Texas, and Forest will of course be there. Beyond that, I'm not sure.

After about an hour, and several drinks, we decide to head back to our neighborhood and stop in at the local bar, George's.

"It was too loud in there to even think." I run my hand through my hair, smoothing out my loose curls. "Why do people enjoy clubs like that?"

Myles holds his head. "I can still feel the thumping in my head. Is that what the kids are listening to these days? Because I'm officially too old."

Raven sits between us in the back seat of the car. "You sound like two old people. It wasn't that bad."

We walk into George's, and it's packed. Music blares from the jukebox, and we find three empty seats at the bar.

"I'll have alcohol, please," I say to the man behind the bar. As soon as it comes out of my mouth, I realize that maybe I should slow down. "And a water."

"She'll have a glass of white wine. And water." Raven clarifies and then shoots me a look.

Raven sits between Myles and me. "I looked up the weather for the Fourth of July weekend. It's supposed to be gorgeous in Montauk. I can't wait to get away. I've been online shopping for some new bikinis."

"That's what Jules said." Miles sips his drink out of a straw. "I feel like we should chip in money or something."

"I don't think it's necessary." I cross one leg over the other. "Maybe I can reach out to Keegan and see if the three of us could be in charge of the food and drinks though?"

Raven licks her lips, and her eyes light up. "Is your brother bringing anyone?"

"Not that I know of," I say very slowly. "Also, you talk about beautiful Dr. Baldwin so much, I figured you were into him."

"I have a feeling he's into someone else." Raven smiles into her glass as she takes her next drink.

"Hello there." I spin in my seat as Dr. Lanson sits next to me.

"Dr. Lanson." I glance up and hold his gaze.

"Again, it's Ian." He smiles at me, then puts his hand in the air to get the bartender's attention.

"Luna. My name is Luna." I poke my index finger into my chest.

He laughs. "Yes, I know your name. Can I buy you a drink?"

I hold up my glass of wine. "I'm fine for now, thanks."

Dr. Lanson, I mean Ian, turns his bar stool in my direction. His gaze starts at my face but works its way down to my bare legs. I pull at my skirt nervously, wishing it were longer. I look around, planning my exit. Being attacked all of those years ago didn't make me scared of men, but it did make me more aware of how certain men make me feel. And when Ian focuses attention in my direction, my skin crawls.

"You're kind of overdressed for George's, don't you think?" Ian leans forward and says into my ear.

"My friends and I went dancing first."

I glance at Raven and Myles who are deep in conversation. They've been having a debate since we moved in about what year a general surgical resident should choose a surgery route. Myles has already decided that he wants to go the cardiothoracic route, which is why he can't wait to spend time with Keegan. Raven thinks residents should explore all options and not hone in on a path until year three at the earliest.

Ian nods. "I see." His leg rubs up against my bare knee. "Well, you look very nice."

"Thank you." I press my lips together.

Ian takes a long sip of his drink but never removes his eyes from me. "I'm hearing great things about you. I told Dr. Parse you could work under me at any time, but I have a sneaking suspicion that you got reassigned purposefully."

"What are you talking about?" I lean in closer because I'm not sure if I heard him correctly.

"I shouldn't be telling you this," Ian says into my ear. "But I heard that Keegan Baldwin asked you to be moved out from underneath me."

"No." The word shoots out of me, and I back up, studying Ian. "He wouldn't do that."

I look up, and spot Forest, standing next to Keegan, which makes this situation that much worse. I didn't even see them, but now they're here, in front of me and towering over Ian and me.

Forest glances at Ian. "Ian."

"Hello. Forest. Keegan." Ian shakes both Forest's and Keegan's hands.

Ian then looks at me. "I was talking to Luna about all the good things I'm hearing about her."

"Yes, I'm sure you have heard good things." Forest is pleasant, but his tone is also clipped.

"Well." Ian looks at me. "It was good to see you, Luna."

He gets up from his bar stool, and Forest takes a seat. "You blew off dinner with Keegan and me so you could come and drink at George's?"

Keegan puts his hand on Forest's shoulder, but his gaze locks with mine. "Let it go."

"I did have plans." I look at Forest, then up at Keegan, who stands, studying me, his hands now tucked in his pockets. "Raven, Myles, and I went dancing. And then we came here."

"You're still good for the Fourth of July, right?" Forest asks. "Or are you blowing us off then, too?"

I roll my eyes. "You already asked me that. Yes, I'm good."

Forest looks at a group of women who walk into the bar. "I have to go say hi to someone. Keegan, will you order me a drink? My regular."

Keegan nods and takes the seat next to me. I spin my stool so instead of looking out, I now face the bar. I hold my glass up to my mouth and take one, long sip. Feeling Keegan's gaze the entire time.

"How was dinner with Forest?" I keep my eyes averted elsewhere. "Let me guess. You suggested something to eat, but then he decided on Indian food anyway."

Keegan barks a laugh, turns his head to the side, and glances at me. "You're remarkably spot on. I once again wanted to try the new sandwich shop, and yes, we ended up having Indian food."

The bartender hands Keegan two drinks, and I turn to him. "I don't know why you don't stick up for yourself. Now you're never going to get to try that sandwich shop."

"Because I don't care about small things like what food we're going to order." Keegan takes a sip but looks at me over his glass. "Forest missed you tonight."

"Yeah, well." I shrug. "Do you even want me to go to Montauk anymore? I understand why you wouldn't."

"Why would you ask me that?" Keegan puts his glass down and runs his finger around the rim of it. "Of course, I want you there."

Keegan continues to gaze at me, and I grab my wine glass and empty the rest into my mouth in one long gulp.

I cross my legs. "Because I had a breakdown in your office and then kissed you. I just figured you wouldn't want to be around me."

"Luna." Keegan narrows his eyes. "About that."

I look to the side, and Raven and Myles are no longer seated there. I finally spot them together by the jukebox, feeding it money. And then I lock eyes with Dr. Ian Lanson, who watches me from across the bar. Ian starts walking toward us before Keegan has a chance to say anything.

"Would you like another glass of wine?" Ian asks when he reaches me. He points to the empty one on the bar. "It looks like you've exhausted that one."

"She's good," Keegan says in a very clipped tone before I can answer.

"Keegan, there's something I've been meaning to discuss with you," Ian says, leaning against the bar. "Will you step outside with me?"

Keegan stands. "Anything you'd like to say to me, you can say here."

"If you insist." Ian glances at me, and then back to Keegan. "Why did you ask that Luna be reassigned to another attending?"

"Do you want to have this conversation in front of an intern?" Keegan says. My eyes widen, and Keegan's face reddens as he balls his fists. "If you want to set up time with me, feel free. I'd be happy to discuss this matter with you."

"You said I could say anything here." Ian laughs and waves his hand dismissively. "What I don't understand is what you think I did wrong, when every time I look in your direction, you're sniffing Luna out."

Keegan shoots up from the stool. "This is a very inappropriate conversation to be having here, Dr. Lanson."

Ian takes a step toward Keegan, and for a moment, I'm worried that he's going to take a swing at him. I jump up and wrap my hand in Keegan's. He glances down at where we're connected, and then I pull him toward the door, and we spill out onto the sidewalk. Forest comes out about five seconds after us.

"What the hell was that all about?" Forest looks at Keegan, then me. "What did he say to you?"

"It's not important." Keegan glances at me, his face a deep crimson.

"No." Forest steps between us. "If someone doesn't tell me what's going on, I'm marching in there, and will ask Ian myself."

"Forest," I say, gripping his elbow. "No."

"He said something about Luna," Keegan says.

Forest jerks his head in my direction. "What did he say about my sister?"

"Please, can we drop this?" I plead.

Keegan looks at me, then Forest. He takes a deep breath. "I saw him cross a line with her at the hospital. I had him reassigned to male residents only."

"I'll fucking kill him," Forest says, charging the door. But Keegan is too strong for him and pulls him back.

"Did you ever pause and think you should have talked to me first?" I say to Keegan. "I don't need a man to come in and save the day. We women deal with this shit all the time. I could have handled it myself. This is why I didn't want to end up at the same hospital as either of you."

"Luna," Forest says, stepping toward me, but I back away. "Keegan was trying to help."

"By creating a huge mess," I say.

"I'm sorry," Keegan says, folding his arms over his chest. "I should have talked to you first."

"Do you think?" I rub my eyes. "You act like you're supportive of women in medicine, but the moment you have an opportunity, you swoop in and try to take over. You're no better than Ian."

Keegan and Forest stare at me as if they can't form the words for what to say next. I shake my head, turn on my heels, and go in the direction of my apartment.

Chapter Fourteen

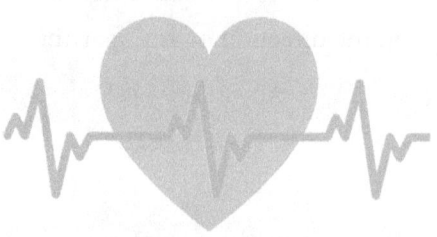

From: Keegan Baldwin <Keegan.Baldwin@med.cornell.edu
To: Luna Oliver <Luna.Oliver@umn.edu

Date: April 24

I'm not sure if you heard, but I'm coming to MN for a long weekend. I get in on Thursday and leave Sunday. I fly to Minneapolis and thought about staying in the city for the night. Are you free? It would be great to see you and catch up. Dinner maybe? I'd head up to Cherry early Friday morning. Let me know either way.

From: Luna Oliver <Luna.Oliver@umn.edu
To: Keegan Baldwin <Keegan.Baldwin@med.cornell.edu

> Date: April 24
>
> I leave for Cabo Wednesday and don't get back until the following Wednesday. We miss each other once again. Safe travels and give my parents a big hug for me.

A couple of days later, we drive two cars to Montauk. Keegan takes Forest, Raven, and me. Myles drives the other car with Jules, who arrived last night from Texas. Raven and I figured they have a lot to catch up on without an audience. And although I've managed to avoid it for the past month, Raven finally meets my brother.

The mood is icy at best, but Raven keeps everyone talking with her questions and singing along to every song that comes on the radio. Keegan, Forest, and I haven't talked about the other night, and I'd rather enjoy this short getaway than focus on it. I considered more than once staying back in the city, and not going to Montauk. But I'm the bridge between my roommates and Forest and Keegan, so I decided to come.

As we make our way down the winding road toward the house, anticipation builds inside me. I've needed a break from the city. And then as we turn the final corner and pull into the driveway, my jaw drops in awe. In front of me stands a magnificent home, an architectural masterpiece. The house is situated right on the water with a breathtaking view of the beach and the ocean beyond.

"Holy shit." Forest breaks the silence as he also stares at the house. "This house is insane."

We go inside, and Raven and I get a little excited and run from room to room. I claim one on the lower level with stunning views.

"Dibs," I say, so everyone else in the house can hear me.

"There's a room in its own wing of the house. Let's give that one to Myles and Jules. They'll be the only ones having sex," Raven says.

"Where are you?" I ask Raven as she stands in the doorway.

"I'm way down the hall. Keegan is next to you, and Forest chose a room a floor up."

The four of us unpack, and after we've been here for about thirty minutes, Myles and Jules walk in.

"This place is incredible." Jules' Texas accent drips off her tongue. "I mean, is this real life?"

Myles puts his arm around her waist. They are the same height, and their eyes take in their surroundings.

"There's this great seafood restaurant I've been dying to try. Is anyone up for that?" Forest says, studying his phone. "It's right on the water. I figured we could start our night there and then see what we're feeling like."

"Sounds great." Keegan, Raven, and I all say at once.

Myles looks at Jules. "We signed up for a sunset cruise tonight. But we'll catch up with all of you later."

We head out to the restaurant, and it's only about a five-minute drive. Forest called ahead and got reservations, and we have a table on the patio and I can smell the ocean salt in the air.

"Keegan." My eyes dart to him as a thought comes my way. "I didn't even give you first dibs on the bedroom. I'm sorry. Switch with me. I have ocean views. I only laid on the bed a little, but I was clean."

"I wouldn't dare." He shakes his head, half of his mouth turning up in a smile. "And I love the bedroom I got."

"You're sure?" I press on, remembering that he spent twenty-three thousand dollars on this weekend, and it should all be about him.

"Completely. Enjoy waking up to the ocean," Keegan says. "You deserve it."

We order lobster rolls, calamari, mussels, and clams for an appetizer, and then we all end up ordering the sauteed sea scallop. Our drinks are the kind that comes with fancy umbrellas, and it feels good to be out of the city and in the open air again.

"We don't have seafood like this in Minnesota," Forest says, bringing me back to reality. "This is literally to die for."

He then turns his attention to Raven, who sits across from him. "Where did you say you're from?"

She whips her hair off of her face with a flick of her hand. "South Carolina. So don't be jealous, but our seafood is amazing."

My eyes meet Keegan's, and then we both look at the water. The ocean before us is alive with color, mostly shades of orange and gold, as if paying homage to the setting sun. The light is diffused, casting an ethereal glow over the water that makes it look like it's on fire. It's a moment of pure magic.

"It's weird that Luna hasn't introduced us yet," Forest says, glancing at me and then Raven. "Or that we haven't ended up at George's on the same night."

"Agreed," Raven says. "What's your story, anyway? Luna acts like you're a secret she doesn't want to share."

"Not true," I say, rolling my eyes. "We've been a little busy since moving here, don't you think?"

Forest leans forward on his elbows, full attention on Raven. Keegan and I exchange knowing glances.

"Well, I'm from the same place as these two," Forest says. "And then I did my undergrad at Dartmouth, Medical School at Boston College, and am a year out of my cardiology fellowship. I'm single and enjoy romantic walks on the beach. Let's see. What else?"

"Funny," Raven says, blowing off the latter part of his comments. "And why didn't you want to go the surgery route like Keegan and Luna?"

Forest smiles. "Because unlike Keegan and Luna, I'm good with people, and I like my patients awake when I'm with them. I love getting to know their stories. I wouldn't get that as much if I was a surgeon."

"Maybe I shouldn't be a surgeon either. I'm also good with people." Raven leans forward too, hanging on to his words before changing the subject. "You being a surgeon, Luna, makes sense. You're always putting your foot in your mouth."

Everyone, including me, laughs at that very true statement.

Forest smiles at Raven, and I see goosebumps travel up her arms. She's putty in his hands, like so many before her who aren't immune to the charm he exudes.

"There are some great bars here," Forest says, breaking the silence. "We should go. What do you guys think?"

I check the time on my phone. "I want to enjoy the house. Maybe read a book. Chill. You guys go."

"Me too," Keegan says, glancing at me. "I thought it would be nice to have a fire. We never get to do that in the city."

"Oh, a fire sounds nice," I say.

"Do you guys mind if I stay here and check out a few bars with Forest?" Raven says.

"Go for it," I say, and Forest's smile somehow grows wider. "Just be careful. He's a real smooth talker."

"Really, Luna?" Forest rolls his eyes.

The bill comes, and I grab my card and put it in the center of the table.

"Forest and I have it covered," Keegan says, holding his hand out.

"No. I'm paying my part." I fold my arms over my chest.

Forest tries to shove my card back in my direction, but I don't let him. "Why are you always so stubborn, Luna?"

"I'm not stubborn," I say. "But I'm not going to let you guys pay for everything."

"Fine," Keegan says, and he and Forest put their cards on mine and we wait for the server.

Keegan and I take the car back to the house and leave Forest and Raven out on the town. Myles and Jules are still out, so I go to my room, change into pajama pants and a tank top, grab a throw blanket from the bed, and wrap it around my shoulders. When I get outside, Keegan has already started a fire, but he's nowhere in sight. There are four Adirondack chairs, and I take one where I can also see the moon glistening off the ocean.

"Hey." Keegan's voice rings out, and I glance at him. He has two glasses in his hand. "I made you a drink."

"Oh. Thanks." I take it from his hand and smell it. "I haven't had a mojito in ages."

Keegan sits in the chair next to me so he can also see the ocean. The night has turned cool, and the fire not only smells like back home, but it warms every inch of me.

"I don't think I'll go back to the city," I say. "I'm going to become a squatter in this house. It's big enough that they won't even know I'm here."

Keegan laughs. "The hospital would miss you."

"I bet no one would even notice I was gone." I look at him through the side of my eye.

"Look at tonight's moon." Keegan moves his gaze to the sky. "I love everything about it. It's so beautiful."

"Really? The moon?" I ask.

Keegan picks at something on his shorts but watches me. "Why not?"

My namesake. When I was born, the moon was full, and my parents were dead set on naming me after it because the moon is the symbol of mystery and feminine energy. Or something like that.

I turn and face the fire and breathe in the scent. I close my eyes for a moment and pretend I'm back on the Iron Range, with the Minnesota forests all around me. I love being here, but I also miss home.

"Keegan."

"Luna."

We say each other's names simultaneously.

"I'm sorry about the Ian thing," Keegan says quickly. "I didn't know how to navigate it, weighing our relationship with the fact that you're an intern. I should have treated this in a strictly professional manner and not like a protective big brother."

"Meaning?" I shift on my chair.

"Professionally speaking." Keegan inhales a breath. "Ian Lanson has a reputation. He's received formal complaints from female residents. It's the worst-kept secret at the hospital. I should have reported it and let leadership handle it however they saw fit."

He pauses and looks down at his balled fists. He narrows his eyes when he glances back at me. "I reacted emotionally, and I'm sorry. I couldn't stand the thought of him touching you. . ."

Keegan looks down again. "That wasn't fair of me. You are a professional, and I shouldn't have stepped around you. That wasn't fair to you. I'm sorry, Luna."

"Thank you." I pull the blanket tighter around my shoulders. "Apology accepted."

"Were you going to say something?"

"I'm sorry too." I look at my folded hands in my lap. "About the other day. I too acted emotionally and crossed a boundary."

I breathe in sharply, finally finding my courage. "I hope you know that your muscles didn't get to me, and I still think you're rather boring. I was delirious from lack of sleep."

"And don't forget I'm also slightly gross." Keegan leans against the side of his chair. "But I get it. You have no idea how many times that's happened to me."

"What?" I jerk my head toward him. "Are you serious?"

"Totally." Keegan raises his eyebrows. "Interns and residents always throw themselves at me after long shifts at the hospital. If I turned everyone in, it would be quite the HR file."

My mouth hangs open, but then Keegan starts to laugh.

"Oh, really? You think that's funny?" I throw my blanket at him as he continues to laugh.

"I'm sorry, Luna," he says. "I was trying to make you feel better. I'm afraid you're the one and only who's ever done that."

Heat pricks my face, and then trickles down my body. Keegan sits, watching me, and then brushes his hair back. And because he doesn't say anything, I fill all the space. Like I always do.

"In my defense, I was having the worst day. And you were so nice. Nicer than you usually are. Because most days, you stare at me like I'm some sort of math equation that's over your head. Literally, you look at me like everything that comes out of my mouth is the stupidest thing you've ever heard. You're doing it right now, actually. And then I decided that maybe I was curious. I didn't think. I never think. It was so stupid. Can we forget it ever happened?"

Keegan doesn't speak at first. He lowers his head and knits his eyebrows together. "Luna," he finally says, leaning forward in his chair. "That's not what I think of you. Nothing you say—"

The sliding glass door opens, and Forest and Raven walk out. I feel both relief and frustration that I won't have a chance to hear what Keegan was about to say.

"We went to the most incredible bar." They both take a seat, and Forest continues. "It was the best hole in the wall. And there was Karaoke. It was epic."

"Your brother sang." Raven looks at me and laughs. "Well, I should clarify. I put his name and the song down without him knowing, but he went up there and did the dang thing."

I glance at Keegan, who still watches me, and Forest and Raven fade into the background. The moment is gone, and the mood and everything else has shifted, as they replay their night out on the town. Usually, I'd want to hear it, but tonight, I only want to finish the conversation with Keegan.

Instead, I say goodnight to the group and go inside.

Chapter Fifteen

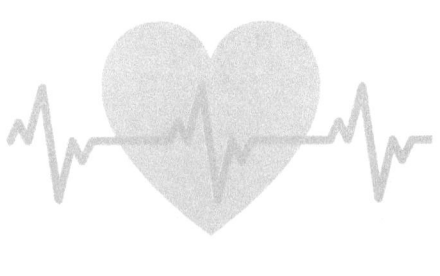

We all sleep in. When I get up, I put on my orange and pink bikini, and then pull over my translucent blue-and-white cover-up that looks more like an oversized men's button-up than anything else. I get to the main living area, and everyone is standing around Jules. When I make eye contact with her, she holds her hand out, and I rush over.

"Oh my gosh. You guys got engaged?" I look between Myles and Jules. I give her a big hug and then Myles. "Congrats."

Jules beams, and Raven pours us all a mimosa. We all hold up our glasses, and Raven leads us in a toast.

"That's where you guys were last night?" I go back to studying the beautiful emerald-cut ring.

"This is amazing. We need to celebrate all day. And look at that ring. Nice work, Myles," I say.

"I'm engaged!" Myles declares to no one in particular and throws back a shot of dark liquor.

Keegan clears his throat. "Everyone is welcome to do what they want today, but I chartered a yacht. And there's room for all of us. I say we have a little engagement party."

"Yes," we all say simultaneously.

"Thanks, Keegan." I drop Jules' hand finally. "I don't suppose you'll let me chip in on the yacht?"

He deadpans me, crossing his arms over his chest, staring at me so deeply I feel like he can see through me. "No."

We all head to the marina and get on the most beautiful boat. And the day couldn't be more perfect. There isn't a cloud in the sky, and it's hot out, with a small breeze coming off the ocean. I get comfortable on the back of the yacht and unbutton my cover-up.

"Oh, I love your suit," Raven says, pulling her dress over her head. "And look at that cute little body of yours that you waste hiding under scrubs."

"Sorry, Raven." I hit her on the arm. "Required dress code and everything. And look at your suit. It's fabulous."

She spins for me.

Raven, Jules, and I lounge on the netting that stretches out over the water, the gentle rocking of the yacht lulls me into a state of pure relaxation. The sound of the waves lapping against the hull is a soothing backdrop to our conversation, and the sun overhead is warm on our skin.

As I roll onto my stomach, my eyes roam over the length of the yacht. The men are gathered near the front of the boat, their voices hushed as they chat amongst themselves. And then my gaze falls upon Keegan.

He's shirtless, and it's as if his chest muscles have been intricately carved out of the purest stone. I knew he had strong arms, but I had no idea what the rest of him looked like. And now that I've seen, I can't take my eyes off him. I squint to try to get a better view of his tattoo. It's on his upper left inside bicep, and there's a shape with a couple of lines of scribbling underneath. I squint my eyes, but he's too far away for me to see it.

As he turns to face me, our eyes meet for a brief moment, and a shiver runs down my spine. My heart rate picks up, and it's suddenly hard to breathe.

"Do any of you ladies want a drink?" Forest comes to the back of the boat.

"Yes," we all say. Forest nods and reaches into a cooler and grabs something for all of us.

"I appreciate you no longer talking about how hot my brother is," I say to Raven.

She starts fanning herself with her hand. "He's cool. It's all good."

"Honestly, I thought I was walking into a couples' trip," Jules says. "I assumed you were with Forest, Raven. And I was sure that you and Keegan were an item, Luna."

Raven and I look at each other, and my face reddens. "No. Definitely no couples here except you and Myles."

Jules raises her eyebrows at me but then drops the subject.

I flip again and let the sun warm my face, and then I get up from my spot to see the scenery all around us. The houses spread across the beaches are expansive and beautiful. I walk to the front end of the yacht, where the men are all in conversation. They look at me when I approach, and then Forest and Myles look away and continue their conversation.

As I shift my gaze toward Keegan, his eyes fix on mine, and I can't help but feel a flutter in my chest. And then, just as I'm about to look away, he wets his lips with a quick flick of his tongue.

My cheeks flush with heat as I become suddenly self-conscious. I glance down at my body, wondering if there's something amiss. And then, when I look back up at Keegan, I realize that his eyes are slowly raking over me. Does he not realize he's staring?

We cannot look at each other like this.

"I never had you pegged as a tattoo kind of person." I grab his arm, but he pulls away. "What is it?"

"It's nothing." He holds his arm flush against his body, hiding it from my view.

"Come on, Keegan." I reach for him again. "Let me see it."

"Luna." He grips my elbow. I grab his arm again. and fling myself against him. He holds my arms down. "Please."

"But I have so many questions." I laugh. "If you didn't want people to see it, why'd you get it in on your arm?"

Keegan grabs his shirt that is dangling off the railing of the boat, turns away from me, and puts it on. The sleeve is long enough that it covers the tattoo.

"You're seriously no fun." I pout. "Boring Baldwin."

"Please drop it," Keegan says, pressing his palms into his temples, and looks at me with frustration.

"Fine," I say. "But I will see your tattoo at some point."

"There's this great beach up ahead." Keegan points over the blue water but is now talking more to Forest and Myles than me, blocking me out. "I told the captain to anchor. It's hot. We could all swim there. Have a couple of drinks. Lie on the beach."

The captain drops us off near the shore. The water is warm, and the salt washes over my body, immersing me in the ocean water. We swim the short distance to the beach, which is filled with people.

"Come to the bar with me?" Raven grabs my hand and pulls me ahead. She grabs money from her waterproof pack around her waist. "I'm in the mood for something light and citrusy."

As soon as we grab our drinks, Raven takes off in another direction, leaving me on my own. Without a destination in mind, I wander along the shoreline until I come across a secluded stretch of white sand.

I sink into the soft grains of sand and stretch out until I make a Luna-sized imprint in the sand. The heat from the sun is intense, but it feels good against my skin. I close my eyes and submerge deeper into the sand, allowing the warmth to envelop me completely.

For a few moments, I leave behind the stresses of the city and the demands of work. I breathe in deeply, and my lungs fill with the salty ocean air. The waves crashing against the shore are a soothing backdrop to my thoughts, and I simply exist in the moment. The sand covers every inch of my skin until I'm one with the beach.

A shadow casts over me, and Keegan is standing there.

"We're all ready to get back on the boat," Keegan says. "Think you can tear yourself off the beach and join us?"

I brush the sand off and reach my hand up so Keegan can help me to my feet. He walks to the edge of the water, and I follow him, and let the waves crash over my toes. His silence fills me with curiosity.

"Are you thinking about all the bacteria found on sandy beaches?" I nudge Keegan with my elbow lightly, and he looks at me.

"Well, you wouldn't believe the amount of Staphylococcus species that we are most likely standing on." Keegan digs his feet deeper into the wet sand. "But no, that was not even remotely what I was thinking of." His eyes flick to mine.

"Then what were you thinking of?"

Keegan opens his mouth to answer, but then Forest runs up, with Raven, Myles, and Jules in tow. Once again, I leave our conversation with so much left unsaid.

Chapter Sixteen

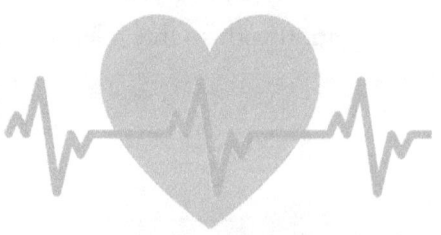

From: Keegan Baldwin <Keegan.Baldwin@med.cornell.edu
To: Luna Oliver <Luna.Oliver@umn.edu

Date: May 30

You are the most beautiful woman I've ever known. I'm so in love with you.

From: Luna Oliver <Luna.Oliver@umn.edu
To: Keegan Baldwin <Keegan.Baldwin@med.cornell.edu

Date: May 31

Umm, dying. Literally. Assuming this was meant for Stella? LOL.

From: Keegan Baldwin <Keegan.Baldwin@med.cornell.edu
To: Luna Oliver <Luna.Oliver@umn.edu

Date: May 31

Mortified. I am so sorry. Stella's last name is Olson. I didn't realize I had sent this to you instead of her. Sorry again.

After hours on the boat, we get back to the house. My skin is sun-kissed, and my freckles have popped out. The house is quiet, and I seem to be the only one here. I unbutton my cover-up and head to the bathroom. My skin is sticky from the salty ocean and sunblock. I reach for the handle, and at the same time, the door flies open, startling me. I take a step back and put my hand over my chest.

Keegan stands there, in nothing but shorts, water beads dripping from his hair.

"You scared me," I say breathily. "I thought I was here alone."

"I'm sorry." Keegan slowly blinks before his eyes pop back open. "Forest and Raven went to a farmer's market, and Myles and Jules are at the harbor to rent jet skis. I decided to hang back."

"Yeah, I see that." I take a deep breath, and my heart starts to regulate. I drag my eyes off his tanned chest and force them up. "What are you going to do?"

Keegan releases his hand from the door and steps toward me. "I was thinking about grabbing a book and sitting on one of the patios of this massive house."

"Speaking of patios, have you seen the one off my room?"

Keegan shakes his head, and I grab his arm and pull him toward the room I've been staying in. "I think it has the best views in the house."

Keegan follows me into the room, and he walks to the French doors leading to a beautiful patio that overlooks the ocean. It's paved with stones and has two chairs and a table between them. I sit at the foot of the bed and watch Keegan take it in.

"Is it too late to switch?" Keegan walks toward me and smiles.

"It's your house for the weekend. You say the word, and I'll move my stuff out of this room immediately."

Keegan starts looking around at my clothes, sprinkled all over the floor. He glances at a pair of underwear on top of the pile. They are red, and on the rear, it says, *I found this humerus*, with a picture of the humerus bone. Keegan raises an eyebrow, and I put my head in my hands and shake it. I gesture for him to sit on the foot of the bed beside me, and he obliges. His eyes stay glued to the panties on the floor.

"Quit looking," I say, nudging him in the arm. "They were a gift. From a friend I went to medical school with. I have so many more. Like, the ones with an EKG that says, *stay calm, but not that calm. My surgeons do it on the table* are pretty cool too."

He scrapes his hand down his face. "You are so bizarre."

Keegan raises his arm and brushes a strand of hair out of his face, and I get the best glimpse of his tattoo that I've managed. I shoot across the bed in an attempt to grab his arm. But he anticipates my move and somehow flips me until I'm flat on my back, and he hovers over me.

"Let me see it." I try to turn his arm so I can see the inside, but he's too strong.

"Luna," Keegan says, pinning my hands above my head. "Why do you want to see my tattoo so bad?"

"Why does someone get a tattoo and not let people see it?" I pout my lips. "The more you hide it, the more curious I get."

"I lost a stupid bet, and I don't like people to see it," Keegan says, and because he has me pinned down, I can feel his breath on my cheek when he talks.

Keegan loosens his grip slightly, and I try to shoot my hand up, and he tightens it again.

"I'm going to see your tattoo at some point," I say. "You know that, right? I'm very persistent."

Our faces hover inches apart, suffocating in the tense air. The weight of his body bears down on me, and his bare chest rises and falls with each breath and it feels like a rhythmic reminder of this new tension between us. Keegan's tongue darts out to moisten his lips, a subtle yet charged gesture. He tilts his head, and it feels like an invitation to dive deeper into all of my recent curiosities.

Keegan glances at my lips, and then rapidly shakes his head like he's trying to erase whatever thought came to it. He releases my hands and then sits up. "You and all of your curiosities are going to get you into trouble."

I sit too. "We're supposed to be curious. We're doctors."

Keegan rubs his palms against his thighs and looks into his lap. The color on his cheeks deepens.

"Yeah," he says. "I suppose we are. Trust me, I have my own curiosities."

"Yeah? Like what?" I turn to him.

Keegan glances at me and then runs his hand down his face. "I keep replaying it in my mind, what would have happened if I had kissed you back."

I raise an eyebrow, surprised at how forward he's being. "I guess we'll never know."

I go to push off the bed, but Keegan reaches for my arm and pulls me closer to him.

"Hmm," Keegan says.

"Hmm," I put my finger up to my lips, imitating him. "I dare you to find out. Because honestly, I don't think you have it in you."

"You dare me?" Keegan reaches inside my cover-up, and his fingers spread against my hips. His pinky finger grazes the sensitive skin beneath my suit, and I manage to feel both thrilled and terrified.

"Yeah," I say, feigning confidence. "I dare you. I think you like teasing me about that one stupid moment in your office. If you kiss me, you'll have nothing to hold over my head. And that bothers you."

"I don't like teasing you." Keegan tightens his grip on my hips and drags me across the foot of the bed and toward him. "But as you can see from my tattoo, I never pass on a dare."

Keegan's gaze sharpens, and with purpose, he bridges the gap between us. I shake my head, and all the rational thoughts that attempt to flood my brain, telling me that we're in dangerous territory and most definitely should not kiss, get pushed way back. It won't mean anything, I tell myself, but it still could change things. And maybe this is what I need to get it out of my mind forever. Because Keegan isn't the only one who's wondered what would have happened had he kissed me back that day in his office.

He reaches out and firmly grips the nape of my neck with his hand, sending shivers down my spine. We move our heads toward each other, calling each other's bluff. But then his lips meet mine, and they are full and plush. He initiates a slow, seductive kiss, and blood rushes to places it shouldn't because I'm not supposed to enjoy this as much as I already am.

As our tongues entwine, I let out a low, guttural moan of pleasure. I reciprocate by placing my hand on the back of his neck, pulling him closer. Keegan grabs me around my waist and lifts me onto his lap.

"Shit, Keegan." My legs are on each side of his torso. We lock eyes and breathe heavily. I hate how much I love the sensation of his taut body between my hips.

"We're kissing." He leans forward, moves my hair out of the way, and drags his tongue down my neck. "Just this once."

"Just this once," I repeat. "For curiosity purposes."

I pull back again and study his features. He has a sprinkling of freckles on the bridge of his nose, and somehow, his eyes manage to be even bluer up close. I start having a mini freakout and pull away even farther. Because although this feels really good, it's Keegan.

"Is this too much?" Keegan asks between kissing my neck, sending blood directly between my legs. "What are you thinking?"

"Nothing." I'm incredibly turned on by this man's body and the way he touches me, even though I'm hyper-aware that it's Keegan. "What are you thinking?"

Keegan takes his thumb and presses it into my bottom lip. He holds it there until his lips connect with mine again. "That your bottom lip is fucking incredible."

Oh.

He shifts me, moves his hand under my cover-up, and spreads his long fingers across my back. My breasts press against Keegan's bare chest, and he wraps his arms around me tightly. His touch makes my body tingle everywhere. Blood pumps to every area of my body, and then I feel

Keegan's erection against my core. My hips roll instinctively, but Keegan presses down on my thighs, stopping me.

"Luna," Keegan says into my mouth. "Slow down."

"Yeah. Okay." I run my fingers through his luscious locks, and he watches me. "Slow."

His hand slides under the loose fabric of my swim cover-up, tracing down my spine and sending tingles through my body.

"You feel incredible," he tells me and deepens our kiss. Our tongues dance. His breath is warm and minty. I can't get enough of his mouth, and the way it dominates mine. "And taste like cherry ChapStick."

I place my hand on his chest, feeling the firmness of his muscles. As my hand travels down his arm, I give it a gentle squeeze, taking in the sensation of his skin against mine.

My thoughts become hazy, and my mind wanders to another place entirely, consumed by the electricity between us. His tongue dips in and out of my mouth, and I gently pull his hair, and the warm breath of his groan fills me. I want to forget all the talk from earlier about only doing this once. Because right now, I'd let Keegan have all of me.

A door slams somewhere down the hall, and then Forest's voice rings out. "Where is everyone?"

Keegan stops our kiss and looks toward the door. His breath is heavy, and we stare at each other, his eyes wide.

"Let me check in Luna's room," Forest says.

Keegan lifts me off of him, dragging me along his length, and both of our breath catches in our chests. It's so heavy against my abdomen, and now I'm wrecked more than I already was. He places me on the bed and then gets up and looks around, before ducking into the closet.

I lie back on the bed, shut my eyes, and my door swings open.

"There you are. I've been calling your name."

I sit up and rub my eyes. "I must have fallen asleep."

"Have you seen Keegan?" Forest raises his eyebrows like he can't quite figure something out. He steps in a foot and looks around. "And why do you look so hot and bothered? What were you doing in here?"

"No. I haven't seen him." I shake my head and run my hand over my still swollen lips. "Maybe he's out exploring somewhere."

"Raven and I picked up a lot of food at the market. We're going to start cooking shortly, and we'll eat in about an hour or so."

"Great." I try to steady my shaky voice. "I'm going to hop in the shower and wash this saltwater off of me, and then I'll be there."

Forest shuts the door behind him, and I jolt up, close the door, and lock it. Keegan walks out of the closet, more composed than when he entered it a couple of minutes ago. He runs a hand through his tousled hair, and we both look toward the French doors in the room that leads to the outside.

"There's your escape." I point.

Keegan doesn't move. His lips are a darker shade of pink, my kisses tattooed all over him. "Luna. That was—"

"At the same time that Keegan goes to speak, I say, "That was a huge mistake. We should not have kissed, even if we were curious. We can never speak about this again. Let's pretend it didn't even happen."

Keegan's face goes blank, and then he knits his eyebrows together. It feels like I've said the wrong thing. Again.

"Luna." Keegan sits back on the edge of the bed, and I follow. He glances at me. "You frustrate the hell out of me."

"I've noticed." I push him on the arm, trying to get back to a place where I don't know what it feels like to kiss Keegan. Or to know the way his body responds to mine. Or be aware that he thinks my bottom lip is incredible. To know these things feels life-altering somehow, so I need to go back to not knowing these things. Because sometimes, a kiss is just a kiss.

He glances at his arm where my fist just contacted him, and then his eyes dart back to mine. Something goes through his mind. I can see it all over his face. I'm a liar. But he doesn't need to know that. Because what just happened did the opposite of conquering my curiosity. Now my mind is busy wondering what it would be like to be under his heavy body. What it would be like to have our bare chests pressed against each other's.

Keegan stretches his long fingers over his tan legs and presses into his flesh. His hair is a mess in part due to my hands combing through it a few minutes earlier. He finally looks at me, and I wish I were better at reading facial expressions or having the ability to get inside someone's head, but I don't.

He points toward the door that leads to a patio. "I guess I'll go."

"Yeah, okay."

Keegan stands, but my legs feel too wobbly so I stay seated a moment as he walks out.

Before I'm able to catch my breath, there's a loud knock, and I jump and run to the door. Raven's on the other side, holding a drink for me and one for herself.

"You haven't showered yet?" She looks at me and peers into the room. "We're going to grill, and then head to this place Myles and Jules want to try. There's this huge outdoor party thing tonight. It's called Montauket. You in?"

I glance at myself in the full-length mirror attached to the closed closet door. The one Keegan had been hiding in only a few minutes ago. Sand still clings to my body, and my hair is in a messy bun on top of my head. And my still swollen lips are a reminder that I'm not going to forget that kiss any time soon.

"I'm going to shower." I take a sip of my drink. "I'll be ready in thirty minutes."

Raven nods. "I'll be upstairs. See you soon."

Only the coldest shower that ever existed could get Keegan Baldwin out of my head.

Chapter Seventeen

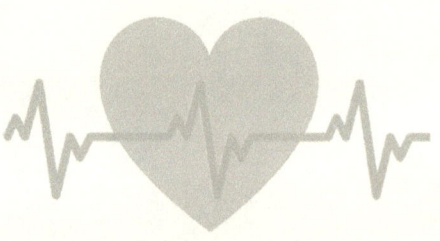

We arrive at the Montauket, and everyone is in front of the hotel and restaurant on the beach, enjoying drinks and listening to live music. A breeze comes off the ocean, and I smooth out my white sundress that lifts with a gust of wind.

"You got some color today." Forest puts his arm around my shoulder, and we look at the crowd. He watches Raven walk across the sand to one of the outdoor bars.

"It's been a great weekend." I blow out a heavy breath, riddled with a million heady thoughts. "I like the escape that this place offers. I don't want to face real life tomorrow."

Keegan stands at the bar and Raven says something to him, and he nods. He looks across the sand to me. When he sees me staring in his direction, Keegan bobs his head but then looks away.

"It was pretty great of Keegan to invite us along," Forest says. "He seems like he enjoyed himself."

"Yeah. I think so." I smooth out my hair, but let myself glance in Keegan's direction.

Forest nudges me on the shoulder. "I always worry about him. His life feels so small sometimes. Like I'm all he has."

I hold my hair out of my face as the ocean breeze circles me. "I don't know. He seems okay to me."

We watch as Raven walks our way. "That's the thing about Keegan. You'd never know one way or another."

"How beautiful is this?" Raven gestures toward everyone standing around, and then we all look toward the sun that is low in the sky. "This place is amazing. Do we have to go back tomorrow?"

"I'm not going to think about tomorrow yet." I hold my plastic cup up and walk toward the ocean. "I'm going to dip my toes in the water."

I've always been obsessed with the ocean. And living in Minnesota, I felt worlds away from one so it's nice to live in New York and be able to drive a relatively short distance and smell the salt in the air and feel it against my skin.

A wave comes up, and I let it crash over my toes and bare legs. I shut my eyes for a moment and try to clear my mind of everything. But instead, it flashes to my childhood. I'm a twelve-year-old, watching eighteen-year-old Keegan pack up his bags, because he graduated high school, with an associate's degree already in his back pocket, thanks to this thing called postsecondary education, and now will be starting Harvard as a Junior due to all of his transfer credits.

His jeans are three inches too short and tight on his thin frame. His baggy sweatshirt looks like it's a hundred years old, and his baby face is almost completely hidden by his oversized glasses held together with black tape. I remember thinking that the world is cruel to people like Keegan. He always seemed too big for Cherry, as if staying there would hold him back and force him to stay small.

My mind starts playing the film again, and this time, I'm seeing Keegan at his graduation from Harvard. The entire family went to Boston, and I was fourteen and way more impressed to get to see such a historic school than I was to see Keegan. He was still a tall, thin man, but I admit, his clothes fit him more. He had a girlfriend, and I remember thinking it didn't seem possible that a girl would like him. What do fourteen-year-olds know?

The last time I saw Keegan before this summer was at his medical school graduation. He was twenty-four, and I was eighteen. He had a different girlfriend this time. But instead of spending time with her that evening, Forest and I helped him pack boxes at his small Boston apartment because the next day, he was driving to New York City to get ready for his residency program. He and Forest let me drink, and I remember being tipsy, verbose, and drunk on the possibilities of adulthood. Forest passed out, and Keegan and I stayed up all night talking.

Our six-year age difference seemed to disappear that night. We liked some of the same music and were interested in similar things. Hell, I was about to start studying medicine, just like him. It occurred to me that evening how much age loses relevance the older we get. That night, we talked for hours, and for the first time in my life, I felt like Keegan and I were developing a relationship outside of Forest or my parents.

I left Boston, feeling like we'd become friends. And then so much time passed. I went to college and studied pre-med. He did a residency. I attended medical school. He did a fellowship. We kept up with email the best that busy people can do, but our lives couldn't have been going in more different directions.

I catch sight of Keegan walking toward me. He emerges from the dazzling rays of the setting sun, his entire being bathed in the warm glow of the dusk. The colors of the sky seem to saturate him with an otherworldly aura, and I can't help but stare. It's as though he's walking out of the sun itself, and for a moment, I'm transfixed, unable to move or look away.

"Hey," his low voice rings out. He puts his phone in his back pocket and gazes at me.

"Care for a drink?" I go to hand him my tepid, flat beer in a plastic cup.

"No, thanks." Keegan holds his hand up to me. "I don't drink beer out of plastic cups."

"Of course, you don't." I shake my head. "I can't see an ocean and not dip my toes in it."

Keegan rubs his hand along his jawline, and it tenses under his touch. "You were the same way with lakes back home."

"Yeah," I say, smiling. "I remember."

"About earlier." Keegan reaches his hand out and gently touches my elbow. "It's all—"

"Keegan Baldwin." I pull my arm back. "I really don't want to talk about it."

His grip tightens on my arm. "Luna Oliver. Please."

I'm scared about what he wants to say because I don't know what I want to hear. But whatever he says, things will shift between us, even more than they already have, and I don't know if I'm ready for that.

"Where have you guys been all night?" Forest stumbles up to us and puts one arm around Keegan and one around me. "I think I may be a little tipsy."

"Do you think?" I shake out of Forest's grip. "What'd you do? Have all the alcohol at the bar?"

"Oh, Luna." Forest pinches my cheeks. "You're so cute when you try to mother me."

"Please." I swat Forest's stomach.

"And you." Forest turns to Keegan and pokes his arm. "What are we going to do with you? I just want you to be happy."

Raven walks out of the crowd, and her face lights up when she sees us. "There you guys are. Myles and Jules took a car back to the house, and I couldn't find you three anywhere."

Forest points to me and then to Keegan. "I was about to ask Keegan about his dating life."

Keegan's head darts in Forest's direction. "It's non-existent at the moment. That's all you need to know."

Raven studies the three of us. "Okay, there's something I've been dying to know."

She steps closer to us to speak over the music. She glances at me first, and then Keegan. "Have you two ever—"

"No," Forest says, putting his hand over Raven's laughing mouth, not letting her finish. "Do not say it. Don't even think it." He then starts singing nonsense and covering his ears.

But Raven can't get enough of it and throws her head back and laughs. "I think I hit a trigger point. What would be so bad about Keegan and Luna—"

"No. No." Forest cuts her off again, and I look down at the sand, avoiding any eye contact with Keegan. My face boils.

"I don't think you fully get it." Forest puts his arm around me again. "Keegan grew up with us. Like, he pretty much lived with our family. And the pact that we have. Right, Luna?"

"Whatever, Forest." My face somehow gets hotter. I look anywhere but at Keegan. "We were kids when we made that stupid pact."

"You see, Raven," Forest says. "I kind of hooked up with Luna's college roommate. And then she kind of hooked up with my medical school friend."

Raven's eyes grow large.

"To be clear," I say. "Your friend kissed me at midnight on New Year's. You slept with my roommate in your childhood bedroom, knowing she was obsessed with you and knowing that you weren't interested in anything more than a one-night stand."

"Wait," Keegan says, looking at me. "You only kissed Forest's friend at midnight? Nothing else happened?" Keegan looks at Forest. "Sorry, bro, that is different."

"See," I say. "I told you."

"I don't know about that," Forest says. "But yes. I wasn't very sensitive to your roommate's feelings. I thought we were just having a good time."

"Back to this pact though," Raven says. "Are you both serious?"

"I didn't mean the pact literally at all," I say. "I just meant don't be mindless about hooking up with each other's friends. He knew Kelsie was obsessed with him, and that it would be nothing more than sex. That's what bothered me."

"So, wait?" Raven presses on. "I'm confused. Can you date each other's friends or not?"

Forest and I look at each other, and I shrug. "If he actually liked my friend and wasn't leading her on, I'd have no issues with it."

"Luna can date my friends if we discuss it first," Forest says. "But going back to your earlier comment, Raven. Keegan doesn't count in any of this. He's family."

"That's too bad for Luna." Raven laughs but then turns her attention to Keegan. "Because you seem so perfect."

"Keegan? Perfect?" I shake my head. "No. Definitely not."

"Wow, Luna," Keegan says, narrowing his eyes. "You sure didn't hesitate."

"I want to hear all the ways he's not perfect," Raven adds. "Because I have yet to find a flaw."

"Hmm," I say, thinking, and then look toward Keegan, unable to think of anything off the top of my head. He tilts his head, studying me. Waiting.

"He's not very spontaneous," I finally say. "And he worries too much."

"You'll have to do better than that, Luna." Raven goes and stands by Keegan and places her hand on his shoulder.

"What about when you accidentally sexted me when I was in college?"

Forest backhands Keegan's arm. "You sexted my sister? Why am I only hearing about this now?"

"It was meant for Stella," Keegan says. His eyes glance at me, and then he looks at the sand.

"Huh." Forest scratches his chin. "Stella doesn't seem like someone who would have been receptive to that. She was your most boring girlfriend to date."

"Wait." I put my hand up, a memory coming to me. "Is that the girl you called missionary?"

"The one and only." Forest grabs his stomach as he laughs, looking at me. "But let's not even start on you. How many boyfriends did you go through in college?"

I grab Forest around the shoulders and squeeze him, but he's too strong, puts me in a headlock, and starts messing up my hair. Keegan tries to step in to help me, but Forest pushes him back and I somehow end up flat on my back in the sand. My dress flies up but I quickly adjust it until it's back in place.

Raven laughs so hard, and we all turn to her. She puts her hand on her side like it's aching with our humiliation. "You three crack me up. Seriously."

Forest and Keegan reach out to me and pull me up. I smooth out my hair.

"We should go." Keegan's words cut through this new silence. "And I'll drive. The rest of you are straight losing your minds."

When we arrive back at the house, I pour myself a tall glass of water and head to my bedroom. Keegan steps out of the bathroom and glances at me. We pause, my hand on the doorknob and his on his doorframe. He takes a deep breath, then goes into his room, and shuts the door.

Chapter Eighteen

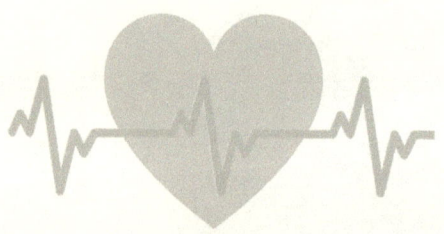

From: Keegan Baldwin <Keegan.Baldwin@med.cornell.edu
To: Luna Oliver <Luna.Oliver@umn.edu

Date: July 12

I'm coming home for an entire week the last week of July. Will I get to see you? I'm staying with your parents. I have to move my mom.

From: Luna Oliver <Luna.Oliver@umn.edu
To: Keegan Baldwin <Keegan.Baldwin@med.cornell.edu

Date: July 14

I haven't heard from you since you accidentally kind of PG-style sexted me. Still dying over that. LOL. I leave for Italy on July 26th and don't come back until August 8th. My boyfriend's parents have a place on Lake Como. Will Stella come with you?

From: Keegan Baldwin <Keegan.Baldwin@med.cornell.edu
To: Luna Oliver <Luna.Oliver@umn.edu

Date: July 14

No. That ended.

Once I get back in the city, I have shifts for ten days straight, and my time is mainly focused on preoperative and postoperative care of the patient. Days bleed into nights, and I barely see my apartment because it's easier to crash in one of the resident rooms at the hospital.

"Hey there, Roomie," Raven says as she walks down the hallway toward me. "I feel like I haven't seen you in days."

"I know," I say, leaning against the nearest nurse's station. "But after my shift, I have the next two days off and can't wait to sleep in my bed and see daylight again."

Raven squeezes my arm. "It almost makes me regret taking time off for the Fourth. Almost." Her lips turn up in a grin, like she's remembering a happy memory.

"Do you want to get all dressed up tomorrow night and go out to eat at a restaurant we can't afford?" I grab my charts from the nurse's station desk and hold them in front of me. "We could see if Myles is free too."

"That sounds incredible," Raven says. "It's a date."

Even though it's the middle of the week, the rest of my shift feels like the Friday before the holiday break. But instead of getting a week off, I get two consecutive days, and I couldn't be more excited about it. I'm starting to feel so comfortable at the hospital, but I miss my crappy, cozy little apartment too.

The rest of my shift drags on. I monitor surgical patients on the step-down floor who are ready to be released. I check vitals, and stitches, ask a million questions, and for those who are ready, I sign off on their release.

When my shift ends, I change out of my scrubs and have a smile plastered on my face when I walk out of the room to leave for the day. My excitement is cut short when Forest approaches me with a concerned look on his face.

"Hey, Luna," Forest says, glancing at his phone and then back at me. "Keegan just called me. He's sick and asked me to stop by. He never asks for anything. But I'm about to start my forty-eight-hour on-call shift."

"I'm sure he's fine," I say. "He probably has a little man cold."

Forest runs his hand through his hair. "I don't know. He never asks for anything. He sounded terrible."

"What do you want me to do?" I look at my watch. If I leave now, I can be home in fifteen minutes and have my first Netflix show queued up as I order dinner.

"Could you stop over there and check on him?"

"Forest, I'm sure he's—"

"Please, Luna," Forest says. "Besides us, he doesn't have anyone. And it's rare enough for him to call me. He's definitely not going to ask anyone else for help."

I blow out a breath. "He's probably fine and doesn't want to be bothered."

"Maybe," Forest says. "And if it's nothing, good. but it will give me peace of mind."

"Fine," I finally say. "I'm sure it's nothing, but I'll let you know."

Forest hugs me and then texts me the address to Keegan's apartment building. He lets me know that he'll call ahead to the doorman to explain that I need to be let up.

I trudge in the direction of Keegan's building, and it's pretty much equal distance to the hospital that mine is, only in the opposite direction. I talk to the doorman, show him my identification, and then he lets me up the elevator. I text Keegan that I'm coming, but I don't get a response.

The elevator stops on the fifteenth floor, and I knock on his door. I wait a few moments and then knock again. When he still doesn't answer, I use the key card that Forest gave me to let myself in.

"Keegan, are you here?" I call out but am met with silence. "Keegan? It's Luna."

I toss my bag on the huge kitchen island, and my mouth nearly hangs open as I take in his place. I've been in the city for nearly six weeks but haven't ever been here. Everything looks new. The counters are white marble, and the living area is expansive. Sunlight pours in from the floor-to-ceiling windows, and the floors are a beautiful light wood.

"Keegan," I say again as I head down a long hallway.

The walls are white, and the only thing hanging on them is a large painting of the spoonbridge and cherry from the Minneapolis sculpture gardens. I pass a bathroom on my right and a room with the door cracked open. I peek inside, and it's a library full of books. There is a lone room on the left at the end of the hallway.

"Keegan." I reach the closed door and slowly open it. "Are you in here?"

His bedroom is dark, but I can see the outline of a massive bed that is centered in the room. I reach his bed, turn on a lamp, and Keegan begins to stir. He's sound asleep, and I consider tiptoeing out of his room like I was never here, but instead, I put my hand on his shoulder and slightly squeeze.

"Hey, Keegan."

One of his eyes pops open, and then he tries to sit up. He's got a sweatshirt on with the hood covering his hair. He looks a little green. I take the back of my hand and press it against his forehead. The man's burning up.

"Am I dreaming?" Keegan says, rubbing his eyes. "Is that you?"

"It's not a dream." I sit on the edge of the bed. "Forest said you aren't feeling well. You're burning up."

"You didn't have to come," he says, leaning back against the headboard. "I'm sorry."

"Do you have a thermometer?" I wave him off.

"Medical bag. Top drawer." Keegan points to the nightstand. "But Luna, I'm fine. You can leave."

"Yeah, okay." I shake his hand off of me and open the drawer. I try to ignore the pile of condoms and reach for the black bag. I open it up, grab a thermometer, and stick it in his mouth. Keegan moans.

When it beeps, I pull it out. "104.3. Damn, Keegan."

I then grab the stethoscope. I try to reach down his shirt, but he has it pulled too tight, so I enter from the bottom. His skin is lava beneath my touch.

"It's so cold," Keegan says as he shivers.

"Compared to your skin, I'm sure it is," I say. "I'm going to listen to your lungs. Take a deep breath."

Keegan inhales and then blows out a breath.

"Rhonchi," I say, hearing the crackling sounds as he breathes. "Keegan, we need to get you to a doctor. I think you have pneumonia."

"No, no." Keegan waves me away. "I'll call in an order of Amoxicillin."

"Keegan," I protest. "For being the smartest person I know, you're acting stupid."

"Luna," Keegan says my name slowly, and I remove the covers and pull him toward the edge of the bed. "My entire body feels like I've been run over. I can't make it to a doctor."

"I'll help," I say, using all of my strength to pull him up. "I'd feel better if you get checked out."

"That's too much of me to ask." Keegan whimpers as he stands.

"You didn't ask," I say. "I'm demanding that I take you in for a chest x-ray."

He leans on me as we walk toward the door. He sits and slips on a pair of sneakers. It's ninety degrees outside, but Keegan looks like he's dressed for winter.

"My friend works at Presby's general clinic," he says. "I'll call ahead and see if they can get me in right away."

Dr. Keegan Baldwin carries a lot of clout at Presby, and as soon as we walk in the door, the two of us are brought to an exam room. I don't ask Keegan if he wants me to stay with him. His tight grip on my arm tells me he doesn't want me to leave. The doctor does a blood test and orders a chest x-ray.

When the doctor leaves the room, Keegan turns to me. "I'm so sorry you have to be here. Forest shouldn't have asked you."

"You know you could have called me and asked for help," I say.

"Lu—"

"If Forest hadn't told me," I interrupt, "you'd still be in bed, miserable."

After a couple of hours at the clinic, the diagnosis is confirmed. Bacterial pneumonia. And on top of that, a case of Influenza A. On the way out, we stop by the pharmacy to grab his prescription for antibiotics. When I get Keegan back in his apartment, he's exhausted and feels miserable.

"Let me grab you some water." His fridge is almost empty. I grab the water jug and pour him a tall glass. "Drink all of this, and let's get you back in bed."

"You can leave, seriously," Keegan says, already walking down the hallway. "You've been so helpful. I don't want you to catch what I have."

I pause, wondering if I should follow him, or say goodbye and leave. My heart grows seeing Keegan like this. I have this strong urge to take care of him and make everything better. My heart breaks knowing he's alone, feeling this way, with no food in his fridge.

"Should I call someone?" I step toward him. "Elise? Anyone else?"

"No. Definitely no." Keegan walks into his bedroom and I follow. "Honestly. I'm good."

Again, my conscience pulls at me. I could leave now, and still get a couple of episodes of my show in. But I don't think I'd enjoy myself knowing that Keegan is here all alone, feeling as miserable as he does.

I grab his arm as he reaches his bedroom. "Do you want me to leave?"

Keegan turns. His face softens, and he slowly blinks. "No. But I don't want you to get sick either."

"Well there you have it," I say. "I'm staying. And I've already been exposed to what you have, so it's too late to worry about that."

"Thanks." Keegan squeezes my hand. He then gets under the covers, turns on his side, and shuts his eyes.

I jump into caregiver mode. I buy groceries for him online and then order a few pints of chicken noodle soup from one of my favorite soup shops in the city. I write out his medicine schedule, sprinkling in plenty of opportunities to give him fever and pain relievers. I stock up on vapor rub filled with menthol, eucalyptus, and camphor. I scrub down every surface that Keegan could have touched. When the groceries arrive, I put everything away, and am proud of all the fresh produce and healthy food options that stare back at me.

After everything is organized, I tiptoe into his room, sit in his comfy chair in the corner of the room, and wait for him to wake up.

Chapter Nineteen

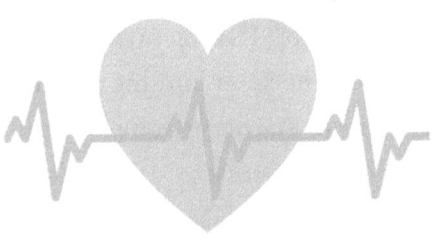

"Luna?" A couple of hours later, Keegan's head shoots up.

"How are you feeling?" I sit on the edge and once again feel his forehead. Then I reach for more meds on the nightstand and hand them to him along with a glass of water.

"You're still here." Keegan sits up.

"I'm not going anywhere," I say.

"You really don't—"

"I know, I know." I wave him off. "You can quit trying to get rid of me, though. I'm staying."

His face softens. "Thanks, Luna."

"Plus," I say. "I need to feed you."

I leave the room, warm up the soup, and bring it to him. "This is the best soup you'll ever have."

"You got me soup?" He studies the bowl in my hands as if he doesn't believe me.

"And a few other groceries as well," I say. "Your fridge was pretty bare."

"You didn't have to," Keegan says.

Keegan spoons the soup into his mouth as I look on. His coloring is already starting to improve, as some pink has started to form on his cheeks.

"When I was young," Keegan says between spoonfuls. "No matter what I was sick with, my mom would make me homemade soup and let me have a can of Sprite."

"It's okay to ask for help, you know." I bend my knee and tuck my foot underneath. "You don't have to go at things alone all the time."

Keegan slowly blinks. "Asking for help isn't a strong suit of mine."

"Can I draw you a bath?" I ask. "Get you into some clean clothes?"

"No bath," Keegan says. "Sitting in my filth and sweat does not sound appealing to me."

I chuckle at this. "Fine. But you should go shower, and I will change your sheets."

Keegan nods and then looks at my outfit. "Sheets are in the linen closet in the hallway. And feel free to go through my clothes and put on something more comfortable."

Keegan goes to his ensuite bathroom, shuts the door, and a steady stream of water turns on. I strip the bedding and throw it in the washer, and make up Keegan's bed. I go back to his room and do a little snooping. His top drawer is filled with perfectly folded underwear and athletic socks. The next drawer down is full of cotton shirts. I smile as I see one from Cherry that says Mathletics across the front. I decide to put that one on, then grab a pair of scrub bottoms, and cinch them tightly around my waist.

The shower is still running, so I explore the rest of his place. The library is beautiful, with two blue velvet chaises pointed in the direction of the books. There are so many of them on floor-to-ceiling shelves. I run my hand along the spines of his countless anatomy textbooks.

Then I stroll to the kitchen, which is a chef's dream. The island is massive and opens up to the inviting living room. I walk over look out a window and take a deep breath. If I lived here, I'd never leave. I heat more soup for Keegan and grab an orange from the bowl on the island to bring to him.

Keegan startles when I walk into the room. It's as if he's forgotten he's not alone. He had time to pull on flannel pajama bottoms that hang off his hips, but he holds a gray shirt in his hand. Water drips down his taut chest. I pull my lips into my mouth and glance at Keegan, who I'm pretty sure catches me staring.

"I brought more food," I say, holding out the bowl. "And while I have you shirtless, let me put some vapor rub on your back."

His skin is sun-kissed and golden brown, and his muscles come together perfectly in an intricate pattern of perfection. I shake my head when I realize I'm staring again.

"Okay." Keegan's eyes rake down my body until they settle on the food in my hand. "I like your shirt."

"It's always been my dream to wear someone's Mathletics shirt, so thank you."

Keegan tries to laugh but ends up having a coughing fit instead. He sits on the edge of the bed, and I stand over him, putting the vapor rub on his upper back. I then move to the front, standing between his legs. His skin is aflame beneath my touch, and his muscles are hard and well-defined. I start by rubbing the vapor rub behind his ears and over his lymph nodes, but then spread my fingers and rub more over his hard chest. I relish feeling his muscles beneath my touch.

"There," I say. "That should provide some relief."

Keegan studies me, his brows knitted together. He then lets out a deep breath, pulls his shirt over his head, and gets under the covers.

"It's really late," Keegan says, yawning. "And my entire body aches."

"Let me grab some meds," I say. "We need to get your fever down."

"I always knew you'd make a great doctor," Keegan says, gripping my hand. "Even if you are terrible at math."

"Thanks." I rub my eyes but smile. "I really appreciate your vote of confidence."

"You should stay with me," Keegan says, patting the bed beside him. "My bed is too big for just one person."

Before I have a chance to answer, Keegan's eyes are closed. I exhale a deep breath and consider folding the covers down and getting in. But then I decide that this isn't the time to overcomplicate things, and I walk out and sleep on the couch for the night.

Chapter Twenty

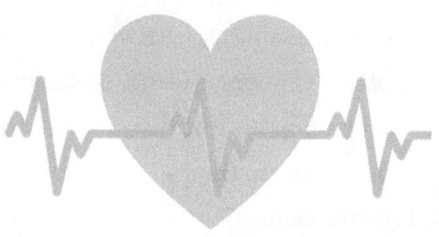

"We have to get your fever down," I say to Keegan when he comes out to the living room and sits on the couch at my feet. I can tell just by looking at him that he's burning up. "I'm going to start rotating between aspirin and Tylenol, and I'm getting you a cold cloth."

"Yeah, I feel like shit," he says.

"You should get back in bed." I stand and reach my arms out for him, to pull him up.

"I'm not tired," Keegan says.

"You look miserable," I say. "Come on. Back to bed."

"You're right." Keegan stretches his arms above his head as he yawns. He finally grips my hands that have been outstretched for him. His skin burns beneath mine. "Do you need to leave?"

"I can." I drop Keegan's hand, and he glances at me as we walk toward his room. "But I don't have to."

"Stay." Keegan holds the door open for me. "We could lie in bed all day and watch shows."

"My pick, right?" I fold the covers down and nod for Keegan to get back into the bed.

Keegan raises an eyebrow. "Do you have a show in mind?"

"I do," I say. "A romance. Obviously. It's what I'd be watching if I were at my place on a day off."

"A romance?" Keegan pulls the covers over himself and raises an eyebrow. "I guess that's only fair."

Keegan grabs his laptop, and I make a cup of mint tea for both of us. He places the computer on his lap, so I have no choice but to move directly next to him to see the screen. Now that I think about it, his apartment doesn't have a TV. He hands me the laptop, and I queue up the show I want to watch.

Our arms press against each other's, and there is something intimate about watching the same laptop as someone else. If I were home and not caring for Keegan, I'd never allow myself to sit in bed all day and watch a show. But after working ten straight shifts, this is exactly what my body needs.

"Those two are clearly going to end up together," Keegan says through a yawn. "Can't you just fast-forward to the good parts?"

"That's not how this works," I say, nudging him. "Of course they're going to end up together, but why fast forward and not enjoy the process?"

"I guess," he says. "It just seems really predictable."

I reach over to the nightstand to give him his meds. Besides pausing for a while when I made lunch, we've been at this all day. And the sun is starting to get low in the sky.

"So wait," Keegan says, a few episodes later. "They're supposed to get married now? Just because they kissed?"

"It was a different time. And it's fiction." I turn to Keegan, and he looks amused. "Keep up."

"Thank gawd those aren't the rules anymore, or I'd be married to Mary Strumble," Keegan says, turning to grin at me.

"What?" I say too loudly and grab his arm. "Your first kiss was Mary Strumble? Tuba Mary? Mathletics Mary?" I can't stop laughing.

"Okay, 'too cool for school,'" Keegan pushes me back. "Who would you be married to?"

"No one you probably know," I say, but Keegan pauses the show, turns to me, and waits.

"Tell me." He smiles.

"Andy Yetts," I say, putting my head in my hands. "Yes, the current town cop in Cherry."

Keegan puts his hand on my shoulder and laughs.

"Wait," Keegan says. "Wasn't he just a grade below Forest and me?"

"Yes," I nod. "He never left Cherry. When he got back from the academy, he was at a high school party, and yeah, we kissed."

"Of course he hung out at high school parties," Keegan says. "He gave me a speeding ticket the last time I was in Cherry for doing thirty-five in a thirty. If I would have known you had a past with him, I would have mentioned your name to get out of the ticket."

"It wouldn't have helped," I say. "I may have broken his heart just a little."

Keegan slowly blinks as he nods. "That is not surprising at all."

Time has no meaning in Keegan's room, where we're transported to the nineteenth century. We're just two friends, spending a couple of days together, forgetting about all the pressures and expectations of the outside world. In here, he's just Keegan, a person who I like more, the more I get to know him. I can pretend he's not my brother's best friend, nor is he the boy I once knew. There is no past or future. Just today.

At some point, we must both doze off. When I open my eyes to the soft glow of Netflix asking if I'm still watching, my head is tucked into Keegan's side, and his arm is slung over me. His long eyelashes sway from the breeze of the ceiling fan, and my hand is spread against his chest. The soft cotton of his shirt a contrast with the hard muscles underneath. Outside, the morning light peeks through the window, which means I slept in his arms all night. I should be worried about catching what he has, but for some reason, I'm not. My desire to take care of him outweighs any fear.

I turn my head slightly to the arm tightly holding me. I glance at Keegan again, and he is still fully asleep. I maneuver out of his grip and turn his arm to see his tattoo better.

"Luna," Keegan says groggily, his eyes slowly opening. "What are you doing?"

"You should have woken me up," I say. "I could have slept on the couch."

Keegan nods. "You fell asleep, and I didn't want to move you."

I don't remember ever sleeping as well as I did last night or waking up this well-rested. The smell of Keegan is so intoxicating to me. The fresh scent of detergent with hints of eucalyptus from the vapor rub.

"I told you I was going to see your tattoo someday, and you're going to let me." I scrape my teeth against my bottom lip and push his sleeve farther, looking at him, prodding him to not stop me. He slowly blinks but then nods.

"This is so not what I was expecting," I say when the tattoo is fully visible. Keegan's face flushes. "When you said you lost a bet, I was pretty sure you had a penis on your arm."

Keegan's tattoo is a crescent moon, and there is a circle of text that surrounds it. *The moon was so beautiful that the ocean held up a mirror.*

"It's actually kind of pretty. Almost romantic." I put space between us, suddenly aware that I'm practically lying on Keegan. "Of all the tattoos your friends could have chosen, why this one?"

Keegan props himself up in bed. "Their first option was a penis, but I was given three vetoes," Keegan says. "So they went with a moon."

"If you're not going to tell me why a moon, I may have to contact your friends myself." I pull the blanket over myself. "You said you have two tattoos? Where's the other one?"

"The second one was also a dare." Keegan scratches his day-old stubble on his face.

"You need to be smarter about your dares, Keegan Baldwin," I say.

"Not all my dares have been bad," he says. His voice is low and gravelly. He's talking about our kiss in Montauk.

"Quit trying to change the subject. Where is this other tattoo of yours? Cause I saw you in your swim trunks in Montauk, and besides the one on your arm, there were no other tattoos."

"You don't want to know," Keegan says.

"I actually kind of do," I say. "Why didn't you want me to see your tattoo?"

"I'm weird about my tattoos and what they reveal about myself." Keegan runs both hands through his hair and hangs his head low before looking at me. "I've just always loved the moon."

"Huh." I knit my eyebrows together. Sometimes when Keegan and I talk, I'm not entirely confident that we're not talking about something much deeper.

Keegan rubs his temples and then brushes a finger over his lips. "The sun is so obvious. Too obvious. Everyone loves the sun, even though it's painful to look at."

Our eyes lock, and he puts his hand on his tattoo but continues looking at me. "But the moon is a compass. It gives light to a dark world. It's so powerful that it determines the tides in the ocean."

"And, well, the moon is beautiful," he says, looking at me. He then reaches over to the nightstand and puts his glasses on.

I furrow my brow even further. "You know, my name means moon in Latin. Of course, you know that. You seem to know everything. It's kind of a coincidence that you have a moon tattooed on your arm, don't you think?"

Keegan shakes his head. "I don't believe in coincidences. I'm a scientist."

"Then how do you explain your tattoo?"

Keegan's mouth opens as if he's about to say something, but then he snaps it shut.

Several moments pass between us, and then Keegan pulls the blanket down. "I'm starting to feel so much better, so don't feel like you have to, but any interest in finishing the first season today? I'm highly committed at this point."

"Good job changing the subject," I say, jumping out of bed. "I'm going to grab your meds, make some tea, and then we can queue it up."

We once again sit in bed, bodies pressed against the headboard, and watch our show. I'm regretting continuing because when I fell asleep last night, it was the wedding scene. Now it's the honeymoon episode and seeing the intimacy on screen makes me think of all the unsaid electricity between us. Neither of us moves or dares to glance in each other's direction. My face heats up as the intimate scene unfolds before us.

"Okay," Keegan says, breaking the silence. "Now I think I understand why women like romance so much."

"Umm," I say, having difficulty forming actual words. "That was something."

Keegan presses pause when the episode ends, shuts his laptop, and puts it on the nightstand. Neither of us moves, but when he turns to me, he inhales a sharp breath. His hand moves to my face, and his fingers delicately push a strand of hair behind my ear. I move my hand to his arm and feel the hardness beneath my touch.

"Luna," Keegan says softly. His tongue wets his lips.

We inch closer together, and then he grips the base of my neck, where he squeezes, sending shivers throughout my body.

Keegan nods as if he's asking my permission. I slant my head to the left, as we close the gap between us. We're so close that I can smell the mint on his breath. He tilts his head, and I close my eyes, breathing him in.

"Keegan, Luna, where are you guys?" Our heads turn toward the door as Forest's voice rings out from down the hall.

I jump out of bed, putting as much space between me and Keegan as possible. I shake my thoughts out of my head because if Forest hadn't shown up, I'd be kissing Keegan. And not because of a breakdown, or a dare, but because it feels like what's coming next for us.

"There you guys are," Forest says, standing in the doorway of Keegan's bedroom, holding a large box in his hand. He looks at me. "Luna, you're officially off duty. Keegan and I are going to play video games all day. Just like the good ole days."

"That sounds…" Keegan's voice trails off, as he steals a glance in my direction. "Great. Thanks for picking up a console."

"Yeah, I'm glad you came," I say, trying to hide the shakiness in my voice. "I have a million things I need to get done before I'm back on the clock tomorrow."

"Are you feeling any better?" Forest says, glancing at Keegan.

"I am." Keegan looks at me, then toward his feet. "Thanks to Luna."

"You're the best, kiddo," Forest says, messing up my hair. "Thanks for stepping in."

"Keegan, help me get this set up," Forest says. Keegan pauses for a moment, looking between us, but then follows Forest out of the room.

When they're gone, I put my hand on my chest, trying to steady my breath. I'm partially relieved that Forest showed up when he did. My senses start to come back to me, and I remember that my life isn't as insulated as it's felt the past couple of days, and there are real consequences to kissing Keegan outside of a dare. But there's an even larger part of me that wants to be underneath him right now. To know what that feels like.

"Hey," Keegan says, stepping back into his room. He leans against the doorframe and brings me back to reality.

"Hey," I say.

"You have to promise me you won't finish the show without me."

"That's a lot to ask." I fold the shirt and scrub bottoms I was wearing and put them on Keegan's bed. "But I'll do my best."

Keegan pushes off the frame and walks toward me. He puts his hand on my cheek. "Thanks for everything."

"It's not a big—" I begin to say.

"It is. To me," Keegan interrupts. "There are very few people who would. . ."

He stops talking, leans in, and brushes his lips against my cheek. We hold each other for a moment and then let go. A rare melancholy starts in my stomach and spreads through my chest. I can't name this feeling. I only know that I'm disappointed to be leaving.

"Let's go, man," Forest yells from the living room. "It's all ready for us."

"Keep taking it easy," I say. "You're still not a hundred percent."

Keegan inhales a deep breath, nods, and walks out of the room.

Chapter Twenty-One

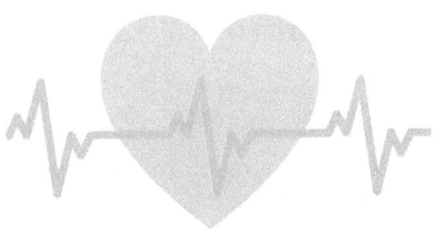

From: Luna Oliver <Luna.Oliver@umn.edu
To: Keegan Baldwin <Keegan.Baldwin@med.cornell.edu

Date: August 25

My boyfriend and I are going to visit Forest in Boston over Labor Day weekend, but we want to spend a couple of nights in NYC as I've never been, and he wants to show me the city. Are you around? It's been forever.

From: Keegan Baldwin <Keegan.Baldwin@med.cornell.edu
To: Luna Oliver <Luna.Oliver@umn.edu

Date: August 27

> We miss each other again. I'll be out west at a CME event for residents and fellows. Enjoy the city and say hi to Forest for me.

"So much for our fancy night out," Raven says, walking beside me as we round on the step-down unit.

"Trust me, no one was as bummed as me," I say. "But what was I supposed to do when Forest basically begged me to help out Keegan?"

Raven puckers her lips. "You spent two nights with the guy, and you're still telling me nothing happened?"

"That's exactly what I'm telling you." I stop walking and turn to Raven. "He was so sick. And that's just not our relationship. Sorry to disappoint you."

"I'm rarely off about these types of things," Raven says. "The guy is into you."

"Dr. Parse is coming our way," I whisper to Raven, relieved by the distraction. "No more boy talk."

"Craik. Oliver," Dr. Parse says as he reaches us. "I need you both to stay on the step-down unit for a few hours. They're backed up."

Today is a short, ten-hour shift, and when I glance at my phone afterward, I have a text from Forest asking if I want to meet him for a drink at George's to catch up. I tell him I'll join him for one, but then I must get home and sleep before another long day tomorrow.

Soft music plays when I enter the dimly lit place. I immediately see Forest sitting at the bar. I put my hands on his shoulders and hug him from behind. "Hey there."

"Hey, Kiddo," Forest says. "I've missed you."

When my drink comes, we clink our glasses together. His face turns serious, and he starts tapping his finger against the bar.

"Luna, I've been wanting to talk to you about something," he says, dragging a finger around the rim of his glass.

"Out with it. You're making me nervous." The number of possibilities fly through my brain.

Forest holds his hand up. "It's not serious or anything. But yeah. I figured we should chat."

"Okay," I say slowly.

"Remember that stupid pact we made? Your roommate. My friend. Even though so many years have passed since then."

"We've talked this to death. Why are we still discussing it?"

Forest takes a long sip of his drink. "Well, when we were in Montauk, you said that your interpretation of the pact is that as long as I wasn't reckless and looking for a fling, you wouldn't care if I dated your friends."

Thoughts fly through my mind. Me kissing Keegan in his office. Our makeout session in Montauk. The two of us almost kissing the other day at Keegan's place. I hold my breath, waiting for Forest to interrogate me.

"Okay," I say, raising my eyebrows.

"You need to know something." Forest folds his hands. "After you said that, I went back to the house, and Raven and I kissed."

It isn't about me. Relief reaches every orifice of my body.

"You what?" I grab Forest's shoulder and squeeze, harder than I intend to.

"Nothing else happened, I promise," Forest says. "And it wasn't this stupid and spontaneous, drinking-induced thing. I want you to know that."

I don't know why, but I manage to be both surprised and not surprised. I saw how well they got along. Both of them have magnetic personalities, and Raven is smart and beautiful. Forest going after a woman like her makes sense.

"Is this a repeat of the Kelsie thing?" I square my body to his. "Where the girl is obsessed with you, but you have no interest in dating? And then I'll be left having to pick up the pieces with Raven. Or I'll do what I did with Kelsie and find a new place to live. Because the crappy apartment I'm in is the only place I can actually afford in this city, and—"

"Damn, Luna. Take a breath." Forest shakes his head. "It's not like that. At all."

"We aren't kids anymore," I finally say. And I think about my kiss with Keegan, suddenly feeling guilty. Even if it was a dare that meant nothing. "You know the risks of getting tangled up in a relationship with someone I live with. But that pact was made at a very different stage of our lives. What the pact should have been is no casual hookups. But if you like her, I'm good. Just don't be an ass."

Am I just like my brother? I've kissed Keegan, and it's not going anywhere. It can't.

"How very mature of you, Luna." Forest puts his elbows on the bar. "And I have no intentions of being an ass."

"So, you kissed in Montauk." I smile. "How romantic."

"She wanted to tell you immediately. I asked her not to," Forest says. "She values the friendship she has with you."

"And nothing has happened since?"

"We've been chatting, but no. I needed to make sure you wouldn't be freaked out by this."

"I'm not," I say and mean it. "Are you going to ask her out?"

"If you're okay with it, yes," Forest says.

"You're going to ask her on a date." I pinch Forest's arm. "Look at you. You're becoming an actual adult."

"It was bound to happen at some point," Forest says.

"Does Keegan know?" I pull my lips into a thin line and wait for a response.

Forest nods. "Yeah. He knows."

"So, I was the only one in the dark?" I shake my head. For some reason, it bothers me more that Keegan knew and didn't tell me.

"He's my best friend, Luna. Of course, I told him." Forest shifts on his barstool. "But I was prepared to walk away entirely if you weren't supportive."

I raise an eyebrow. "That's stupid."

The bell on the door jingles as someone walks through, and Forest waves. "Speaking of Keegan, he's meeting us here."

My gaze cuts to him. I haven't seen him since the morning I left his place to go back home. Keegan gives Forest a bro's hug, and then he nods in my direction.

Forest beams. "Order yourself a drink, Keegan. I'm going to step outside and make a phone call."

Keegan takes the seat next to me and gets the attention of the bartender.

"You look a lot less greenish-gray," I say. "How are you feeling?"

"Like a fully functioning human," Keegan says. "I appreciate what you did for me so much. And so far, it looks like you didn't catch anything from me."

"You knew about Forest and Raven?" I change the subject as I turn my stool toward Keegan.

He lifts an eyebrow. "He finally told you?"

"Why didn't you tell me?" I stare at the bottom tip of the moon tattoo on his inner arm. It's now all I can see. "How long have you known?"

Keegan winces and seems to contemplate how honest he should be. "Since I witnessed the kiss our last night in Montauk."

"Of course you did." I push Keegan's arm.

"Luna," Keegan says in a calm voice and looks down at my hand.

"You've known since Montauk?" I say in a quieter voice this time. "And you didn't tell me?"

"It wasn't my place." Keegan puts his hand on my shoulder. "He's my best friend, and he asked me not to say anything."

"He'll always be your favorite Oliver, won't he?" I move my shoulder to create space between us.

Keegan removes his hand and leans closer to me. "I'll keep your secrets too."

Our eyes meet, and the intensity of his gaze pierces through me. As we stare at each other, my eyes can't help but wander to his lips, the same lips that kissed mine in a passion-filled moment in Montauk. One I won't let him discuss with me because I fear it will open up something we'll never be able to close.

Keegan takes my hand. "Luna?"

"Yeah?"

Keegan drops it. "Our kiss in Montauk." Keegan glances at the door, grips the back of my stool, and leans into me. "Our almost kiss at my place. Are we ever going to discuss it? Or are we pretending that these things mean nothing?"

Heat floods my face because all I've been doing since it happened is pretend. I don't allow myself to think about it, nor do I allow myself to ponder if Keegan ever thinks of it. With science, I want to know every answer, even if it's scary. But with feelings, I'd rather be in the dark than know something that could hurt and disappoint me.

"It didn't mean anything," I finally say. "I mean, seriously, Keegan. Can you even imagine?"

Keegan's brows knit together as he studies me. He leans so close to me, that I can breathe in his scent. "What is so hard for you to imagine?"

"Me." I point to myself. "You. We've known each other our entire lives. We have very little in common. We're pretty much complete opposites. You've always been like a big brother to me."

"Huh," Keegan says.

He folds his hands behind his head, leans back in his stool, and continues to stare straight ahead. His face is freshly shaven, and his square jaw twitches at the corners.

"What do you mean? Huh?" I lean forward to hear him better after the jukebox starts up. "That's all you're going to say?"

Keegan sits up straight and brushes his thumb across the rim of the bar. He looks behind me, moves my hair off my shoulder, and says into my ear.

"You didn't kiss me as if you see me as your brother."

"Keegan Baldwin." I put my hand on my chest, willing my heart to stay inside. For someone who is more shy than straightforward, his candidness takes me by surprise.

The bell over the door jingles, and I can tell by Keegan's face that Forest is back. He glances at me as he pulls away. I'm both thrilled and terrified at the thought of Keegan and me.

"I just talked to Raven. Her shift is almost up, and she's going to join us for a drink," Forest says as he reaches us.

Keegan and I look at each other, but I quickly divert my eyes toward Forest. There is an entire side of Keegan I'm only beginning to know, and it makes me nervous—as much for him as I am for me. I'm not good at relationships, and Keegan is becoming one of my favorite people. But if he ends up like every other guy I've dated, where he'll selfishly put his needs over mine, I don't think I could stomach it.

Chapter Twenty-Two

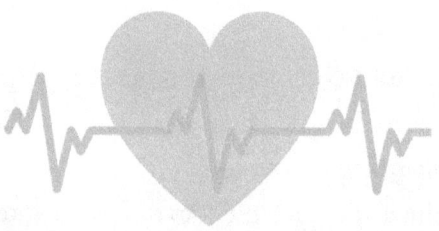

From: Luna Oliver <Luna.Oliver@umn.edu
To: Keegan Baldwin <Keegan.Baldwin@med.cornell.edu

Date: October 1

I wouldn't ask this unless it was VERY important. But O-Chem is kicking my ass. I reached out to Forest first, but we got so frustrated with each other that he hung up on me, and I spent the night crying. What is your patience level with helping someone better understand the reactions and preparations of carbon-containing compounds?

From: Keegan Baldwin <Keegan.Baldwin@med.cornell.edu
To: Luna Oliver <Luna.Oliver@umn.edu

Date: October 1

Isn't your boyfriend premed?

From: Luna Oliver <Luna.Oliver@umn.edu
To: Keegan Baldwin <Keegan.Baldwin@med.cornell.edu

Date: October 1

Boyfriend? What boyfriend? He was insecure and asked me not to be friends with other men. Like, are you kidding me?

From: Keegan Baldwin <Keegan.Baldwin@med.cornell.edu
To: Luna Oliver <Luna.Oliver@umn.edu

Date: October 1:

I'll call via messenger tonight.

The heat is oppressive today and the window units in our apartment aren't able to keep up, so we bought box fans. I would have declined Forest's family dinner with him and Keegan tonight because there is nothing less I want to do than to travel to Chelsea in this heat, but he has central air and his place is so much cooler than mine. I may even ask him if I can crash there.

My sundress sticks to my body as I approach Forest's building. My phone vibrates against me, and I stop walking to look at it. It's a text from Forest to Keegan and me, apologizing that he forgot to reach out sooner, but that he's going to the Yankees game with some friends tonight as the Twins are in town.

"You have got to be kidding me," I say, still staring at my phone, as sweat drips down the nape of my neck.

"So typical," a voice says, and I look up as Keegan also approaches Forest's building, phone in hand.

"If he'd thought to send this about twenty minutes ago, I could still be in my semi-cool apartment, sitting in front of a fan in my underwear," I say.

Keegan squeezes the back of his neck. "That's exactly what I was thinking."

I fan myself with my hand. "Well, do you want to share a car back to the Upper East Side?"

"We came all this way," Keegan says, looking around. "We could eat. Are you hungry?"

"I'm always hungry," I say. "And hot."

Keegan grabs his phone, scrolls through it, and then places it to his ear. "Yes. Hi. This is Dr. Baldwin. I'm wondering if... Yes. For two. Inside. We'll be there in about ten minutes. Perfect. Thank you."

"This is Dr. Baldwin," I say, mocking him, and Keegan chuckles.

"One of my favorite restaurants in the city is two blocks away. I guess you could say I'm a regular," he says.

"Is this your date spot?" I nudge him in the arm as we walk down the sidewalk.

"No," Keegan says, glancing at me. "But if friends come in from out of town, I always like to take them here. I've become close with the owner. I hope you like Italian."

"If the restaurant has air conditioning, I'll like it."

As we stroll down the winding street, the flickering street lights cast shadows on the worn cobblestone pavement beneath our feet. We arrive at a charming Italian eatery tucked away in a cozy corner of the block. The soft glow of warm light seeps through the restaurant's windows.

"Dr. Baldwin," an older gentleman says as he opens the door for us. "It's so good to see you. And what a beautiful date you have."

Neither of us bothers to correct him.

"Mario, I'd like to introduce you to a longtime family friend of mine, Dr. Luna Oliver. Luna, this is Mario Barone. He and his family have owned this restaurant for over fifty years."

"It's the best Italian food in the city." Mario takes my hand and kisses it. "We have your table all ready for you."

The aromas of fresh-baked bread, simmering marinara sauce, and roasted garlic waft out, tantalizing my senses and making my mouth water. The restaurant is cool, a huge contrast against the outside heat. Mario takes us to a table in the back, away from the crowd.

"Your regular table, Dr. Baldwin."

Keegan's table is a corner booth, the walls painted all around us, making me feel like I'm in Italy.

When we're seated, I lean forward on my elbows. "A regular? You're treated like royalty here."

Keegan laughs and color spreads against his cheeks. "It's nothing. Really."

"What's the story?" I say, leaning forward on my elbows.

Keegan releases a breath. "When I first moved to the city, I lived in this neighborhood, and Barone's quickly became my favorite restaurant. I used to come in here with textbooks and study, and I got to know Mario, his family, and a lot of the staff. Mario's personal story is fascinating, and the history of the struggles his family had as Italian immigrants. Then the pandemic hit, and like so many other restaurants, Barone's was on the brink of closure. Long story short, but I became a silent investor."

The server comes by, and Keegan orders a bottle of wine and appetizers.

"Wow," I say with genuine surprise. "And you're telling me you don't bring dates here all the time? That's what I would lead with. A story of saving a restaurant from closure, which also happens to have amazing food."

"You and Forest are the only people I've ever told," Keegan says. "It's not something I openly share with people. I know what it's like to come from nothing. I want to do what I can to help people."

I take a sip of my wine, and it's got to be the most expensive I've ever had. The flavors explode in my mouth, and I close my eyes and let out a satisfied sigh.

"You are so layered," I say, slathering butter on the warm bread that just arrived. "I'm learning so many new things about you."

"Yeah, well." Keegan unfolds his silverware from the cloth napkin and raises his eyes to meet mine. He releases a long and slow breath. "Sorry. I lost my train of thought."

"Why?" I tilt my head.

"Sometimes when I'm around you, I lose my ability to form words."

"Really?" I study his face, looking for hints of sarcasm.

"Really," Keegan says, picking at the bread in his hand. "You make me nervous."

"What?" I glance at Keegan to see if he's teasing. He pulls his lips into his mouth and then looks down at his glass. "But I'm me, nothing—"

"Precisely." Keegan closes his eyes for a moment. "You're you."

"Anyway, " Keegan says. "Now that I've openly admitted that to you, feel free to change the subject.

To shift the conversation in a new direction, I say, "If your dad hadn't died, do you still think you would have wanted to be a doctor?"

"I'm not sure." Keegan stretches his fingers across the table. "I had this teacher, Mr. Verny, who took me under his wing. He got me interested in science, and I realized I loved solving mysteries and that could translate to medicine. I became fascinated. Obsessed really. Not until I was a little older did I realize how much my dad dying in front of me also drove my desire to become a cardiothoracic surgeon.

Maybe in hindsight, it was what I was always supposed to do, but my dad's death provided my why, and Mr. Verny made it seem possible."

Our food comes, and we're silent for a few minutes. He puts his fork down and looks at me. "What about you? You've never told me why you wanted to become a doctor. I remember when you were younger, you were always curious and asking questions, but I never realized how much you wanted to do this."

"Isn't it obvious?" I take my napkin and dab the corners of my mouth. "For the scrubs. I never have to get up in the morning and decide what to wear to work."

Keegan laughs as he shakes his head. He reaches his hand across the table and places it over mine. "Do you always use sarcasm as armor?"

His bright blue eyes stare into mine, waiting for a response. It's easier for me to be funny than to let someone see the real me.

"It's because of you and Forest," I finally say. "You guys were always doing medical experiments in our garage, and I was fascinated. After you guys moved away, I saved up all of my money and bought *The Mayo Clinic Textbook*. It was eighty dollars, which was a lot of money for me back in the day. But I'd study it for hours every night. Memorizing the bones of the body. Different ailments people could have. The anatomy of the heart and brain."

I fork a ravioli into my mouth and nearly moan because it's the best thing I've ever tasted. Keegan still watches me, so I continue.

"But so many people told me it probably wasn't possible because of how bad I was at math. When I was in tenth grade, I met with our high school counselor about colleges, and he asked what I wanted to be when I grew up. It was the first time I told someone at school what I was thinking."

Keegan leans forward on his elbows waiting for me to say more. "The counselor said I needed more realistic goals than that. And that I should look into Executive Assistant roles, or if I really applied myself, I may be able to become a surgical assistant. If I aimed really high, maybe even a nurse. You know, something better suited for women."

"He said that?" Keegan's eyes widen.

"Verbatim." My heart accelerates at the memory. "He was such a dick. I was so mad. It was probably that moment when I realized I may not always be the smartest in the room, but I can be the one who works the hardest. I was going to be a surgeon."

"Luna," Keegan says slowly. "You're the smartest person I've ever met. No matter what room you're in."

I take a long sip of wine, ignoring his compliment, but knowing I won't forget it for the rest of my life. "When I got accepted into medical school, I scanned my acceptance letter, and sent a really pointed letter to the school counselor who was still employed there."

"Sometimes I wonder how many girls are out there just like me," I say, passion filling every cavity of my body. "Bad at math and discouraged to go into medicine for that very reason. It pisses me off honestly. Because I'm going to be a damn good surgeon, and I just needed someone to believe in me. I want to help other girls get into medicine because the field could use more of us."

"You always believed in me, and at the time, I didn't realize how important that was to me," I say. Keegan's eyes soften, and his fingers spread across the table, almost reaching for mine, but then stopping short. "But now I realize how much your confidence in me propelled me forward."

I've been talking for too long, but when I look up from my wine glass, Keegan is staring back at me, smiling.

Keegan's smile reaches his eyes. "I think that's one of the best whys I've ever heard."

After dinner, we step out of the restaurant, and the heat hits us like a physical force, enveloping us in a thick blanket of humidity. The surrounding buildings loom tall and imposing, their concrete facades absorbing and radiating the stifling warmth. Above us, the sky is ominously dark, and the distant rumble of thunder echoes through the city streets, vibrating in our chests.

As we walk, we pass by an ice cream shop, its bright neon sign casting a cheerful glow against the dreary night. I am drawn in by the delicious scent of freshly made waffle cones and the sight of the ice cream, the colorful flavors swirling in their glass cases. I convince Keegan to have a cone with me.

The thunder grows louder, and the darkness is illuminated by a brilliant flash of lightning, painting the sky a vibrant shade of purple. Keegan puts his hand on the small of my back. And then, with a deafening roar, the heavens open up, unleashing a torrential downpour upon us. The rain comes down in sheets, each drop pelting against our skin like tiny pinpricks. We hurry through the deserted streets, laughing and shrieking at the sudden turn of events.

"This way." Keegan picks up his pace, and we jog until we reach a long and narrow alley, nestled between two buildings with a protective overhang, and he pulls me into the space. But it's too late because we're both drenched and my dress clings to my body.

About eight million people live in this city, yet we've found a place where we're the only two people. To the left, down the long alley, is the back of a building, with a service door and a large trash receptacle. And to my right, just a few feet away, the filth of the streets gets washed clean as the rainwater moves rapidly into the sewer. Street lights flicker, and with the next crash of thunder, the block goes dark. My body stiffens. I've never seen the city void of light.

"Hey." Keegan walks closer until my back finds the brick of the building behind me. "It's okay, I'm right here."

"Yeah. No. Of course." I grab his wet shirt and pull him toward me. His hair is soaked, and the water drips onto my face. I'm still scared, but it no longer has anything to do with the darkness.

"I wasn't honest with you at the restaurant." I let my truth slip out, which somehow feels easier when I can't see Keegan's eyes.

"Did you make up the counselor story?"

"Of course not." I swat his arm and keep my hand there. "But there's something that I should have maybe mentioned to you as you were opening up to me."

"Yeah? What is that?" Keegan's voice is shaky.

"You make me nervous too," I say, and his arm tenses beneath my touch. "But unlike you, I talk too much when I'm nervous."

"That's why you talk so much around me." I can hear the smile in his words.

"Whatever." I roll my eyes and playfully swat his other arm.

Keegan takes my hand and places it on his heart, and it's beating so fast that it feels like it could explode.

"In the spirit of all of this honesty between us, that kiss in Montauk meant something to me." Keegan gently slides his thumb along my jawline.

Every few seconds, Keegan's face comes into view with the lightning overhead.

"All of these truths feel like a lot," I say.

Keegan brushes wet hair out of my face. "You are in complete control. We'll go in whatever direction you want this to. If you want things to go back the way they were, that's what we'll do."

"The way things were." I loop my fingers through his jeans buckle and pull him closer. The need for proximity is louder than the voice telling me to be scared of this new thing between us. "As if that's even a possibility at this point."

There was before we kissed and after.

Keegan's face illuminates with the next bolt of lightning, and I can't help but look at his lips. His body trembles beneath my touch.

"Can I kiss you?" There is uncertainty in his voice.

The darkness makes me brave, and I nod. Keegan reaches out and grasps the back of my head, creating a protective cushion between me and the wall. His hands engulf me, and a shiver runs down my spine. His lips come crashing down on mine with such a fierce intensity that I lose myself. I am momentarily breathless and gasping for air, but then he breathes for me, filling my lungs with everything he has.

As he kisses me, his hard body presses against mine. Every point of contact between our bodies is so electrifying, sending waves of pleasure coursing through me, and igniting a fire that I have never felt before. His touch is so tantalizing, so all-consuming, that I am lost in a world of pure sensation.

"This is all I think about." Keegan sucks at my bottom lip as he presses into me.

I run my hands through his wet hair and wrap my arms around him. Keegan pulls at my dress and splays his warm hand against the skin of my upper back. His lips ravish mine, and my legs are weak beneath me, but the pressure of his body keeps me upright.

Keegan smells like a combination of rainwater and soap. I pull his body to me, and he groans as he hooks my leg around him. It's a kiss that feels like it's heading somewhere. It's like a good glass of wine that makes me want to have another so I can be transported to a place where everything feels better and more heightened.

As the darkness around us gives way to the sudden blaze of the streetlights, I'm caught off guard, my eyes squinting and adjusting to the sudden brightness. I feel a flicker of panic as we're now exposed in plain sight, the light casting our faces and bodies into the open.

He takes a step back, putting some distance between us, and I am left feeling momentarily deprived, my hands clutching at his sides. The sudden movement has robbed me of my balance, and I'm left reeling, my head spinning.

As I try to catch my breath, I feel my body sagging, and my head falls forward onto Keegan's chest, seeking comfort in the solid warmth of his body. His chest rises and falls with each breath, and I match his rhythm, trying to regain control of my breathing.

"Fuck. Luna." The rain has all but stopped. Keegan takes my hand and gives me one long kiss. "I don't know what to do with all of this need I have to touch you."

"Yeah," I say, pulling back from our embrace. "I'm finding all of this very problematic."

"I should take you home." Keegan takes my hand and walks me to the street. "It's gotten late."

He goes to hail a cab, but then I grab his arm as I get the attention of a man standing next to a pedicab.

"Let's take that." My eyes shine as I point. He rolls his eyes and puts his hand up again for a cab.

"I am very serious." I grasp his hand, pushing it down.

Keegan lets me get in first, and then I pull him in next, even though he's very reluctant. It's snug back here, and his knees hit the metal post in front of us. I give the bike driver my address, and we take off down the road. I glance at Keegan, and he shakes his head.

"I can't believe you got me on a pedicab," he says. "I can say with certainty, I never thought I'd be on one of these."

"Life's an adventure," I say through a laugh. "You need to start embracing all the things the city has to offer."

We stop at a red light and someone approaches our cart with a bag of mangos, and through Keegan's protests, I buy all of them.

"Luna Oliver," he says, trying to grab them out of my hand. "You cannot eat fruit that you bought off the street."

I hold one up to my mouth and smell it. And then I take a bite, and it's sweet and juicy. I hand it to him.

"If I get salmonella, I'm blaming you." Keegan bites into the mango that I hold, and then I wipe the juice off his mouth.

"It's good, isn't it?"

Keegan puts his arm around me and pulls me toward him. He kisses the top of my head and lets out a long sigh.

I grab his face and turn it to me. "What was that for?"

Keegan holds my chin and then kisses me softly. "You make me see life in color."

"Wow." It's the nicest thing anyone has ever said to me.

Keegan's eyes gleam with radiance as they capture the silvery glow of the moon as it peeks out from the clouds.

"I'm happy that Forest blew us off tonight." Keegan squeezes my knee.

I nod. "Me too."

The pedicab pulls up in front of my building, and when Keegan goes to get out with me, I turn and smile. "You're not going to ride this back to your place?"

He shakes his head. "Not a chance."

We pay the man, and Keegan stands in front of me. I'm not sure if he wants to say something or simply doesn't want the night to end. But he's silent, watching me.

"You know we're stepping in it, right?" I finally say, even though the words have been on the tip of my tongue all night. "We're crossing every line."

"Yeah, I know." Keegan takes my hand, kisses the top of it, and then intertwines our fingers.

"We should probably start behaving better," I say. "Before anything else happens."

"Yeah, maybe," Keegan says, turning his head, searching for something in my expression. "Do you want to stop things now? Before they get complicated?"

"I don't know," I say honestly, squeezing his hand. "Do you?"

"No," Keegan says as he grabs me by the waist and pulls me flush against his body. "My muscles and non-boring life are finally changing your opinion of me. I wouldn't want to lose all of this ground I've gained."

"I'm rubbing off on you." I put my hand on his arm, on the muscles he speaks of. "I thought deflection was more of my thing."

"You want me to be serious?" Keegan traces the strap of my sundress with his finger.

"You have no idea how long I've. . ." Keegan's voice trails off, and he takes a long blink. "But we'll do whatever you want. Or don't want."

"I want to take it day by day," I say. "See what happens."

Keegan takes my face in his hands and kisses me. His mouth opens mine, his tongue exploring, and if he asked me again, I would give a very different response. I'd tell him that I want so many more nights like tonight.

"Day by day it is," Keegan says into my mouth and then pulls away and kisses my forehead.

"Goodnight," I say, moving to my toes to give him one more kiss.

I go into my building before Keegan walks away. Even though I don't say anything, I'm confident that we both understand that this has to stay between us for now.

Chapter Twenty-Three

From: Keegan Baldwin <Keegan.Baldwin@med.cornell.edu
To: Luna Oliver <Luna.Oliver@umn.edu

Date: October 15

Luna, how was your test?

From: Luna Oliver <Luna.Oliver@umn.edu
From: Keegan Baldwin <Keegan.Baldwin@med.cornell.edu

Date: October 15

I was literally just about to email you. I aced it! You are seriously an incredible teacher, and I couldn't have done so well without you spending the past few nights online with me. I owe you.

Tonight, we are headed to a rooftop in Midtown for the monthly Relationships in Residency social event, and it's an eighties karaoke theme. It was highly suggested that we dress the part. Raven is decked out with a Madonna look, and I go with a teal and purple prom dress that I found at a thrift shop. And sadly, Myles doesn't look much different than he usually dresses in faded jeans and a t-shirt.

Raven finishes applying my blue eye shadow, and when I look in the mirror, we both start laughing.

"I'm not going to lie," I say. "Part of me hopes no one recognizes me. I work with these people."

Raven smacks her lips together and ties a ribbon in her hair. "Are we ready, guys?"

"Here you go." Myles pops into the bathroom and hands us both a drink. "After we finish these, I'll call a car."

"You have the patience of a saint." Raven grabs the drink from Myles with her free hand. "It must be horrible living with women."

"You're mostly cleaner than men." He walks away but yells back at us. "Well, not you, Luna."

"I am not that bad," I yell over Raven's loud laugh, and I then look at her. "I've been getting a lot better at picking up my stuff."

"You have." Raven shifts her hips into mine. "You even put away clean dishes the other day. Although you did leave your clothes in the washer for three days and stunk up our place."

"The car will be here in ten minutes." Myles taps a finger along the kitchen counter. "We should think about heading downstairs."

We pile into a car and head to Midtown. One of my favorite things about New York is that no one looks in our direction. The city is diverse and eclectic. There isn't one type of person that doesn't belong here. Three people dressed in their most ridiculous eighties outfits don't garner us any attention. It's probably my favorite thing about the city and something that Cherry could never afford me.

When we arrive at the venue, a sign near the door tells people from Presby to head to the rooftop for a private party. We go up a flight of stairs, and then our peers come into view. The rooftop is packed with both residents and attendings who usually show up at these things to foster relationships. Two people stand behind the karaoke machine and belt out Whitney Houston's "I Wanna Dance with Somebody."

"This place is nuts." Raven loops her arm in mine. I grab Myles, and we grab drinks. "The entire hospital seems to be here tonight. Who's working?"

A couple dancing bumps into me and apologizes, and I survey the crowd. The doctors I've met put their all into everything, whether it's saving people's lives or partying. None of us seem to have an off switch. We're all former class nerds who finally arrived and have a seat at the table.

I release an audible gasp as Forest walks my way. He's never met a theme party he didn't like. He strides toward us in an oversized blazer, matching pants, and big sunglasses. His eyes meet mine, and he pulls his sunglasses down to wink and then puts them back in place. Being the center of attention is his comfortable place.

"Are you singing with me tonight, kiddo?" he asks as he reaches me and pulls me into a hug.

"I didn't know you were coming," I yell over the loud music. "And that would be a hell no to singing."

He then hugs Raven and gives Myles a fist bump. The crowd screams as a Prince song comes up next, and one of the orthopedic surgeons I've met gets behind the microphone. We all move away from the speakers and huddle up close to a railing.

And then I see him. Keegan emerges from the crowd, and instead of dressing like the theme, he wears his everyday clothes. A pair of dress pants and a button-down shirt. He walks in our direction, and Elise is a step behind him. She loops her arm in his. I touch my lips and think of our kiss.

"Hey." Keegan takes a moment to look at all of our outfits. "You guys look—"

"On point," Forest says and pats his shoulder. "Where's your outfit, man? Too cool or something?"

"I came straight from work," Keegan says. "I had a surgery canceled last minute, or I wouldn't be here at all."

"And I didn't even know I was coming until you called me earlier, Forest, so I didn't have time to put an outfit together." Elise squeezes Keegan's arm, and his eyes flick to mine.

Jealousy and maybe a little of something else course through my veins. Elise stands so close to Keegan. She is effortlessly beautiful in her simple summer dress. Her skin looks like she bathes in milk. And her golden blond hair curls perfectly at the ends. But my lips still tingle from our kiss that happened only two days ago, and I don't want to feel the way I feel seeing him standing next to her.

"Love the outfit, Forest." We all turn as a man approaches. Forest smiles and puts his arm around him.

"Hey," Forest says, looking at us. "This is my friend and colleague, Dr. Matt Theis."

Forest introduces all of us to Matt and waits for me last. "And this is my sister that I've told you about. Luna. She's an intern in the gen surg program."

Matt's face lights up. "Luna. I've heard so much about you." He puts his hand out to shake mine. "Forest tells me you did medical school at the University of Minnesota. That's where I went."

I smile. "Yes. I graduated in the spring. Are you a cardiologist as well?"

"Electrophysiologist." Matt drops my hand and leans against the railing next to me. "And congrats on your residency in general surgery. I hear it's very competitive."

"Thanks. I'm loving it so far," I say. Everyone is engaged in their conversations, except for Keegan, who keeps stealing glances my way.

"I'm going to grab a drink," Matt says. "Can I get you anything?"

"A white wine, please." I point. "A table just opened up, so I'll be there."

Myles leaves us to say hi to a fellow doctor, and the rest of our group moves to a table to sit.

"He is so cute," Raven says, nudging me with her elbow. "Right?"

"Yeah, he's fine."

Matt is attractive. Someone I'd usually be interested in, but all I can think of is Keegan and the way he touches me. His presence envelops me, and thoughts of him invade my brain constantly.

"He's someone I'd be comfortable with you dating," Forest says. "He's the nicest guy. Newer to the city. An excellent doctor."

I raise my eyebrow. But before I can say anything, Keegan speaks up. "I thought you guys didn't date each other's friends?"

"Well." Forest laughs. "I think we officially put that rule to bed, don't you think?" Forest looks at Raven and grips her hand.

Matt approaches, hands me a drink, then sits in the empty chair. Forest grabs Raven and pulls her to the dance floor when the song changes.

"I'm assuming you had Dr. Miller as a professor?" Matt says, turning to me.

"Uh," I moan. "The abra-cadaver guy? Yes. I had him. He was the worst."

Matt starts laughing. "If he said it once, it would have been fine. But it was every time we had labs."

"You're newer at Presby, right?" Elise says, allowing Keegan to raise his brow at me. He stares at me, questioning.

"Yes," Matt says. "I've only been here for about six months. I finished my fellowship at The Mayo Clinic."

"Did you move with your family?" Keegan asks.

"Just me," Matt says. "But my brother lives in Brooklyn, and I wanted to be closer to him. And, well, I've always wanted to live in New York."

"Keegan." Elise puts her hand on his, and he doesn't move it. "I love this song. Do you want to dance?"

"No, you go ahead," Keegan says.

"Please." She cups his face. Elise then stands and pulls Keegan's arm until he gets out of his chair. He hesitates, but then follows her.

When they are gone, and it's only Matt and me at the table, he turns his body towards mine. "Isn't Dr. Baldwin the best? My colleagues and I love working with him."

"He's actually from the same hometown as me and Forest."

"Wow," Matt says. "I had no idea. I knew he and Forest were close though."

Raven comes back to the table, and Matt stands. "I'm afraid I have an early morning tomorrow. As much as I'd love to stay, I probably shouldn't."

"It was great to meet you," Raven says.

"Yes," I say. "And thanks again for the drink."

"I wish I could stay," Matt says, looking only at me. "Hopefully, I'll see you around the hospital or at George's."

"I'm often at one of those places," I say.

"Great to meet you, Luna," Matt says.

I'm finally able to pay attention to Keegan and Elise on the dance floor. Her arms are wrapped around his neck, and when he says something, she leans in to hear him better.

"Keegan and Elise look nice together," I say, resting my face on my hand, a heavy weight in my stomach.

Raven raises her eyebrows and then glances at the dance floor. "How much is it killing you to see Keegan with someone else?"

"What?" My head jerks in her direction. "Why would I care?"

"You care." Raven's lips move to a thin line.

"Raven," I say. "My brother."

"Luna." Raven moves next to me and sits. "What is said between us stays between us."

"It's not that," I say. "It's just that with Keegan, things are overly complicated."

"I know, I know," Raven says. "He's like family. You've said it so many times I was starting to believe it. But girl, he's never looked at you like you're family. And that's not how you look at him, either. If you don't get after it, someone else will. So you're going to have to figure out what you want."

"How do you know all of this?" I pout my lips as I continue to watch him dance with Elise. "I barely mention his name to you."

"I've known it since the first moment I saw him approach you at George's." Raven winks at me. "Maybe you should tell Keegan how you feel."

A slow song comes on next, and Forest finds Raven's hand and takes it.

I look to my right, and Myles stands around with some residents, near the bar, fully engrossed in conversation. Then, I look to my left, and Elise laughs and takes Keegan's hand. She tries to keep him on the dance floor, but he resists. He puts his hand up in the air and waves her off, but she then takes her other hand and practically holds him hostage.

And now I'm stuck, having a front-row seat to them dancing again to one of my favorite songs about that damn small-town girl and this stupid lonely world. There are at least twenty couples, dancing and laughing, as a man and a woman belt out the lyrics, but my eyes fixate on Keegan.

He towers over Elise. She says something to him, and he leans in to hear better. Elise then goes to her toes, and unless my eyes are mistaking me, she leans in and kisses him. On the lips. In front of me. Jealousy and a bit of rage creep up until I feel like I'm going to explode.

Raven approaches me and tries to grab my arm, but I push her off and rush through the crowd until I reach the door of the roof, my heels clanking against the metal stairs as I make my way to the main floor. I hurry outside into the night, and the karaoke music continues to blare overhead. A taxi goes by, and I put my hand up in the air and hop in the backseat.

I don't like how I feel right now. No one I've ever dated has ever left me feeling this out of control and possessive. I've always had a plan, and I'm currently on step four of my five-point plan. The only thing left is to complete a fellowship in trauma surgery. I've vowed that I wouldn't get into a serious relationship until this plan was fully executed. Yet here I am, feeling completely out of control. I crawl into my bed, pull my blanket up to my chin, and try to think of anything but Keegan Baldwin.

Chapter Twenty-Four

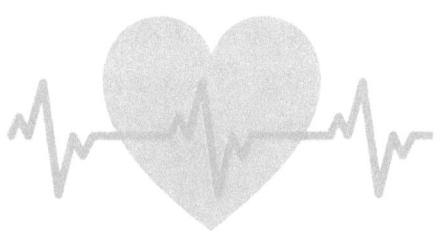

Last night's eighties resident party is all I can think about as I arrive at the hospital the next day. I stop at the good coffee shop on the first floor of the hospital because today is not the day for the cheap, doctor's lounge brew.

"Hey," a voice calls out. I raise my head at the sound of Forest's voice as he approaches with Keegan. "You're going for the good coffee today too?"

"Yes," I say. "It's needed."

"You Irish goodbyed us last night," Forest says. "What happened?"

My eyes meet Keegan's, but he pulls his gaze away from me and looks down. "I was tired. And wanted to get a good night's sleep."

"Well," Forest says, smiling. "You must have made a good impression because Matt texted me and is wondering if I'd ask you if he can have your number."

"Sure. Why not." I glance at Keegan, who crosses his arms over his chest and looks surprised.

Keegan pulls the pager off the waist of his scrubs and looks at it. "I've got to go."

When he's gone, Forest shrugs his shoulders. "He's been acting off since the moment we walked into the hospital together."

"Maybe he and Elise got into a fight or something," I say, digging for information.

"Nah," Forest says. "Keegan made a comment to me this morning, and I have the impression that it isn't going anywhere."

After grabbing my coffee, I go to meet the other residents and await today's orders from Dr. Parse. Myles and Raven are already there, and Raven lets out an exaggerated yawn.

"Luna." I'm brought back to reality. "You are on the cardiac step-down floor today."

"Wait." Dr. Parse stares at me when the words fly out of my mouth, and my mind goes to Keegan. It will be hard to avoid him if I'm on the Cardiac floor. "Can I switch with someone?"

"No, Dr. Oliver. You can't. Every resident has their assignment. Myles. You'll be with Luna on Cardiac."

Myles and I go to the Cardiac floor where we'll be rounding with other residents, and a nurse points to one of the hospital rooms, and we walk in. Keegan is in there with a nurse, examining a patient. Our eyes meet, and he nods while holding his chin.

"Dr Oliver. Dr. Worth." He hands me the patient's chart. "This is Mr. Stanotti. We're preparing the operating room. I originally hoped to do a Transcatheter Aortic Valve Replacement today, but he had some congenital abnormalities so we'll need to do a sternotomy."

With my stethoscope, I listen to the patient's heart. He has an obvious murmur with some palpitations. His breathing is also short as if he can't catch his breath. Myles then listens.

"Aortic Stenosis?" I glance at Keegan.

"Yes," Keegan says. "An irregular heartbeat. The patient has angina, shortness of breath, and constant heart palpitations. A CT confirmed the diagnosis."

"How long will I be under?" Mr. Stanotti asks Keegan.

"The surgery lasts anywhere from four to six hours. You'll be well taken care of sir."

Keegan turns to Myles and glances at me. "You can both scrub in today and observe." Myles grabs my arm and squeezes. If it were up to him, he would shadow Keegan every day.

I need to get my head in the game, but I have a hard time focusing. We head down to the operating room, and the surgery team gets scrubbed in. Keegan pulls on a surgical cap that says you have a pizza of my heart, and it's filled with pizzas and hearts. My mom also made this one for him. Keegan pulls a mask over his face, and I do the same. Then we continue scrubbing up to our elbows.

Keegan makes a six-inch incision down the patient's chest, right between the collarbones. A technician hands him the surgical saw, and he cuts through, starting at the top of the sternum and working his way down.

Keegan then gets the retractor in place, to split the sternum apart. He carefully cuts the pericardium, and the beating heart becomes even more visible. He replaces the valve, talking through the entire surgery. He's calm and soothing, and it's obvious how much he is liked and respected by everyone in the operating room. Surgical teams ask to be with him.

Several hours later, when the surgery is complete, Keegan starts closing the patient up.

"Dr. Oliver." Keegan glances at me. "Take this sternotomy wire and lace it through the needle." Keegan continues. "His bones are a bit hard, so I'm going to use a drill to make small holes for the wires to go through."

Keegan demonstrates, and I lace the wire through the bone. The stainless-steel wires are thicker than I was anticipating. His bones start coming together.

"That's it, Dr. Oliver. You're doing great."

"Dr. Worth." Keegan glances at Myles and hands him more wire. "Now you try."

Myles then laces the wire through and looks at me in amazement that we're getting to be so active in a surgery.

"Excellent job, team." Keegan finishes closing his chest.

Keegan leaves the operating room first, and then we all follow. A technician helps Myles and me get out of our gloves and gown, and I feel the natural high like I always do after getting to be part of something like this.

All of the baggage I brought to work this morning disappears the moment I scrub in. It's a rush of adrenaline, power, and possibility, in every surgery I'm in. I walk to the changing room, done with this shift that ended up going beyond twelve hours, because once I'm in surgery, I'm in it until completion, no matter how long it takes.

As soon as I step out of the changing room, my eyes lock onto Keegan's form. He's leaning casually against the wall, his knee bent up and his arms folded over his chest in a way that makes his arms look massive.

With a fluid motion, he pushes off the wall and falls into step beside me. We head outside and thoughts flood my head, but words remain buried. All day, I've pushed aside my anger toward him, but now that it's just the two of us, the feelings bubble up to the surface.

He goes to touch my arm, but I push him away. "Please don't."

"What's wrong?" he asks, stepping away from me.

I glance at him, and he manages to look hurt, even though I'm the only one with that right.

We get a couple of blocks away from the hospital and I finally turn to him.

"Everything," I say. "I slept like crap last night. This feels too complicated, and I just don't think I can do this anymore."

"Can't do what?" Keegan says as my apartment building comes into view.

"You." I point to him. "Me."

"I'm sorry if I don't understand what taking it day by day means," he says. "I don't know how things are supposed to go."

My mind flashes to last night. I hated how out of control I felt over my emotions. How helpless I was seeing Keegan with Elise.

"I don't know either," I say. "But I don't think you're supposed to parade a woman around in front of me. That part seems clear."

"Elise?" Keegan puts his hand on the wall next to me. "Your brother invited her. I didn't know what to do. She.."

Keegan stops talking, so I fill in the blanks. "Kissed you. Yeah, I saw. Thanks for that."

"I didn't want that to happen," Keegan says. "I sat her down and told her that I have feelings for someone else. Is telling your brother that Matt can have your number your way of taking things day by day?"

We stare at each other. My hands on my hips and his folded over his chest.

"This will always be our problem," I say. "Because we can't be together openly."

"That's bullshit, Luna." Keegan drags his hand down his face. "You're making excuses. If this is about Forest, let's sit him down and have a conversation. We'll tell him we want to be together."

"You're kidding me, right?" I cover my face. "We can't tell Forest. And is that even true?"

Keegan's eyebrows knit together, and then he reaches for me. "It is for me."

"I'm overwhelmed." My body shakes as thoughts flood me. "I don't know what I want. All I know is that I need to show up every day at work as my best self, and that's not how I felt today. I was distracted. I can't afford to be distracted."

I step out of the alley, but Keegan stays put, watching me. He tucks his hands into his pants' pockets. "So that's it, Luna? Really?"

"You and Forest have spent the past few years teasing me constantly," I say. "Wondering why I cycled through men so frequently and refused to settle down. It's because I'm laser-focused on my goals. Men are a distraction. You're a distraction."

Keegan steps toward me. "I wasn't teasing you, Luna. I was—"

"I have to get out of here," I say, tears dangerously close to the surface. I turn from Keegan and rush toward my building.

When I get inside my apartment, I let myself release a breath. I lean against the door and put my head in my hands. This is what I do. I'm a scientifically-minded person, and when it comes to emotions that can't be measured or explained, I panic and walk away. Having feelings for someone means that my feelings are tangled up with theirs, and I'm not in a spot where I can be openly vulnerable.

I can't scientifically explain that of all the men I've met in the city, I only ever think of Keegan. And I sure as hell can't explain why he'd like me over a successful surgeon like Elise. None of it makes logical sense to me.

There's a pounding at the door, and I jump. I slowly open the door, and Keegan's hair looks disheveled and he's sweaty as if he ran up the eight floors to reach me sooner.

"We can't leave things like this," he says as he walks through the entrance.

I hold the door open for him. "My roommates could have been here."

He looks around the place. It's just the two of us here.

"Look," Keegan says, pacing back and forth, and then color spreads across his face. "I like you." Keegan squeezes the nape of his neck as he steps closer to me.

I press my body into the door behind me, relying on it to hold me upright.

"I'm not good at feelings," I say. "I'm not in a place where I can do complicated."

"It doesn't have to be complicated." Keegan's eyes narrow. "I know you don't want anyone distracting you from your goals. I would never do that, Luna."

"Well," I say, blood rushing to my face. But he's known me too long. He sees into me, where all my truths lie.

Keegan places his fingers around my wrist. "Do you have any idea how long I've waited for us to be at the same place in our lives? We're finally here, and when we kiss, I am so damn sure about you. I know you feel something too."

"But what if it doesn't work out," I say. "We're ruining the dynamic of what we've always been. And you hurt me last night."

"That's fair," Keegan says, as his arms press against the closed door, caging me in. I lean back farther against the door. "I don't know how to act in public around you. You've made me so nervous that someone will find out about us, that I've done the opposite and pretend that I barely know you."

"I don't know how to do this either," I say. "Which is why walking away seems easier."

"But what if I don't want to walk away?"

"Don't make this harder than it needs to be." I try to push off the door, but Keegan grips my waist, his hands pressing into my sides.

He pulls me close and kisses me. I don't hesitate, as instinct, and not logic takes over. I wrap my arms around his neck and press my body into his with urgency and relief. His hands grab my hips, holding me steady against him.

My body mocks my words. My sadness and anxiety of the day were because I craved to hear everything Keegan just said to me. I wanted to feel the need he has for me. Keegan holds me against the wall and presses his hard body into mine. He grips my arms above my head, intertwining his fingers with mine. He tastes like a candy cane, and his touch is becoming familiar and very welcomed in my life.

"What now?" I pull back, breathing heavily, needing to stop things before we lose control and Myles or Raven walk through the door.

Keegan steps away from me. He adjusts his shirt and runs his fingers through his hair.

"Let me take you on a date." Keegan grabs my earlobe and caresses it.

"A date?" I pull my bottom lip into my mouth.

"Yes." Keegan kisses me gently.

"I think I can try that," I say, breathily.

I move my arms from his neck and put them around his waist, and we hold each other. I rest my head on his chest, feeling both relief and fear because there is no turning back and erasing all of the new things I feel for this man.

Keegan kisses the top of my head. "According to this calendar, you are off on Thursday night. Can I take you out?"

"Yeah," I say, taking a deep breath. "Okay."

"I'll never hurt you." Keegan kisses me one last time and walks to the door. "But you have all the power in the world to crush me."

"And you still want to try this? Knowing that?"

"More than anything." He squeezes my hand and walks out into the hallway.

Chapter Twenty-Five

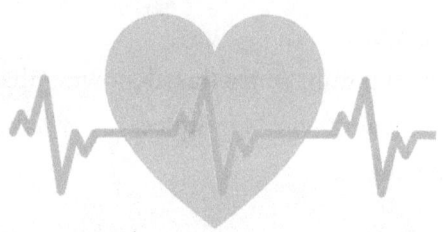

From: Keegan Baldwin <Keegan.Baldwin@med.cornell.edu
To: Luna Oliver <Luna.Oliver@umn.edu

Date: November 15

I can't wait for you and your family to be here for Thanksgiving. Not that I'm keeping track, but I haven't seen you in nearly three years. I've been mapping out all the places I want to take you. I know you've been here once, but never when I've been here.

From: Luna Oliver <Luna.Oliver@umn.edu
From: Keegan Baldwin <Keegan.Baldwin@med.cornell.edu

Date: November 16

> You are going to hate me, but there's been a change of plans. This new guy I'm dating asked me to go to Chicago to meet his family. (Which feels soon, but I'm going with it) I know it's been forever. Sorry, Keegan. But I know you understand.

Tonight, I get ready for my date with Keegan alone. Myles and Raven are both working a twenty-four-hour shift and won't get off work until eight in the morning tomorrow. And I'll be starting my shift shortly after. Sometimes our hours align, and sometimes, they are so polar opposite, that I forget I have roommates.

I texted Keegan earlier in the day to ask about attire. He suggested I dress up a little, so I pull out my reliable little black dress and finish the look with strappy heels.

I've had this dress forever. It's got cap sleeves with a deep V. It's short and has a zipper down the back. I do a nude lip, glance at myself one more time, and then wait for Keegan. There's a knock at my door, and I hate that my building doesn't have a doorman. I open it, and Keegan stands there. His mouth falls ajar as his eyes take me in.

"You look"—he squeezes his neck, which has flushed with color—"beautiful, Luna."

I grab my purse from the counter and peel my gaze off Keegan. Because damn, he looks beautiful too. He wears dark-fitted pants, with a button-down shirt and a blazer, and my heart palpitates in my chest.

"Where are we going, anyway?" I ask when we reach the elevator.

"First, dinner." Half of Keegan's lips turn up in a smile as he places his hand on the small of my back. "After that is a surprise."

We take a car to a Japanese restaurant in Midtown. It's only been open for a short time, and I haven't even tried to get in because I've heard it's impossible. I only know this because I overheard a patient I was treating mention it to her friend.

"We're having dinner here?" I practically whisper as I wrap my arm in his. "I've heard it's amazing."

Keegan and I are seated, and he starts ordering us things. A bottle of Sake, Edamame, Ikura Hummus, Sashimi Moriawase, Toro Tartare, and Koji Shrimp. At some point, I quit paying attention, because I don't know what half of it even means.

"Have you been here?" I cross my legs and fiddle with my hands.

"No." Keegan places his elbows on the table. "I've always wanted to though. I was waiting for a special occasion."

"You don't need to do this for me, you know." I uncross and recross my legs. "Takeout would have been perfectly fine for me."

The sake arrives, and our server pours us both a glass. Keegan raises his glass. "It's our first date," he says with a smile. "I wanted it to be memorable."

"Does this mean you're going to let me pay for half?" I smile and bite my bottom lip.

"How about you buy the dessert." The corners of Keegan's lips turn up.

We leave the restaurant, my stomach happy and full, and walk to the Broadway District.

"Wait. Are we going to a show?" I ask, pulling Keegan toward me.

He looks at me and smiles. "You mentioned once that you've never been, and that you'd like to see one."

"But, Keegan." I pull at his arm again. The sign overhead lets me know what we're seeing. "You're taking me to a Broadway show? On our first date? Where do we even go from here?"

He puts his hand on the small of my back as he leads me through the door. He leans in and whispers in my ear. "When we're old and wrinkly, we'll always remember tonight."

I glance at Keegan through the corner of my eye, wondering where we'll both be in thirty or forty years and if, I'll still know him and remember tonight. His comment is presumptuous but somehow carries no arrogance.

We take our seats, and it's only a few rows from the front, in the very center.

"Have you been to a show before?" I lean over and ask, just as the lights start to dim.

"Yes." He intertwines his fingers in mine and places our hands on my leg. "But never with you. So, it feels like my first time."

WHEN HEARTS ATTACH

A hush falls over the crowd, and slowly, a red curtain opens, and the first song comes on. Emotions wash over me in ways that I wasn't expecting. The tightness starts in my chest, and I'm so happy it's dark because tears start rolling down my cheeks. Because I am among the most amazing talents, seeing one of the best plays in the world, and the voices are beautiful, and the lyrics are powerful. And somehow, I'm in New York City, I'm a doctor, and I feel like, in so many ways, the life I've manifested for myself is happening.

One of the things I've never bent on is where I wanted life to take me. I was young when I created a five-step plan for myself, and I've made it this far and not let anything, or anyone, get in the way of my dreams. I'm proud of myself for that.

I cross my legs and lean in Keegan's direction, and he holds my hand tight in his. I'm aware of his presence and his thumb that circles my knee and runs up my leg until it meets the hem of my dress. I've never felt so comfortable with anyone on a first date, but after all, this is Keegan, and I've known him my entire life.

I'm also transported somewhere entirely different. When the final curtain goes down, and the lights are turned back on, I pull my hand out of Keegan's and clap along with everyone else. The actors all take a bow, and we stand and clap some more. When I look at Keegan, he stares at me, a goofy grin on his face.

People pool onto the street after the show. And we walk, with no destination in mind, but in the general direction of my apartment. We stay silent for so long, and I wipe my remaining tears from my eyes. After seeing something so beautiful, no words seem sufficient.

"Luna." Keegan's shoulder rubs against mine, and he looks at me. "Watching you watch theater might be the best thing I've ever done. Ever."

"There aren't adequate words," I say because there aren't. Seeing this play changed me. It transcended anything I could have imagined or hoped for.

I'm reminded of how the arts can transport us. I've been so busy trying to be a good doctor, that I haven't escaped in so long. But tonight, I felt somewhere else. The farther Keegan and I walk, the less people surround us. We leave Midtown and cut through Central Park, and the city lights seem to disappear.

"You're so quiet." Keegan grabs my hand and brushes his lips across my knuckles. "Are you okay?"

I look up at the sky and can see a few stars. That's what I've missed most in the city. Because back home in Minnesota, I could see the entire galaxy. Venus was always directly above me in the night sky.

"Something feels heavy to me," I say.

Keegan grips my hand tighter. "Are you second-guessing going on a date with me?"

"No, it's not that," I say quickly. "Since being a doctor, I have seen twenty-seven people die."

Keegan stops walking and pulls me to him. He places his hands on my face. "Do you know how many lives you've saved?"

I shake my head. "I haven't counted those."

He leans forward and gently brushes his lips against mine. It's a featherweight touch. He pulls away and cups my face. "Remember that day you came into my office?"

"The day I accidentally kissed you? No, I've blocked that out."

Keegan laughs. "Well, I had a similar breakdown in week two of my internship year. I was doing a pediatric ER rotation, and three young kids, one still a baby, were brought in with fatal gunshot wounds. Their mom had a psychiatric episode and murdered them. When the dad arrived in the ER, I had to tell him all three of his babies were gone."

"Keegan," I say, gripping his hand tighter.

"After my shift, I somehow made it back to my apartment, and I closed the door and cried for hours. I even started typing up my resignation letter. I was done, Luna. I didn't think I could do it."

"What changed?"

"Your brother called me to chat," Keegan says. "I tried to play it off like I was fine, but he knew better. He said that instead of focusing on the things I couldn't change, like saving those three babies, I should think about how I can be the most compassionate doctor in how I interact with others, like the dad. He told me to find a way of being someone's light on their darkest days."

"Forest said that?" A tear runs down my cheek. I wipe it away and chuckle. "That kind of wisdom came from him, huh?"

"That's probably why I love the moon so much. It's my light during dark times," Keegan says. "And I'm sorry if I didn't provide the right words to you that day."

"Well," I say, "the kiss may have derailed the rest of our interaction."

"The truth is." Keegan squeezes my hand. The moon above us illuminates Keegan and he looks like he's glowing. "I wanted to kiss you too."

"Really?" I shake my head. "You don't have to say that to make me feel better."

"I don't want to be a temporary distraction to make you forget. I want to be your light too. And I didn't want to question if our first kiss was just to transport you. I wanted to know that you wanted me. The same way that I want you."

"I. . ." I stop talking, unable to form the appropriate words. Keegan wants me. Has he always wanted me?

Keegan pulls me toward him and wraps his arms around me. "We are going to see some of the worst things that life has to offer. Being doctors, we sign up for it. But I'm going to be compassionate, empathetic, and whatever the outcome is for my patients or their families, I'm going to be someone they remember that made them feel a little better during the worst day of their lives."

"You have muscles, aren't boring, or gross, and you're really wise," I say, and Keegan laughs. Our conversation teeters so much on truths, that I have to provide levity.

We exit Central Park, and things start to get familiar to me and I recognize where we are. But like every other night I'm with Keegan, I don't want it to end. My building finally comes into view. And my feet should hurt, but they don't. Instead, I feel this release of euphoria. From the play. From Keegan. From everything. We stop in front of my building.

Keegan looks at me, searching my face for something. He glances at the building. "If it's not too late, should we go down the block to that twenty-four-seven ice cream shop? I could go for something sweet, and you promised me dessert."

"The Icy New Yorker?" I glance down at the street. "Because I happen to have ice cream from there in my freezer."

Keegan pauses. But I push forward. Because tonight made me feel brave. Tonight, I'm going to carve out my piece of happiness. I stand on my toes and kiss his jawline. Keegan sucks in a deep breath and holds it.

"Do you want to come up?" I may sound confident, but I'm shaking inside.

Keegan opens his mouth, but before he can say anything, I add, "Raven and Myles are on call. All night."

"Luna." His voice sounds hoarse all of a sudden. "I can't believe I'm saying this to you, but we should probably take things slow."

I grasp Keegan's waist and pull him toward me. "Let's go slow then." I take his hand and nod toward the door.

Keegan hesitates, but only for a moment, and then he follows me inside. We get into the elevator, stand on opposite sides, and take the ride up. I want to tell him that it's just ice cream, but I'm hoping it's going to be much more than that.

Chapter Twenty-Six

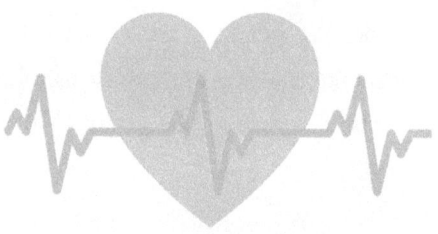

From: Keegan Baldwin <Keegan.Baldwin@med.cornell.edu
To: Luna Oliver <Luna.Oliver@umn.edu

Date: June 4

I'm sorry I missed your college graduation, Luna. I can't tell you how intense my residency program is, and until I finish, this is my entire life. I hope you know how proud I am of you. The University of MN Medical School is lucky to have you.

From: Luna Oliver <Luna.Oliver@umn.edu
From: Keegan Baldwin <Keegan.Baldwin@med.cornell.edu

Date: November 16

Thanks, Keegan. Graduation weekend was a blast. Wish you would have been there. Not that I'm keeping track, but how's it been nearly four and a half years since I've seen you?

From: Keegan Baldwin <Keegan.Baldwin@med.cornell.edu
To: Luna Oliver <Luna.Oliver@umn.edu

Date: November 16

Too long.

We get inside my apartment, and I flick the lights on and peer down the hallway to make sure that Myles and Raven are gone. Their rooms are dark. When I come back to the combined kitchen and living room area, Keegan has taken his sports coat off, and it now hangs on the back of a chair.

He undoes his cufflinks and pushes his shirt up his forearms. When he glances at me, he catches me staring. I shake my thoughts out of my head, go toward the freezer, and bring out a few pints of ice cream.

"Cherry, mint chocolate chip, or rocky road," I say, balancing the three containers, the coolness a contrast from my sweaty hands.

Keegan joins me in the small, galley kitchen. I have to push past him to open a drawer and pull out two spoons. I struggle even looking in his direction because I can't seem to breathe in his imposing and large presence. Being with someone I've known my entire life, on the precipice of that relationship changing for good, is much scarier than getting to know someone new.

"Cherry." Keegan grabs the container from me and leans against the counter. "Always cherry."

"Such a loyalist." I hoist myself up on the opposite counter and open the mint chocolate chip. I squeeze my thighs together and cross my legs at the ankle. Keegan dips his spoon into the ice cream, and I watch as he puts it in his mouth and licks it. Our eyes connect, and Keegan gives me a reassuring smile.

It calms me immediately.

"Do you remember that ice cream shop in Cherry?" Keegan puts the spoon in his mouth, and his tongue lazily darts out to lick the last drop off of it. "They had fifty flavors to choose from, but when I find what I like, I stick with it. So, after all these years, it's only cherry for me."

"Cherry on Top." I nod my head, remembering the shop back home that I haven't been to in forever. "That's what that place was called."

"Yeah, that's right."

My dress is bunched up and Keegan's eyes move to my thighs, and he sucks in a breath. Keegan pushes off the counter, and I unclasp my ankles so he can stand between my legs.

"Can I try the mint chocolate chip?"

I raise an eyebrow. "What happened to being loyal?"

"Well." Keegan grins. "Your moans are selling it for me."

Keegan puts both hands flat on the counter, and his arms cage me in. I dip my spoon into the pint and hold it out for him. But he doesn't even glance at it. Instead, he brushes my hair to the side, squeezes the nape of my neck, and presses his lips against mine.

My mouth falls open, and his cool tongue dips into mine, and I taste an explosion of different flavors. His lips are cold, a contrast against his warm breath. I wrap him tighter in my arms. He squeezes my hips over my dress and pushes his body into mine.

"Mmm," Keegan says into my mouth, never letting up from our kiss. "Mint chocolate chip tastes good."

He takes the pint from my hand, dips the spoon in it, and rubs a streak of ice cream down my neck. In one swift motion, he licks it off. His tongue drags against my skin, sending shivers to every part of my body.

"It might be my new favorite flavor." He smears some on the other side of my neck, and my body turns to molten ash as his tongue glides down me, awakening my senses and sending heat between my thighs.

I straighten my back and move my hand to his belt buckle. Keegan inhales such a sharp breath, that I fear my touch hurts him.

"What happened to going slow?" he says, breathily.

I've known you for my entire life," I say. "It doesn't get much slower than that."

Keegan inches forward, and runs his hands up my bare legs until he grabs my butt and drags me toward him. I clench his hips, desperate to feel him against me. He hoists me up, my legs squeeze around his waist, and he walks me to my bedroom. I'm frantic to be closer to him. I grab fistfuls of his hair and press my body into his. When we reach my room, he puts me down, and I feel like a baby giraffe learning to walk. My legs are wobbly, and I'm unsteady on my feet.

Keegan is enormous compared to my frame. He reaches his hands around me until our bodies are flush. He is so warm and hard. He then takes my long hair in his hand and pushes it aside. He lays a sweet kiss on my neck, and then the sound of my dress's zipper and the breeze from the fan on my bare back hit me all at once.

He pulls my dress down, and I shimmy my hips until it falls into a pile on the floor. I step over it, still in my heels. Keegan backs away, out of reach, and his eyes drag down my body.

"Fuck, Luna." His voice is throaty, and he runs a hand down his face. He starts slowly unbuttoning his shirt, painfully slow, our eyes never leaving each other's. He removes his cotton shirt, revealing a bit of himself, and then it falls to the floor. His skin is golden, and a vertical line separates all of his toned abs into perfect blocks. His pants hang low on his hips, and he once again closes the space between us.

"You wore the panties I saw on the floor in Montauk. I've had dreams about them."

I reach my hand out and spread it against his taut chest.

He presses on my panties, right in the center, and I jolt at the sensation. "So hot, Luna."

Keegan drops to his knees in front of me, clasps his hand behind my knee, and removes my heel. He then slips off the other one. He stays in that position, moving his hands to my butt, pushing me toward him. He kisses my stomach, right above my panty line, and then he buries his face in my panties, his face pressing against my core.

"Keegan." I pull his hair, as he kisses me over the thin, wet fabric. My nerve endings go into overdrive with the pressure of him against me.

"You have no idea how long I've fantasized about this." Keegan kisses me once more, and then I pull him to a standing position.

Without my three-inch heels, I strain my head to look at him. His fingers brush against my arms, and then I reach for his pants' buckle because I don't think I've ever wanted anything more than to see where his ab muscles lead. I unzip them, and they fall to the floor. I don't look away from the bulge in his boxer briefs.

Keegan lifts me, with seemingly little effort, and I wrap my legs around him. He lays me on the bed, and the weight of him presses into me. Keegan's movements are all so fluid, that I don't even feel him reach behind me to unclasp my bra. But then he's pulling the straps down, kissing me where they once were, and then he yanks it off completely.

"You're beautiful, Luna," Keegan speaks into my chest, and then with his thumbs, circles the swells of my breasts. He glides his tongue down, pausing at my very alert nipples, watching me the entire time.

"Beautiful, Baldwin," I say, jerking forward as his teeth scrape gently across my breast. Keegan's eyes flick to mine, and half of his mouth turns up, and he chuckles against my skin.

His hand roams down my stomach until it reaches my panties. He fiddles with the tiny bow, and then his thumb hitches beneath the elastic. I arch my back while grabbing his shoulders for support.

"Can I touch you?" Keegan asks.

"Okay." It comes out weakly. "Yes."

"Luna," Keegan says as his hand stretches beneath my panties. "I can feel what I do to you."

Keegan dips a finger, then two, into me, his knuckles brushing against my core. I curve my back, already so close to an orgasm.

"How do you like it, Luna?" His tongue darts out, and he licks his lips.

"Like this," I moan, gripping at the sheets beneath me. "Exactly like this."

I pull his head toward me and kiss him deeply, and his fingers dip into me with a new intensity. He pulls away, holds my chin, and watches as my toes curl underneath me, and I dig my nails into Keegan's arms.

My legs fall farther open. All the earlier nerves I felt now gone, only replaced by pleasure, and a sense that life was always meant to lead me to this exact moment.

"Keegan," I say again, and he smiles against my lips, as warm liquid pools low in my belly, and then the pressure continues to build. I jerk my hips into him, and bite my closed fist, as pleasure pulsates through me. Keegan pulls my hand away and kisses me as I climax, whimpering into his neck.

"I want to taste you," Keegan says as he pulls his hand out of my panties, and my body morphs into the mattress. I'm complete liquid. "But my desire to be in you outweighs everything else."

Keegan's lips bring me back to the present. He kisses my neck and then moves to the few freckles that are sprinkled along my shoulders. He looks at them like they are the most precious thing he's ever seen. He moves down to my breasts, and my stomach, and then he slides my panties down my legs. I sit up and help take his boxer briefs off, and then I see it. Right below his abdominal muscles, low on his hip, is a tattoo of two bright red cherries, connected by a thin green vine.

"Keegan Baldwin." My eyes go wide, and I lean forward and rub my fingers against his ink. "Another dare? It's like I never even knew you before."

I can't take my eyes off of it, or the size of his erection. He stands in front of me, so confident, and lets me take all of him in. I kiss his tattoo and then run my tongue along it. I take him in my hand and continue dragging my tongue down his length.

"Luna, please." Keegan grips my chin. His fingers shake against my skin, and for the first time, I can see how nervous he is. "If you do that one more time, this will be over before we start, and I really don't want that."

"Sorry," I say, smiling. "I just really love your tattoo."

I wrap my hands around Keegan's arms and pull him on top of me because I need the weight of him more than I need air. I press my lips against his, and the heaviness of his erection presses against my core.

He stops kissing me and looks into my eyes. "Are you sure you want this?"

"Yes," I say, moving his hair out of his face. "Are you sure?"

"More than I've ever been sure about anything." His voice is shaky, and it makes my heart swell for some reason.

"Top drawer," I say. I don't know why I have a supply there. I haven't used them. But maybe it's because, from the moment I arrived in the city, I hoped for this.

Keegan opens my nightstand, pulls out a condom, and spreads it down his length. He hitches his hand under my knee and kisses me with a new intensity. He sweeps my hair back and looks so deeply into my eyes. No one makes intense eye contact like Keegan, but seeing his blue eyes as he lies on me, is an entirely different thing.

"If this is a dream, I never want to wake up." He gently squeezes the back of my neck.

I grip him around his hips, not wanting to delay things any longer. I'm ready for him. Keegan takes my hand in his and raises them over our heads.

"Please, Keegan." I seize his hips, pull him closer, and gasp at how full I feel when he slowly pushes into me. My body begins to adjust to him.

"Are you okay?" Keegan cups my face and then kisses my forehead. "Is this okay?"

"Yes." I nod. "It's perfect. You're perfect."

"Hey." Keegan kisses me so tenderly that I feel the emotions in my toes. His lips cover mine, his mouth still tasting like cherry ice cream. He lies over me, not moving, as if he knows my body isn't used to his size.

Keegan rolls over me, and the pressure soon turns to pleasure with each thrust, as we find a rhythm, our bodies connected. His hair tickles my face as he glides over me. I kiss his salty neck which glistens with sweat.

"You feel like silk." Keegan continues holding my hand, but his other hand grazes the inside of my thigh before he hooks his fingers around my knee. "So fucking incredible."

I dig my hands into his back and feel the movement of each muscle. I then grab his arms. There is nothing soft about Keegan, but his tender touch takes me by surprise. The way his finger grazes my core, and then grips my butt. The featherlight touch of his hand moving down my arm, until he circles my hip. The dirty things he whispers to me, are in complete opposition to how I imagined him as a lover. Because if I'm being honest with myself, I've wondered so many times what Keegan would be like.

In my dreams, Keegan was mostly a shy lover. But the reality is, he's a little bit of everything. He is shy, especially when he holds my gaze, his eyes fluttering. But he's also so masculine and says things that make my body blush. More than anything, he's thorough. There is no part of me that he hasn't touched and adored.

"Keegan." The feeling of a growing tidal wave hits me again, and I rip my hand out of Keegan's, and grab his waist, pulling him closer. He cages me in with his arms, each muscle tightening with each movement. I roam my fingers down his back and grip his butt, causing a whole different level of friction between us. He quickens his pace, and my ceiling fan does very little to drown out the sound of our flesh slapping together.

"I love this lip of yours." He bites my bottom lip and scrapes his teeth down my neck.

It's not a tidal wave that comes next. It's a tsunami this time. A surge of blood rushes to my core. At first, it seems so far away, but then it's here, crashing into me and building pressure until I have no choice but to be taken out to sea. I squeeze against Keegan's pulsating erection and bite into his shoulder.

"Luna." Keegan's eyes roll back, and when he tries to back off of me, I once again pull his hips toward me.

Keegan holds me close and mumbles something unintelligible into my neck, and a guttural sound escapes him. I hold him close to me as his entire body trembles. His weight falls on me, and I'm pinned beneath the weight of him.

His heart beats against my chest. A fast staccato. Keegan props himself up on his elbow. He brushes my wild hair off of my face. He kisses my eyelid, then my other. Keegan moves to a sensitive spot behind my ear before his lips press against mine.

"You are incredible," Keegan says, pulling out of me until I'm once against empty.

"You," I say, and even that word takes more energy than I have right now.

With his thumb, Keegan starts rubbing circles over my left breast. He presses his lips to mine and then kisses the spot his thumb is tracing, right over my beating heart.

My heart doctor.

We lie in each other's arms, taking deep breaths. He's known me my entire life, and I trust him, almost more than I trust anyone. He allows me to be myself—to be silly and make mistakes. To say the most ridiculous things, without judgment. I cuddle up to Keegan, and he drags me farther into his body.

Keegan kisses my forehead. "If you would have told me that this would someday be my reality, I would have spent a lot less time feeling sorry for myself that I was never going to get the girl."

"Keegan," I say, closing my eyes, all of a sudden shy.

"I'm being serious." He hooks his hand around my hips, and in one swift motion, pulls me on top of him in a straddle. "You are my dream girl."

Keegan's face turns serious, and he sits up with me on his lap and starts kissing me like it's our first time all over again.

*****

My alarm goes off at seven the next morning and I pat the bed next to me, but it's empty. Keegan's dress shirt is crumpled in a pile on the floor, and I pull it on. Some big emotion washes over me. It's not regret. It must be the realization of inevitability. Or of the door we tore wide open last night.

I rub my eyes as I walk to the kitchen. Keegan is dressed in only his white undershirt and jeans and stands in the kitchen, flipping eggs.

"Good morning." Keegan turns from the stove to look at me. His hair is tousled, and there are hints of the boy I once knew. The blue of his eyes shines bright, and then his mouth turns up in a smile.

"I thought you needed a good breakfast before today's shift."

I wrap my arms around him from behind, until my palms lie flat against his chest. I rest my head on his back.

Then I reach around him where the bacon is and bite into the crispy and salty meat.

"You have to be at the hospital at eight." He puts scrambled eggs and bacon on my plate, grabs the pans, and starts washing them.

He walks to the bedroom, and I fork some food into my mouth but then follow him. He then kisses me so softly on the lips, that ditching work and staying tangled up with Keegan all day crosses my mind.

"Your presence would be hard to explain to my roommates," I say. And even though his tattoo is now covered by his pants, I trace my thumb over it, excited to know it's there. It will always be a little secret that we share.

"My shirt looks good on you," Keegan says, as he grabs my legs, places me on the bed, and lies over me. He unclasps the one button, and it falls open, revealing all of myself to him.

"But it smells like you." I cup Keegan's face and pull his lips to mine.

"It's yours," Keegan says as he kisses the skin above my heart. "It looks much better on you."

"Are you sure we can't play hooky today?" I pull his mouth to mine and deepen our kiss. I wrap my legs around him so he can't go anywhere.

"You have no idea how hard it is for me to walk away from you right now," Keegan says, pushing into the bed and putting space between us. "But I have a surgery at nine."

I pull his shirt tightly around myself and sit next to him at the foot of the bed. Keegan takes my hand in his and kisses the top of it. He draws in a sharp breath and releases it slowly. He finally turns and faces me.

"Forest needs to know."

"That we had sex?" I shake my head. "Should I tell him it was three times or leave that part out?"

"Please don't use humor to minimize this." Keegan releases my hand.

"Okay. I'm just not so sure." I grab his arm, and he turns to me. "Shouldn't we wait to see what happens from here? What if I sit him down and tell him, and then you decide that you're not interested or I figure out I can't keep up a relationship and my residency? Or what if we realize that we're actually annoyed by each other and want to call it quits? We need to think this through better and figure out what last night even meant for us."

"The last thing I need is time." Keegan pulls me onto his lap, and I tuck my head into the nape of his neck. "I know exactly what last night meant for me."

I move his hair back and kiss him. His mouth is sweet and possessive. I clench his hair, but he pulls away from our kiss, out of breath.

"Luna. We need—"

"I'm not ready to let anyone into this thing between us." I hold my hand over his heart, interrupting him. "Especially Forest. Not yet."

He kisses my neck and gently pushes me off his lap. "The longer we wait, the harder it will be."

I stand and pull him up. "I need a little time."

He nods. "I'm going on the record to say, waiting to tell him doesn't feel right, and if the situation was reversed and Forest was hiding something from you, you'd feel shitty about that."

"I hear you," I say. "Let's just give it a little time."

"Okay." Keegan pulls away from our embrace. "And you have thirty-seven minutes before you need to be at the hospital, so I suggest you get moving."

Chapter Twenty-Seven

The emergency room is chaotic today. A family of four comes in with third-degree burns. Then a man in his early thirties comes in after suffering cardiac arrest playing basketball at a local gym. Once we get him stabilized, I'm assigned to a college woman who has a foreign object stuck up her vagina after a night of partying.

The emergency room is both a devastating place and somewhere that reminds me I wouldn't do college again. I am happy to be in the early years of my late twenties, where I'm on the other side of some of the things I regularly see here.

Myles stands next to me at the nursing station, looking at a chart. "Today has been nuts."

He looks at me and shakes his head. "Yeah, you know the college girl you're treating? I'm dealing with the boyfriend who also has a foreign object up him."

"What is wrong with people?" I turn and lean against the counter. "Apparently, I was at the wrong parties when I was in college."

"Are you kidding?" Myles finishes his chart and hands it to me. "I never went to college parties. I was that guy."

"Trust me." I place the chart on the counter. "I wasn't at many either."

"Hey." Myles turns to face me. "Just a reminder that Jules will be here around eight. And you're sure you don't mind her staying with us for an entire week?"

"Myles," I say. "It's all good. I'm excited to see her. And it's not like I'm home much anyway."

"Great." He looks back at a new chart he grabbed. "We only have to make it to May and then we'll have our wedding back in Texas, and she'll move here for good."

My pager starts going off. "See you later."

I walk down the corridor to my college patient's room, but then Raven reaches me and loops her arm in mine.

"Hey, Luna. What are you doing tonight?"

I glance at her, and a mischievous grin is all over her face.

"Why?" I raise an eyebrow.

"Forest and I were talking—"

"You and Forest?" I cut her off mid-sentence. "You're a we now, aren't you? Oh my gawd. My new best friend and my brother are a we."

"Anyway." Raven puts her hand up to stop me. "We're going to George's for a drink. You should come. I miss that face of yours."

"I won't be off until seven at the earliest."

Raven smiles. "I know. Plus, this will give Myles and Jules time to be in the apartment alone for a while."

Her final statement is what pushes me over the edge. Myles hasn't seen Jules since she was here for the Fourth of July weekend, which was only two and a half weeks ago, yet somehow feels like a lifetime ago. I'm going to guess they wouldn't mind having the place to themselves to catch up.

"I'll meet you guys there," I say as my pager goes off again, and I head down the hallway.

The rest of my day goes by fast. I'm able to scrub into the surgery of my female college patient, who after Xray, is found to have a travel-sized electric toothbrush in her vagina that requires surgical extraction. It's an interesting procedure, but also enough to confirm that I have no interest in going into gynecology.

After my shift, I change into my clothes and head across the street to George's bar. I walk through the door, and before I have a chance to spot Forest and Raven, Forest puts his hand up so I see him, and he walks in my direction.

"Hey, Luna. A booth just opened up in the back corner." He squeezes my shoulder. "We were waiting for you."

I lean in so Forest can hear me. "Is the entire hospital here tonight? It's packed."

"Raven and I were just saying the same thing." He grabs my arm and leads me to the back of the bar. "It's good to finally see the white of your eyes. Where have you been lately?"

It's a question I can't easily answer, and thankfully, Forest doesn't wait for me to respond before leading me to a booth in the back of George's. I spot Raven, and next to her is Matt from Eighty's Night.

"Luna. You remember Matt," Forest says. "He decided to join us for a drink and bite."

He sticks his hand out to me. "It's great to see you again, Luna."

"Yes, you as well," I say. "I'm glad you recognized me outside of eighties clothes."

He laughs. "Well, I have seen you around the hospital, so I had a good point of reference."

"I'm so happy you could join us, man." Forest points to the booth, and Raven slides in, and Forest sits next to her. Matt motions for me to sit first, and then he takes a seat.

"There you are." Forest raises his hand to wave, and I look behind me where Keegan is walking towards us. He pauses when he reaches our booth, but then Forest moves out of the way and Keegan slides next to him. "Is it just you tonight?"

"Who else would I be with?" Keegan responds.

"I don't know. Your mystery date," Forest says. "You mentioned going on the best date of your life and I—"

"I'm alone tonight," Keegan says, cutting Forest off.

Forest raises an eyebrow in Keegan's direction, and I stare straight ahead.

"Great to see you, Matt." Keegan sticks out his hand to shake Matt's.

"You as well," Matt says. "Forest gave me a call, and I thought coming out instead of going back to my apartment seemed like a good thing to do."

"Well." Keegan drops his hand, and then his eyes flick to me, before quickly looking away. "Thanks for thinking of me too, Forest. I need to unwind after the day I had."

It's my first time seeing Keegan since he left my apartment in the morning, and my body blushes as I replay last night in my head. I put my fingers on my lips, still tingling from how he kissed me. I had to put lip gloss on for work today to hide the ecchymosis on my bottom lip, the only outward evidence of our night tangled up with each other.

Matt turns to me, giving me all of his attention. "How are you liking Presby?"

"It's great." I pivot my body toward Matt and cross a leg over the other. "My Chief Resident is amazing, and I was lucky enough to find good roommates. Present company included." I gesture toward Raven.

"Is New York overwhelming after spending your entire life in Minnesota?" He studies me as he pushes back his longish, blond hair. "Because I spent most of my life on a farm in Iowa, and this city seems otherworldly to me."

Somehow, I can sense Keegan's gaze burning into my skin, and it sends a shiver down my spine. I can't meet his piercing gaze because it would reveal all the things that I'm not ready for anyone to know. My heart races and my palms grow sweaty as I attempt to remain composed and focus on whatever words are coming out of Matt.

With Keegan so close, it's hard to think about anything but him. My mind cuts to the way he touched me, and the words he whispered into my ear. I glance at his hands, and heat floods my body once again as I remember all the things that transpired in the past twenty-four hours. I blush thinking of his cherry tattoo, adjacent to his magic penis.

Before I can answer, Forest puts two glasses down on the table. "Luna, Matt and I were talking about how we Midwesterners need to stay together in the big city."

I put my glass down. "Yes. I just learned Matt was from Iowa."

"Yeah." Matt smiles and puts his arm on the seat behind me. "It's always so nice to meet fellow Midwesterners here. I feel like we're the same speed."

"I think I mentioned this to you, but Keegan is from our same hometown back in Minnesota," I say, attempting to shift some attention his way.

"Why'd you want to practice out East?" Keegan asks him, and we all turn. Keegan then pushes his hair out of his face, and it's hard to look away from his bright, blue eyes. "I know you did your fellowship at Mayo, and not many people choose to leave such a great institution."

"I prefer big cities, and like I said the other night, my brother lives around here." Matt picks up his napkin. "After my internal medicine fellowship at Mayo, I realized that Rochester wasn't a place I wanted to stay and raise a family. It started feeling too small."

He shifts his body and ends up a little closer to me, once again giving me his undivided attention. "How about you? Was Presby your first choice for residency?"

"It was." I rest my elbow on the table. "Besides the obvious reason for Forest being here, their gen surg residency program is one of the best in the country."

"And," I continue, "I love the culture of the city. It's so diverse, and there's so much to do."

Raven leans forward. "You know what you need to do? Get to a Broadway Show. We could go together. You mentioned you've always wanted to go to one."

My eyes dart in her direction, and I have to hold myself back from sharing that I happened to see one the night before. I can see Keegan out of the corner of my eye, and his hands are folded on the table and he moves from studying them to his eyes burning holes into me. I'm a prisoner on the inside of this booth, and I want to get out of it and be alone so I can process the past day.

"Yeah," I continue. "Someday for sure."

"It must be nice having your brother here." Matt looks at Forest, and then Keegan. "And a friend from back home."

Forest laughs. "I'm sure Luna loves having her big brothers hovering all the time." Forest puts his hand on Keegan's shoulder and starts to push him out of the booth. "But why don't the three of us go check on the pizza order? It should have been here by now."

Keegan raises an eyebrow and pushes his shoulder into Forest's. "I'm sure it will be up shortly. We don't need to check on it."

"Okay." Forest clears his throat and looks at Keegan with curiosity. "Raven, will you check with me?"

They slip out of the booth, and it's just Keegan, Matt, and I. Raven glances back at me and shrugs before Forest takes her hand.

"We'll be back shortly." Forest taps the table, and he and Raven walk away.

"Do you guys get to work together much?" I ask, trying to divert Matt's attention off of me.

Matt's eyes glance away from me and look toward Keegan. "I've referred patients who have needed surgery to Keegan, yes. I just recently read your paper on the aortic arch dissection. Stellar work."

Matt once again looks at me before Keegan can respond. "It's always nice to meet people new to the city. This place can be overwhelming."

"Yeah," I say. "It's definitely not the easiest city to make friends."

"Luna." Matt looks at his half-full beer on the table, and then back at me. "If you're up for it, maybe we could explore this new city together. I'd love to take you to my favorite coffee shop. Show you around to the few places I've discovered."

I glance across the booth, wanting to look at Keegan, to reassure him, but he's looking away as he slides out of the booth without saying anything.

Matt once again turns to me. "No pressure if you're not interested. You're new here. I'm new here."

"Oh," I say, as thoughts flood my mind. "It's just that—"

"I'm probably coming on too strong." Matt cuts me off. "As friends, of course."

"Yeah, maybe." I press my lips into a line and rub them together. "It's just that I started seeing someone, which is why I hesitated."

He holds his drink to his lips and takes a long sip of it. He then looks at me and smiles. "I completely understand. I did not mean to be too forward."

"Don't be sorry." I shake my head. "I appreciate the offer, and I'm always up for exploring the city as friends."

"Yes. Of course." Matt says. "As friends."

I see movement out of the corner of my eye and turn as Keegan walks out of George's.

"Matt, can I squeeze past you?" He slides out of the booth so I can get by.

"I need to get out of here, but it was really nice meeting you." I stick my hand out and shake his.

"Yes, it was great seeing you."

I have to find Keegan.

Chapter Twenty-Eight

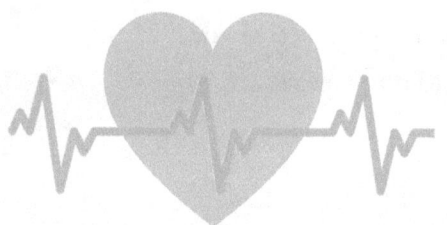

From: Luna Oliver <Luna.Oliver@umn.edu
From: Keegan Baldwin <Keegan.Baldwin@med.cornell.edu

Date: April 2

Keegan!

From: Keegan Baldwin <Keegan.Baldwin@med.cornell.edu
To: Luna Oliver <Luna.Oliver@umn.edu

Date: April 2

Hi Luna. What's up?

From: Luna Oliver <Luna.Oliver@umn.edu
From: Keegan Baldwin <Keegan.Baldwin@med.cornell.edu

Date: April 2

You never email anymore. Why?

From: Keegan Baldwin <Keegan.Baldwin@med.cornell.edu
To: Luna Oliver <Luna.Oliver@umn.edu

Date: April 2

I'm really busy.

From: Luna Oliver <Luna.Oliver@umn.edu
From: Keegan Baldwin <Keegan.Baldwin@med.cornell.edu

Date: April 2

As long as you're not avoiding me.

The darkness envelops me like a shroud, suffocating me and filling me with a sense of illogical fear. I walk briskly in the direction of Keegan's apartment, looking around me at every turn. I quicken my pace, trying to keep my eyes focused ahead, and resisting the compulsion to look over my shoulder.

Every voice, rustle of leaves, snap of a branch, or siren in the background, sends my heart racing. It's probably not the dark that scares me, but the things people do to other people in the dark that cause me to run the last half block to Keegan's building. Nighttime makes me remember that one night in college like it happened yesterday and not years ago. I haven't had an episode like this in years. They always happen when I least expect them—when I think the trauma of that night no longer lives in me.

When I reach the glass front door, I have his doorman ring him, and after showing identification, I'm waved in. The elevator opens on his floor, and I don't have to knock because Keegan stands in his doorway, waiting. He's already changed out of his clothes and is now in one of his Cherry shirts with a pair of joggers.

His expression changes when I fully come into view after stepping out of the elevator. He pushes off the door and in one large step, is in front of me, his one hand cupping my face and his other on my shoulder.

"Luna." Keegan turns his head to the side, studying me. "You're pouring sweat. What's wrong?"

All the stress from the short walk in the dark, and how affected I still am from being attacked years ago, catches up with me. I wrap my hands around his waist and bury my face into his shirt. I focus on my breathing, trying to slow it down. I hold him so tightly, that there's going to be a Luna-sized imprint when I let go.

His hand presses into the back of my head, pushing me farther into his chest. My heart begins to regulate as his pounds against my ear. Keegan's other hand caresses my back.

"Everything's okay, Luna," Keegan says. "You're safe. I'm here."

Keegan's chest goes up and down with each breath, and when I've finally caught mine, I release my grip around his waist and step back. He grabs my hand and pulls me inside his apartment. I'm finally able to take a deep breath.

"Panic attack." I lean against Keegan's kitchen island and continue to focus on my breathing. Keegan goes into his freezer and pulls out a pint of ice cream. He then grabs a couple of spoons. "They come out of nowhere."

"Color is returning to your face." He nods at the barstools around the island. "Come here."

Keegan grips my wrist as I sit next to him, and I know he's taking my pulse. We doctors are never fully off-duty. Keegan takes the lid off of the ice cream and then pushes it in my direction. Mint chocolate chip. I dig my spoon into it and take a big bite, before offering some to Keegan.

"You left." I spoon more ice cream into my mouth, and it's cold against my tongue.

"I should have said goodbye," Keegan says, looking into his lap. "I didn't want to interrupt."

With a deep sigh, I slump forward and press my palms firmly against my forehead, my fingers entwined as I bury my head in my hands. I then shake my head slowly from side to side. My hair falls messily around my face as I let out a breath.

Keegan takes another bite of ice cream, and I do the same, before securing the lid on it. I push off of the stool, grab the pint, and then bring it back to the freezer, out of sight, so I won't be tempted to eat more.

I make my way back to where Keegan waits, anticipation etched across his face. As I draw near, he turns his body to face me, his eyes locking onto mine with a gaze. Instead of sitting, I position myself between his parted legs. Leaning forward, my fingertips graze his hair, gently brushing it back and savoring the softness of each strand. Keegan's hands find their way to my hips, his fingers pressing against my skin as he pulls me closer.

"I'm sorry, Luna." Keegan rubs the skin on my hips in a circular motion. "But I was in the way. And Matt was taking his shot with you. Anyway, why wouldn't he? He'd be a fool to not try."

He closes his eyes and swallows. "But I didn't need to watch."

"Keegan." I put my hands on his upper arms.

"Dr. Theis is a decent guy, Luna," he says. "I respect him a lot."

"Yeah," I say, nodding my head. "He wants us to go sightseeing together."

"And?" Keegan's hands drop to his side. "Do you want to?"

"Well." I step closer and go back to running my hands through his hair. "I told Matt that there's this boy I like, so I probably shouldn't."

"You like a boy?" The corners of Keegan's lips twitch, and he pulls me closer. "I want to hear everything about this guy."

"Well." I shrug. "He feeds me. A lot. And good food too. From nice restaurants."

"He feeds you?" Keegan's chest shakes as he laughs. "Is there any more depth to him than that?"

"He's smart." I grip Keegan's shoulders and then trail them down his arms until I settle my hands on the back of his muscular thighs. "He's like this brainiac surgeon guy. At least that's what he told me he did for a living. I can't know for sure. It could have been a line he fed me."

Keegan's head falls forward with his next laugh. He rests it on my chest and wraps his arms around my waist. "He feeds you and may or may not be a surgeon. Sounds like a real keeper."

"Correct." I pull his chin up.

"Does he have any special skills or anything?" Keegan tilts his head.

"I don't tell everyone this," I whisper into his ear. "But this boy, well, he has magic fingers. You wouldn't even believe what they're capable of. They do so much more than just operate on people."

"There it is." Keegan grips my hips and lifts me onto his lap, and my legs wrap around him. "Forget feeding you and maybe being a surgeon. I would have led with magic fingers. Do not let that guy go."

Keegan presses me into him, and I need his mouth on mine like I need to take my bra off at the end of a long shift at the hospital. With a sudden, swift movement, Keegan stands, my thighs tight around him as he carries me. My heart pounds in my chest, and I can hardly catch my breath as he pushes me against the wall. His effortless strength makes me dizzy with desire.

"I don't plan to," I say the words quietly into his mouth, words that at this moment, I fully mean.

Kegan responds by intensifying the kiss, his mouth parting mine.

Cold, mint chocolate chip kisses are my new favorite. We undress each other, and I run my lips along his chest, and then push Keegan back on the bed and kiss the muscles along his stomach. Everywhere Keegan touches me, a fire ignites. He flips me so I'm on my back, and he hovers over me.

"I want to show you another skill that this boy you like has," Keegan says, pulling my pants down and tossing them on the floor.

"Wait," I say, lifting my head. "You didn't bring out all of your skills on our first night? I'm intrigued."

He lifts my shirt over my head and then kisses my breast, stomach, and hip bone.

"I've been thinking about what you taste like all day," Keegan says. "It's all I've been able to think about."

"Keeg—" I begin to say but find myself without words as moisture pools between my legs.

Keegan hitches his arms under my thighs, lifts my legs, and then buries his face against my core. The sensation ignites every one of my nerve endings, and I call out his name while fisting the sheets for something to hang onto.

"Luna." Keegan presses against my thighs until they open further for him. "So sweet. I knew you would be."

His tongue works its magic, as a finger, and then two slides inside of me. I shut my eyes, and let myself feel what he does to me. I try to clear my head and not think about where this thing with Keegan is heading. I reach down and intertwine my fingers with his as my body starts to shake until I erupt from pleasure.

"I need you," I whimper. "In me. Now." I say between breaths.

Keegan lowers his joggers, and I grip his hips and pull him to me.

"Luna," Keegan says, breathily. "Condom."

"No," I shake my head. "Pill."

I don't need to tell Keegan again, as he presses into me with urgency and desire.

*****

"My mom called today." Keegan rolls onto his side, breaks off a piece of chocolate, and hands it to me.

The covers are only pulled up to his waist, and I run my hand over his arm and then chest. I plump the pillow beneath me and then rest my head on my hand.

"Is that a good thing?"

"Honestly, I don't know," Keegan says. "This is our pattern. Her love and availability have always been very inconsistent."

His fingers twist my hair into curls, and then he releases his grip. "It's been an emotional fuck, if I'm being honest."

"And now she's reaching out again?" I say.

"Yeah," Keegan says. "Almost daily. And we talk about our days, and it's like nothing has ever happened between us."

Keegan releases a long, slow breath, rubs his eyes, and then moves to his side. He tells me about his mom's boyfriend she had after his dad died and how he used to beat Keegan until he was black and blue. He opens up about the drugs, alcohol, and time she's spent in rehab. He admits that she missed every big moment in his life, including all of his graduations. I realize why I can't even recall what Rain Baldwin looks like. She was never around.

"Forest hates her," Keegan says, grabbing my hand and kissing it. "If he knew she was calling me again—"

"Forest probably doesn't hate her." I run my hand along Keegan's jaw, and he closes his eyes and leans into my touch. He takes his hand and hooks it on my hip, bringing me closer until I'm pressed up against him. I nuzzle into the warmth of his chest.

"He just really loves you," I say.

Keegan kisses my forehead, sits up, and leans against the backboard of his bed. He pulls the sheet up with him, and it hangs at his waist.

"I once asked your dad how many more times I should continue to forgive my mom."

"What did he say?" I sit too and hold the sheets over my chest. Keegan extends his arm and holds me close.

"He said I should forgive my mom at least one more time than she's hurt me."

"That is such a Tom Oliver thing to say."

"I have this very real fear that I'm not going to have her for long," Keegan says. "And I need there to be peace between us. She is the only family I have left. Well, besides you guys."

Keegan presses his palms into his eyes and then with his eyes closed, reaches for my hand.

"Luna," Keegan says, releasing a breath. "Forest has been the best friend in the world to me. And here I am, going behind his back, and it's so shitty and—"

"Keeg—"

"I feel sick about it." Keegan puts his hands on my shoulders.

"I hear you," I say. "I've never talked to him about guys I've dated. Why should I now?"

"Because it's me," he says. "And I know you get that important distinction."

Keegan is right. I'm inexperienced when it comes to all of this. I haven't had very long relationships because I've never met someone who seemed worthy of fitting into my life. I purposely kept dating casual, knowing that nothing was going to get in the way of me moving to the city and becoming a doctor.

Things with Keegan feel very different than with any other guy though. My desire for him to experience only good things, to be around him constantly, and to be his person is something I've never felt before. But what if I'm wrong? I can't blow everything up with Forest for something that won't last anyway.

"It's the lying he won't get over," Keegan says.

I move to my side and take a deep breath before my next words. "Do you want to stop this thing between you and me before anyone finds out or gets hurt? We can take it to our graves."

"No." The word shoots out of Keegan's mouth like a rock out of a slingshot, and he props himself up on his arm. "And if I'm being honest, it scares me that your default is always to end things instead of facing something difficult."

"I'm sorry." I inch closer to Keegan. "That's not what I meant."

Keegan raises an eyebrow, and I'm not sure he believes me. He is right though. Forest will never forgive the lying.

"It's getting late," I say, covering my yawn. "I should really get going."

"You can stay here." Keegan grips the sheet covering me and runs a finger along its edges. "I'd love it if you would."

He squints his eyes, waiting for a response. I rest my hand on his face and softly kiss him.

"I would," I say. "But all of my stuff is back at my place, and I work early tomorrow."

Keegan nods, and I kiss him again. This time, he presses his hands along my cheekbones and deepens our kiss. He doesn't want me to leave. I feel like I'm already disappointing him, and that thought makes me scared. There is something about being with Keegan that allows me to dream of the future I always envisioned for myself. The way he kisses and holds me makes me believe that life isn't all about science and absolutes. I want to get lost in it, but I don't know if I can.

"I really need to go," I say, pulling away from his kiss.

I jump off the bed and start putting on my clothes. Keegan stands, gets dressed, and then holds his hand out to me.

"Come on," he says, kissing the top of my hand. "I'll walk you home."

Chapter Twenty-Nine

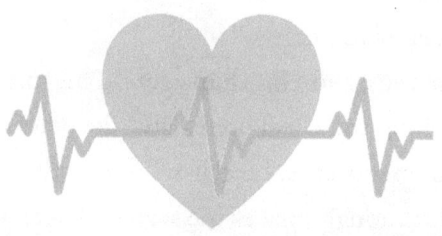

Today starts so early that when Raven, Myles, and I head through the hospital door, it's still dark outside. A few times a month, our schedules align, and we end up on the same rotation, and today is one of those days. We start our early morning doing discharges for patients on the general surgery wing. I jot down drain outputs, follow up on morning labs, and then glance down at imaging recently received for patients undergoing small bowel protocol.

"Hey there, Scarlett. I'm Dr. Oliver." I grab the patient's chart. "How are you feeling?"

My voice startles her, and she sits up. "Please tell me I get to go home today."

"You get to go home today." I put her chart down and grab my stethoscope to listen to her heart and lungs. "It looks like you had a Sigmoidectomy. And you've had a bowel movement?"

"Yesterday, late evening." I study her labs and then pull down the blanket covering her legs and lift her gown to observe the few laparoscopic incisions on her abdomen.

"Everything looks good. Your blood work is great and you can start on solid foods today, but I'd still like you to take it easy."

"Will I feel better after this?" Scarlett lays back down on the bed and pulls the blanket up to her chest.

"People have had great outcomes after this surgery." I smile and pat her knee. "I'm giving you the go-ahead, but before we release you, your physician needs to sign off on the chart. It shouldn't be long."

"Thanks, Dr. Oliver," Scarlett says and waves as I walk out of the room and go to the next patient on the floor.

"Morning huddle is in fifteen minutes," Dr. Parse says as he passes me in the hallway. "Go up to cardiac rehab and complete sign-outs there first. They're backed up this morning."

"Got it." I take the stairs up a level, and as if they were expecting me, a nurse behind the desk hands me a chart.

"Room eleven, Dr. Oliver."

I study the chart of the young male. Heart transplant. Noah Anderson. Why do I know that name? I knock once, walk in, and recognition spreads across my face immediately. It's Keegan's patient who he implanted a ventricular assist device in earlier this summer.

"Hi, Noah." He sits up and smiles when he sees me. "I'm Dr. Oliver. It seems like my final exam is the only thing left before you're discharged."

"Hey, Dr. Oliver," Nurse Lex says, giving me a side-eye. She starts checking on the patient.

"Noah," I say after listening to his new heart and then moving onto his lungs. "I saw you a couple of months ago when you got your VAD. You look like a different person."

"Are you sure I met you?" he asks, and the nurse raises his bed. Noah leans back. "I think I would have remembered you. You're kind of hot."

"Noah." We all look at the door as his mom walks through, her forehead bunched up in annoyance. "She is your doctor. Show some respect."

"It's fine, Mrs. Anderson." I open Noah's gown to look at the large incision down his chest. "If Noah's flirting game is this strong, it must mean he's feeling better."

"See, Mom?" he says as Lex comes to his bedside and pulls down the dressing covering the incision. He then looks at me. "You're kind of young to be a doctor, aren't you? You can't be much older than me."

"Well." I go back to his chart. "I'm an intern, and before we let you go for good, your attending physician is going to pop in." The chart confirms what I already suspected—that Keegan did the heart transplant.

"For the next six weeks, Noah, you need to stay within thirty miles of the hospital at all times." I pull his blanket up to cover him again. "No driving and you'll have weekly follow-up appointments."

"Your nurse Lex will get you set with all of the medications you'll need," I add. "And go through instructions on when to take what."

"How's my favorite patient?" Keegan comes through the door with a big smile and walks to Noah. "You look great."

"I feel great, Dr. Baldwin." Keegan sits on the edge of Noah's bed. "I was about to ask Dr. Oliver out on a date. But my mom keeps getting in the way."

Keegan glances at me and laughs, and Mrs. Anderson once again scolds her son. "Noah, seriously. That's enough. Leave this nice doctor alone." She then looks at me. "I am so sorry, Dr. Oliver. It must be the meds."

"I almost died. This is the new me." Noah crosses his arms over his chest.

"I'm just relieved that your heart transplant didn't affect your eyesight, Noah," Keegan says, looking at me through the corner of his eye, and my face flushes with heat.

"His vitals and blood work look great," I say as I hand Keegan the chart. "He's been up and walking. Lex is going to sit down with him to go over the medications and six-week protocol."

Keegan flips through the paperwork and then takes out his stethoscope. He listens, and the room falls silent. "That is one strong heart you have, Noah. Do you want to hear it?"

Noah's chest expands as he holds a breath, but then he nods. Keegan removes the earpiece, places it in Noah's ears, and lets him hear his new heart. Mrs. Anderson and Noah's eyes fill with tears. Keegan stands, and Mrs. Anderson rushes toward him, wrapping her arms around him.

"I know this is your job," she chokes out a sob. "But thank you for everything you've done for Noah. There just aren't enough words."

"I feel like my embarrassing mom took me out of the running with you," Noah says. I glance at him, and he winks and then laughs.

"Take care of yourself, Noah. Treat that heart well." I squeeze his blanket-covered foot and head towards the door, as I'm already late for the resident's morning meeting. Keegan excuses himself and then steps out of the room with me.

"Hey," he says. The overhead fluorescent illuminates the blue in his eyes. "Pretty incredible, right?"

"That was a full circle moment." I squeeze Keegan's elbow. "One of my first memories of being an intern was talking to Mrs. Anderson about Noah's condition."

Keegan follows me into the stairwell, and the heavy metal door slams behind us. The musty scent of old concrete and stale hospital air fills my nostrils. He grabs my wrist as I go to walk down the stairs, bringing me back to his level.

"And the guy has impeccable taste in women." I go to laugh, but before I can, Keegan presses his lips against mine. One hand cups my face while the other wraps around my back. It's a short kiss, but our first in such a public setting. My knees feel weak beneath me.

"I'm on-call in the ER all week, but are you free Saturday night?" Keegan says, fiddling with the stethoscope around my neck."

"I think I am." I pull at his white lab coat.

"I got two tickets to Tchaikovsky's Swan Lake at Carnegie Hall," he says, squeezing my hand. "It's a date."

"It's a date." I press my lips together, suppressing a smile.

Keegan leans in and quickly kisses me again. "Have a great day, Dr. Oliver." He squeezes my hand three times.

Keegan walks back through the door leading to the cardiac unit before I have a chance to catch my breath and say anything back to him. I smile and hold a hand on my chest to slow my heart as I head down the stairs.

Most days at the hospital are harder than they aren't. I spend my time giving bad news to patients, holding the hands of people as they take their last breath, or hugging family members of those who didn't make it. There have been nights I've gone home and soaked my pillow with tears from all I saw on that given day. The bright light in all of it is that I'm experiencing life with those walking a similar path to mine. Raven, Myles, Forest, and Keegan all feel this too.

Some nights, Raven, Myles, and I will sit in the living room, all scrolling through our phones not saying a word to each other because after what we saw that day, there's nothing left to say. We still choose to be around each other, but the physical presence of someone who knows what this feels like is what makes us all get up the next day and do it again.

"Luna." The sound of Forest's voice brings me back to reality. "What's going on? Do you always walk down the hall with a goofy grin on your face?"

"It's been a good morning, that's all." We stop in the hallway, and Forest adjusts the stethoscope around my neck. The one that Keegan was just playing with.

"I don't suppose you're on call tonight?" Forest asks.

"Actually, I am. Why?"

He checks his pager and then walks in the other direction. He looks back at me. "I am too. Let's try to meet up for coffee or something if it's slow. I miss you."

The rest of the day is more uneventful than the morning. We do morning rounds with our Chief Resident, Dr. Parse, and a new attending physician, Dr. Zahra Badawi. I then scrub in for a perforated viscus case. The afternoon is slow, so I have some time to study for the intern exam. At the end of the day, when most are leaving, including Raven and Myles, I greet the night interns, residents, and attendings.

At ten in the evening, Forest comes walking down the hall, with two coffees in hand. "You're a sight for sore eyes," I say as he hands me the cup.

"It's been slow." Forest opens a door to one of the on-call rooms.

I take a sip of coffee and then lie down, and Forest lies on the bed next to me. "It's been like this all day. I got so much studying in."

Forest turns to his side, and I do the same. "In my head, when you moved here, we'd see each other all the time. But lately, I feel like I've barely seen the whites of your eyes."

"Yeah." I look down and spread my fingers across the thin blanket beneath me. "It's an adjustment, this being a doctor thing."

"I remember it well," Forest says, squeezing his temples. "Have you talked to Keegan recently?"

"Well," I begin to say, feeling so wrong that I'm hiding things from my brother. "I mean, of course we talk. Why?"

"He's been acting kind of strange," Forest says. "He's always busy when I want to hang out. And when I ask him if there's a girl in his life, he gets all weird."

Breath catches in my throat, and I swallow down the emotion. "Yeah?"

"Yeah." Forest rubs his temple. "It's probably nothing, but I'm very aware that our family is all he has. He and his mom haven't spoken in a long time."

Guilt hits me squarely in the chest, and I know I need to be the one to tell him. Regardless of the million reasons I want my relationship with Keegan to stay private, Forest deserves better than this. I've been monopolizing Keegan's time, and I know that he and his mom speak daily, and Forest deserves to know these things too.

"Anyone special in your life, Luna?" Forest sits up on the bed and looks at me. "Did Matt ever ask you out?"

"Well—" I begin to say, but Forest cuts me off.

"Oh there is, isn't there?" Forest ruffles my hair and laughs. "What happened to getting through your internship year?"

He has handed me an opportunity to come clean and be honest on a silver platter. I sit up too, knowing that this is the perfect time to let Forest know that I've fallen for his best friend. I can't hold off any longer. I love Forest, and he deserves my truth.

"There is something—" Forest holds a finger up to me as his phone vibrates against the bed. He mouths something to me and then rushes out of the room.

A minute passes, and then two. I sit on the bed and glance at my phone and pager, neither of which is trying to get my attention. Then Forest walks through the door, and the minute I see his face, I push off the bed and rush to him.

"Forest, what is it?" I place my hands on his shoulders.

His face crumples before me, and then he wraps his arms around me and pulls me close. His chest heaves against me, and I rub his back.

"What happened?" I ask, pulling away, so I can look at him.

Forest rubs his palms into his eyes. "A patient of mine. Ended up in the Emergency Room tonight."

I grab Forest's hand, lead him to the bed, and sit beside him. Forest looks at me and wipes a tear out of the corner of his eye.

"She plays college basketball and has been having episodes of syncope." Forest puts his head in his hands. "She was referred to me, and I did all the tests, and everything was okay. But then after a few more fainting episodes, she recently came back to see me."

Forest takes a deep inhale, holds his breath, and then releases. "I ran more tests and discovered that she had long QT intervals. I saw her last week. I told her we were going to continue to follow this closely, and that it was most likely from the anti-depressant she was on."

Forest glances at his hands, which are now shaking. I take his hand in mine.

"But today, she was on campus, having basketball practice, and collapsed." He looks at me, his face looks broken. "She went into cardiac arrest. They did everything they could, Luna. But her heart was stopped for too long."

I grab Forest and pull him to me. I wrap my arms tightly around him and try to take an ounce of his pain from him. I've only ever seen Forest cry once in our lives, and it was when our dad was diagnosed with cancer over a decade ago.

"She was twenty," Forest says into my shoulder. "And all I can do is replay what I should have done when I detected the long QT interval. I should have done something."

"Forest, you can't." I hold his face in my hands. "You ran the tests. You were going to follow up. You can't go down the path of what-ifs."

The weight of what we do and the pendulum swing of emotions we experience daily hit me. Some doctors can separate themselves from the patients we see, but that isn't Forest and it's not me either.

"I should go to the ER and talk to her family." Forest wipes his eyes. "I'm sorry, Luna. Was there something you wanted to tell me?"

There was, but he's at the capacity of what he can hear tonight. I shake my head. "Come find me after, Forest. I'm here for you."

He nods and then rushes out of the room.

Chapter Thirty

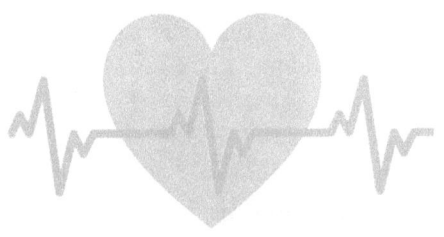

From: Keegan Baldwin <Keegan.Baldwin@med.cornell.edu
To: Luna Oliver <Luna.Oliver@umn.edu

Date: March 23

Congrats on matching.

From: Luna Oliver <Luna.Oliver@umn.edu
From: Keegan Baldwin <Keegan.Baldwin@med.cornell.edu

Date: March 23

Well, if it isn't Keegan Baldwin. I figured you'd forgotten about me. I haven't heard from you in ages and haven't seen your face in nearly eight years.

From: Keegan Baldwin <Keegan.Baldwin@med.cornell.edu
To: Luna Oliver <Luna.Oliver@umn.edu

Date: March 23

Well, we're about to live in the same city, so I'm sure that will all change.

From: Luna Oliver <Luna.Oliver@umn.edu
From: Keegan Baldwin <Keegan.Baldwin@med.cornell.edu

Date: March 23

Yeah? But don't rope me into joining your NYC branch of Mathletics. I'm going to be way too busy.

From: Keegan Baldwin <Keegan.Baldwin@med.cornell.edu
To: Luna Oliver <Luna.Oliver@umn.edu

Date: March 23

I'll just be happy if you can find time in your busy schedule to see me once in a while. You've always been so much cooler than me.

From: Luna Oliver <Luna.Oliver@umn.edu
From: Keegan Baldwin <Keegan.Baldwin@med.cornell.edu

Date: March 23

It's the duct tape on the glasses Keegan.

From: Keegan Baldwin <Keegan.Baldwin@med.cornell.edu
To: Luna Oliver <Luna.Oliver@umn.edu

Huh. Who knew?

Tonight, Forest and I are having dinner, and no matter what, I'm going to tell him. Which means today is the last day of normal. I want to think he's going to be okay, but I'm not sure he will be. And this isn't because of a stupid pact we made years ago about not dating each other's friends. His issue will be that it's Keegan. Because Keegan has always been his. And never mine.

It's a slow day in the emergency room, so Raven and I spend some time updating charts. It's rare for us to have so few patients, and I've witnessed how quickly that can change, so for now, I'm enjoying that I get to sit down for a moment.

"Hey, girl." Raven puts her chart down and rests her feet on the chair across from her. "The charts are pretty much updated."

"I know." I look toward the door. "Where are all the sick people today?"

Raven also glances toward the door. "Right? Even the step-down floor is pretty empty."

"Well." I put the charts down on the desk. "Dr. Parse asked me to go through the exam rooms and do an inventory check. Page me if you need anything."

"Will do." Raven spins in her chair. "I wish they would cut one of us. Time feels like it's standing still."

The first exam room I go into is a mess. I bring in a supply cart and start stocking the room with the necessities. There's an enormous amount of peace in the mundane. The hospital is not a place I usually find it, and ever since

I started my residency, this is the first day that's ever felt like this.

When I open one of the cupboards in the exam room, I see a binder, grab it, and hoist myself onto the foot of the bed. I flip through the pages, and it's a guide to all of the different protocols for a variety of scenarios that can happen at the hospital.

The soft glow of natural light filters in from the hallway, casting delicate shadows on the sterile walls. As I glance up, my eyes meet Keegan's, who stands at the doorway, silhouetted against the brightness outside. He leans against the frame and then steps inside. With a gentle click, he closes the door behind him.

He slowly moves toward me, a half-smile spread across his face. His beauty is the in-your-face kind. His scrubs cling to his toned frame, accentuating his every curve and muscle. A pristine white coat completes his professional ensemble.

"I'm Dr. Baldwin," Keegan says, and a corner of his lip curves up. "And what brings you in today?"

"Oh, really?" I scrape my teeth along my bottom lip. I put my finger up to my temple, thinking. "Dr. Baldwin, is it?"

Keegan nods.

"Well," I say. "My heart has been tachycardic all day." I point to the left side, playing along.

"Tachycardic?" Keegan pulls the stethoscope off his neck and puts it in his ears. "That's a big medical word for a patient. Do you have a medical background?"

I shake my head.

Keegan untucks my scrub top and rakes the cold metal against my skin until it's firmly over my heart.

"It's pounding," he says, pausing to listen further.

He's not wrong. My heart always speeds up in his presence. I learned all about it in medical school, and I know there's a scientific explanation for it. The brain sends signals to the adrenal gland, which secretes hormones such as adrenaline, epinephrine, and norepinephrine. What my books didn't teach me is how my brain knows that Keegan is the only person who causes this reaction in me.

"I better listen to your lungs." Keegan reaches over me, his face hovering an inch away from mine, as he moves the stethoscope to my back. "Are you having any trouble breathing?"

"No." I shake my head. "But my jaw has been tight all day."

Keegan steps back, feels along my jawline, and then drags his fingers down and presses on my lymph nodes.

"Can I ask you something, Dr. Baldwin?" I move my legs apart so he can get closer to me for this examination. "Are you sure you're old enough to be a doctor? You seem a little young."

Keegan smiles and puts his stethoscope back around his neck. "Well, I started college at sixteen."

"A prodigy," I say, pressing my lips together.

Keegan barks a lap and presses down on my thighs with his hands, spreading his fingers across them.

"One more question," I say and point to the red letters that adorn his white coat. "Do you think I could listen to your heart? You know, to learn a thing or two."

"Of course," Keegan says, and I sit up straighter to reach him. I grab my stethoscope.

"Interesting." I move his scrub top out of the way, and he flinches when the cold metal connects with his skin.

It's an intimate thing to get to hear someone's heart so clearly—much different than lying my head across his chest. The lub dub sound comes through the earpiece as his heart valves close and blood pumps in and out of his chambers.

Keegan rests his hands on my shoulders. "What's your diagnosis?"

"Well." I keep the earpiece in, and let the stethoscope hang around my neck. I pull my bottom lip into my mouth and smile. "Your heart is racing. Your skin is glistening. You must be thinking of a beautiful woman who has captivated you."

Keegan laughs and pulls my hips toward him. "Your stethoscope told you all of that?"

"It's a special stethoscope," I say, looking down at it. "With very special powers."

"Gawd, I love you," he says.

My eyes shoot to my forehead, although I quickly convince myself that Keegan used those three words flippantly, and not literally. Keegan's lips collide with mine in a fierce, passionate kiss, before I have a chance to react to his words. I am caught off guard by the intensity of his embrace. I fall back on my elbows, and he rests his arms on either side of me. His lips are insistent, his tongue seeking entrance to my mouth, as he deepens the kiss. Heat radiates off his body, as he presses himself against me.

Light again pools into the exam room, and Keegan takes a dramatic and quick step back.

"What the hell?" We both jerk our heads to see Forest standing in the doorway. All ten units of blood in me feels like it runs to the floor. My body liquifies.

"Forest, wait," I yell. But he turns to leave the room. I jump off the exam room bed and chase after him. I grab his arm, but he shakes me off.

"Talk to me, Forest." I follow him down the corridor, and I practically have to jog to keep up with him. "Please."

Footsteps come up on our rear, and I turn to see Keegan trying to catch up. Forest gets in the elevator, and we follow him to the main floor. Once we get there, Forest rushes outside into an empty courtyard nestled between a couple of the hospital buildings.

He runs his hand through his hair, pulling until his brown locks stand on his head. "How long has this been going on?" Forest then folds his arms over his chest. His face is at first pale, and then when he looks at Keegan, it turns bright red.

Neither of us answers, and Forest furrows his brow with intensity. "How long?"

I try to grab his arm again, but he shakes me away. "I was planning on telling you. Tonight. At dinner."

"How fucking long?" Forest turns from me to face Keegan.

"About a month." Keegan blankly stares at him.

"A month?" Forest rubs his fingers into his temples and takes a step closer to Keegan. "You've got to be kidding me right now."

Forest looks at me, and then Keegan, directing the question to him. "Are you guys fucking?"

It's as if I'm not here—that this entire thing is between the two of them and has nothing to do with me.

"Forest, don't do this." I grab his arm again. Tears spill out of my eyes. "Not here."

"Keegan, I asked you a question." Forest's eyes blaze into Keegan's. "Are you fucking my sister? It's not a hard question."

Keegan looks at him straight in the eyes, his expression blank. "It's not like that."

An older couple walks into the courtyard, and I say in a more hushed tone. "We weren't trying to hurt you."

"I feel so much better." Forest shakes his head. "For fuck sake, Luna."

"It just happened." Keegan takes a step closer to Forest. "We can sit down and talk about this."

"We." Forest rolls his head back and laughs. "There is no we, Keegan. Not between us. You are dead to me."

"Don't do this," Keegan says, putting himself between Forest and the only exit.

Forest laughs maniacally. "I had the decency to tell you the minute I started feeling a certain way about Raven. I even asked your permission. But you guys didn't have the decency to do the same for me?"

"She's my fucking sister." Forest drags his hand down his face and turns to Keegan. "You've had every opportunity to talk to me about it, but I have to find out like this."

"This is all my fault," I say, stepping in, putting my body between the two of them as they continue to step toward each other. "Keegan wanted to tell you immediately. I begged him not to."

Forest snaps his head towards me as if he's remembering that I'm here too. "I know this is all your fault, Luna. It always is. You never think about anyone but yourself. And based on your track record, we all know how this is going to end. And then what?"

"Don't do that," Keegan says, reaching for Forest's arm, but he jerks it away.

Forest balls his fist up and shakes it. I grab his hand, and he finally lowers it and says to Keegan, "You have no idea how much I want to hit you."

"I know," Keegan says, stepping closer to Forest, almost like he wants to be hit. Like that would make him feel better.

"You're better than this," Forest says. "You're both better than this."

His words are cutting, and Keegan stands and takes it and doesn't react. Forest walks away, and Keegan stays firmly planted on the ground like his feet are weighted down by lies of omission. He tucks his hands into his pockets and looks at the green grass below his feet.

Forest walks back inside and I run after him, and this time when I grab his arm, I don't let him shake it off.

"Luna," he says in a whispered tone as action swirls all around us. "How could you?"

Forest pinches the bridge of his nose and takes a long and slow inhale. "How did you think this was going to go, Luna?" Forest chokes back a cry. "Or were you going to continue to lie to me?"

"I didn't do this to hurt you." Tears stream down my face.

"I feel like a fool." Forest wipes his eye with the back of his hand. "I've lost my best friend in the entire world. Because of you. I can't stand to look at either of you."

"No," I say abruptly. "Be mad at me. Not him. Keegan wanted to talk to you. You guys can't lose each other. I'll make this right."

"I don't know if I'll ever look at you guys the same," Forest says.

"What can I do? I'll do anything," I beg, my voice desperate for an answer to make this all better.

Forest shakes his head, brushes past me, and heads down the hallway in the other direction, and I'm left standing there, trying to put together all the pieces of the last few minutes.

Chapter Thirty-One

My watch tells me I'm at almost thirty-thousand steps, which means I've been walking the streets of New York for hours. I've missed about ten calls and fifty text messages from Raven, Keegan, and my mom, but I'm avoiding all conversations. The sun set hours ago, and I can hear Keegan's voice in my ear telling me to be safe. But tonight, my grief is my greatest companion, and even the darkness doesn't make me feel alone. My pain surrounds me like a weighted blanket.

And then I look up and see Keegan's building. Deep down, I knew this was where I was headed the entire time, and I avoided ending up here for hours. I know what I need to say, but they aren't words I want Keegan to hear. I'm in a land of what-ifs, and I can't help but feel that I not only let Forest down but disappointed Keegan too. He asked, no, begged me to tell Forest as soon as things started between us. And now my decisions are at the center of chaos. I created this mess.

The doorman waves me in, and I head up to Keegan's apartment. He's not standing in the doorway like so many other times when I've visited, but instead, his door is open. Keegan leans over his island, studying papers lying there. His hair is wet, and his black-rimmed glasses are back on his tired-looking eyes. When he sees me, he jumps to his feet and rushes toward me.

"Where have you been?" Keegan pulls me into a hug. "I've been worried sick about you."

"I needed time to think," I say, pulling away from his embrace. I study him, surprised that he's acting like nothing has changed between us when everything has.

"I've been thinking a lot about this," Keegan says. "I'm going to sit down with Forest, and then—"

"Keegan, stop." I put my hand up, and he pauses. Anything he says is going to make this one thousand times harder.

"I've been thinking a lot too," I say.

He removes his glasses and pinches the skin between his eyebrows. He watches me as I try to find the words to say next.

"We tried," I say, nervously laughing because it's the only thing keeping me from crying. "The past month has been..." I can't find the words to describe what our time has meant to me.

"But?" Keegan backs up and leans against the kitchen island.

"You heard what Forest said." I inhale a sharp breath. "Maybe I'm not ready for a relationship, and he's probably right that this won't end well. And if we both admit that now and go our separate ways, you and Forest have a chance."

Keegan pushes off the island and clasps my wrist. "For me and Forest to be cool, I have to lose you?"

"You'll go back to being Forest's best friend," I say. "And you and I can walk away while we still like each other. Before either of us screws this up. We'll act like nothing ever happened. You'll be Forest's best friend, and I'll be the younger sister you guys sometimes include."

"You've always been more to me than that," Keegan says.

"Keegan." I pull my wrist away from him. "It's better for us to walk away before real feelings are involved."

"Real feelings?" Keegan says, shaking his head. "What is it going to take for you to understand how I feel about you?"

Keegan escapes down the hallway but returns a moment later with a book. He stands in front of me, opens a page, and then hands me a picture. A photo of Keegan and me stares back at me. It was taken at his medical school graduation. I barely remember someone snapping a photo. My brown hair is pulled on top of my head, and my arms are crossed. I look at the camera, annoyed to be there, and even more irritated that someone is making me take this photo. Keegan though, looks at me. His crimson and black robe hangs off his frame, and he holds his cap and diploma in his hand. I glance at Keegan.

"Why are you showing me this?" I say, holding it up, studying it.

"I don't know how I can be any more clear, Luna. Do I need to spell things out for you?" Keegan shakes his head and then snatches the photo from me. "I have a tattoo of a moon. I carry around my favorite photo of us in a book of poetry."

"Keeg—" I begin to say, but he interrupts me.

"You want to end things before we catch feelings," Keegan says. "But I've been in love with you for the past eight years."

"No. Don't say that." Blood drains from my face at Keegan's admission, and I can't seem to find any of my words. I look down at my feet.

"Why?" Keegan grabs my arm.

"It's just that. . ."

I've been at this point in relationships before, but never this soon into it. No one I've ever dated in the past has ever made me want to try to make things work. Instead, my reaction has always been to run. Relationships require compromise, and I've never been willing to do that. I've always known the path I've wanted to take. College. Medical School. Residency. Fellowship. After that, I'd decide on where I wanted to practice medicine, and I always intended to make that decision independent of any man in my life. This is the point in relationships where I walk away because every man I've dated has felt like an obstacle instead of a partner.

It's hard to see Keegan in the same light, though.

"I didn't know," I finally say. "How could I have known?"

"You've chosen to stay willfully ignorant," Keegan says, lifting my chin to face him. "Luna." Keegan closes his eyes and inhales sharply. When he opens them, they are glossy. "I've been in love with you for longer than is healthy when it's unrequited."

"You don't love me," I say. "You can't."

Keegan steps back from me wounded. "Don't insult my intelligence."

"Then why am I only hearing about this for the first time?"

"When was I going to tell you?" Keegan says. "I fell in love with you, and then the next day, I was moving to New York to start a six-year residency. You were just starting undergrad. And then going to medical school. You were in Minnesota. I was here. Our lives have been going in opposite directions for so long. I have a moon tattoo, Luna. You know I don't believe in coincidences. Short of telling you, and scaring the shit out of you, I feel like I've been very clear about my feelings."

"Keegan." I put my head in my hands. "None of this was supposed to happen. I can't have distractions. I said I wasn't going to date in my internship year because I needed to focus on medicine. I told myself that when I did start dating it wouldn't be someone I worked with. Forest hates us both. And now here I am. I've been in New York for less than three months and have already created a mess."

My heart breaks looking at Keegan. I've never hated hurting someone more than I loathe the pain I can see all over his face. But I'm so focused on Forest and his pain, that I can't focus on mine, and what walking out the door could mean. If I remove myself from the equation, Keegan and Forest may have a fighting chance at their relationship. There is no point in my life when there was one without the other. I refuse to be the reason why.

"I don't want to hurt you." I step toward him, and he backs away. "But I don't know how to navigate this. Taking space from each other makes the most sense. To figure out what we both want."

"You aren't hearing me," Keegan says, and he rubs my arm with his hand. "I know what I want. I've always known, Luna. You are my light. You've always been my person."

I shake free from him and bury my face in my hands. I can't look at him. I've messed everything up beyond repair and seeing the hurt in Keegan's eyes will be the end of me.

After what feels like several minutes of not saying anything, I feel Keegan step away from me.

"Take all the space you need," Keegan says.

"You know how much—"

"I'm speaking as faculty for Heart Divergent in Chicago and leave Sunday," Keegan says, interrupting me. I realize there will be no Carnegie Hall date. "Then I'm going to head to Cherry for a couple of weeks to see my mom."

"I don't know what else to say." The tears become more steady down my face. "What I want more than anything is for you to fix things with my brother. You two need each other."

I think of all the ways they've needed each other in life. When Keegan's dad died when they were only ten years old. All the times Keegan's mom couldn't care for him throughout the years. When Forest's high school girlfriend broke his heart right before their graduation. When our dad was going through cancer treatment. They've been each other's constant through all of it. There is no Forest without Keegan.

"I've said everything I can." Keegan looks at his hands.

"Keegan, please," I say, grabbing his arm. "This is hurting me too."

"Well," he says, stepping back. "I have a lot to do to get ready to leave. You should probably—"

"Yeah, I'll go."

I step toward the door. I decide to look back and immediately regret it. Keegan, who I've never seen show emotion, wipes a tear that fell from his eye. A million words flood me—things I want to say. But instead, I rush out before I let him see too much of me.

*****

There is no time to wallow in the constant sadness that I feel. Work makes me put aside feelings and focus on those that need me the most. I need to put one foot in front of the other and do my job. I keep telling myself that space is a good thing. It will allow me to focus on my job, and look into spending a year or two at Jamaica Queens Hospital, where their general surgery program has a greater focus on trauma, which is where I want to go after my residency. I also need to continue studying for the intern exam. Even so, my chest feels heavy, and I can't think of anything except Keegan and how alone he must feel right now.

"We are so going out tonight." Raven takes my arm as we walk down the hospital corridor. "And we won't talk about men."

I blink away a thought. "I really don't feel up for it."

"I know," Raven says. "But you need a distraction. You aren't eating. You look like crap. You can talk to me, you know?"

"Yeah." I nod my head. "But you're dating my brother. It feels like a conflict of interest."

"Forest is being ridiculous." Raven leans in and lowers her voice. "You're not the first brother and sister who have dated each other's friends."

"It's more complicated than that though," I say. "Forest wouldn't care if I dated any of his other friends. But Keegan doesn't count."

"What do you want?" Raven asks as she squeezes my hand.

"Peace."

Raven laughs. "Sorry, Luna. That's not reality. Life is messy and imperfect, and none of us survive it."

We line up in front of Chief Resident Parse, who starts doling out our daily assignments. "Dr. Worth," he says to Myles. "You'll be on the neuro floor today. Dr. Craik," he says to Raven, "You'll be in gynecology. Dr. Oliver, cardiac."

I trudge up to the cardiac floor, ready to rip the Band-Aid off. Because if it wasn't today, then it would be another day where I'm forced to face Forest, Keegan, or both. It may as well be today.

Dr. Lanson is the first person I see. "Well, Dr. Oliver. I haven't seen you up here in a while."

"No," I say. "I've been mainly in the pit. But this is where I'll be spending my day."

And then a doctor I don't recognize rounds the corner and smiles when she sees me. She sticks her hand out.

"I'm Dr. Aza Farouk. I'm here for a few weeks. I'm usually at Columbia."

The only thing worse than having to see Keegan is not seeing him. Knowing that Dr. Farouk is here instead of him makes this hospital feel empty. Nothing feels right without him here.

"Dr. Oliver." Dr. Farouk stands next to Dr. Lanson. "Do you want to scrub in for your last heart surgery for a while? I hear you're moving on to endocrine and robotics for your next rotation."

"Yes," I say. "Today is my last day of thoracic for a while."

Everything in my life seems to be changing. Forest won't answer my calls. Keegan is gone for a couple of weeks, I'm debating spending years two and three at Jamaica Queens Hospital, and it all feels like too much.

Dr. Farouk looks at me. "The patient is a twenty-six-year-old female. Born with a ventricular septal defect, never requiring repair. She developed endocarditis, and it destroyed her mitral valve. We're going to open her up, give her a new valve, and repair the VSD."

We get into the room, where the patient is being prepped for surgery, and my brother stands at her bedside.

Forest glances at me. His eyes seem tired, and he struggles to look directly at me. Nothing in life feels good when my brother and my relationship is in this state. We've always been close, but as I further examine our relationship, it occurs to me that as much as I love my big brother, we haven't had a lot of real conversations.

"Emmy, this is Dr. Farouk, and she'll be your surgeon today. This is Dr. Oliver, a surgical resident who will also be scrubbing in. You'll be in great hands," Forest says.

"It's nice to meet you, Emmy." Dr. Farouk takes her hand and pats the top of it.

"After surgery," Forest continues, "you'll be brought to the ICU. Your family will be there to greet you, and I'll stop by and check on you as well. Do you have any questions?'

Emmy shakes her head, and we head down to the operating room.

Dr. Farouk is a great surgeon. I stand across from her, observing, and jumping in when she gives me opportunities. My head is both in the game and also with Keegan. I wonder where he's at this very moment. I contemplate if life will always feel this empty and void of color if he's not around. Mostly, I ponder if this heaviness in my chest, the sadness that I can't run from, is love.

Chapter Thirty-Two

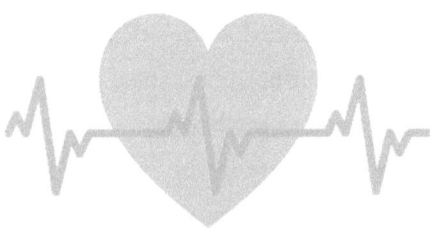

Two days later, I'm awoken by pounding at the door. Myles and Raven both peek out of their rooms, and we all shrug and walk to the door. None of us were expecting anyone, especially at this hour. I throw the door open, and Forest stands on the other side.

"Did you get Mom's text?" Forest walks into the apartment.

Forest hasn't talked to me in days, and my heart speeds up, my mind going to a million different things that could be wrong—things bad enough for Forest to break his silent treatment.

"I was sleeping. My phone's been on silent." I pick up my phone that is on the counter. "Nevermind. It's dead. What's going on?"

Forest glances at Raven. She goes back to her room, and Myles goes back to his. He then follows me.

"It's Keegan's mom." Forest puts his hand over his mouth and shakes his head. "She's dead."

"What?" All the air in me escapes. I get dizzy, sit on my bed, and put my head in my hands.

"They found her body in the river." Forest sits next to me and wipes his damp face with the back of his hand. "Mom called me first thing this morning, and she's been trying to reach you as well."

"Have you called Keegan?" A dam breaks inside of me, and a sob escapes me. "He's in Chicago. All alone."

Forest presses his palms into his eyes. "I've called at least fifty times, and it goes to voicemail each time."

"Is everything alright?" Raven peers through the doorway.

"No." I grab a bag out of my closet and start throwing clothes in it. I rush to the bathroom and grab all of my toiletries.

"Raven, can you let Dr. Parse know that I'll be gone for a couple of days? Family emergency. Maybe you guys could pick up a couple of shifts, or—"

"Luna." Forest grabs my arm. "You don't have the time off."

"He's all alone, Forest." I look at Raven, and she comes and wraps her arms around my waist. "We are literally the only family he has."

"Keegan's mom passed away," Forest says, glancing at Raven.

"Don't worry about anything but getting to Keegan." Raven hugs me tighter. "We'll make sure you're covered."

Forest puts his face in his hands.

"I hope you're getting your ass to Minnesota too," I say. "We don't deserve him, Forest. We've been horrible."

"Luna, please." Forest pinches the bridge of his nose.

"I'm not wrong." I throw a sweatshirt over my shirt. "You say he's your best friend. Your brother. And Keegan has always been there for you. Always. But the minute he does something that you don't like, you take your love away. And I'm no better."

"You really want to do this now?" Tears stream down Forest's cheeks. "I'm hurt. The thought of you two having this secret behind my back. The fact that neither of you trusted me enough. I will always be there for Keegan. But damn it, Luna. You should have told me."

But I wave him away. "We're all he has."

"I was mad." Forest starts pacing. "Don't act like this is all on me."

"Here." Raven shows us her phone. "There's a flight to Minnesota at eleven. But you guys' better book it now."

Forest sits at the foot of my bed, looking at flights on his phone. I do the same and lock in the next flight.

"Booked," I say, quietly.

"Booked." Forest stands. "I need to run home and pack. I'll see you at the airport."

I arrive at the gate as it's boarding. I don't see Forest anywhere, but when I get on the plane, he's already sitting in first class. I walk to the back of the plane with the majority of the people. But when I go by Forest, he grabs my arm.

"I rented a car. I'll meet you outside the gate."

"Okay."

When I get to my seat, I try to call Keegan one more time, but again, it goes to voicemail.

*****

We land in Minneapolis, and Forest and I navigate our way to the car rental terminal and brace ourselves for the car ride ahead of us. I don't know if Keegan's phone is dead or he's blocked my number, but I've called more than twenty times, and each time, his low, husky voice comes on, saying to leave a message.

Forest and I don't speak as he navigates through the Twin Cities traffic. When the road finally opens up, he lets out an audible breath.

"I know I haven't exactly acted like the model big brother." He glances at me sidewards. "But are we going to talk about this? I mean, really talk about this?"

Forest and I have gone through life getting along for the most part. But he's never opened up to me, nor have I to him. We've kept things superficial and focused on the quantity of our interactions instead of the quality of our relationship. Our dad doesn't talk about feelings much either, but my mom has always been open about these things. I don't know where our lack of vulnerability stems from.

"You know when we created that stupid rule about not dating each other's friends?" I blow out a breath. "It was because you were young and reckless, and I knew my friends were going to fall for you and you were looking for nothing but a good time."

"It took me a minute to accept you and Raven, but you aren't the same guy you were eight years ago and I know you actually liked her so I got on board with it. Almost immediately." I move my foot to the dash.

Forest grips the steering wheel with a new level of intensity. "You act like I've been the only reckless one, but you and I are more alike than you care to acknowledge. I didn't make that pact just for me, Luna. I knew my friends would be interested in you, and I also knew that no man that was in my orbit would ever be good enough to fit into your five-point plan."

Graduate top of my class in high school. Finish my pre-med degree in the top tenth of my class. Get into a top

Medical School. Graduate with Latin honors. Get into a top general surgery residency program. Complete a fellowship in trauma surgery.

"Then why were you willing to introduce me to your colleague Matt?"

"Because I don't care about him," Forest says.

"Of all the people though, Luna. Keegan? My Keegan?" Forest says. "I wouldn't care if it was any other friend. But Keegan."

"Trust me, I know," I say. "I was as surprised as anyone. I know you think I'm reckless, immature, and not ready for a relationship. But I didn't enter into this thing with him lightly."

Forest barks out a laugh as he wipes his eye with the back of his hand. Crying and laughing are two sides of the same coin, as are pain and joy.

"I've never thought of Keegan that way," I say, sniffling. "But from almost the moment I saw him this summer, something had shifted. I tried to ignore these feelings and push them down. But I couldn't."

Forest turns the air up in the car and blows out a breath. "When did it start?"

"Do you really want to know?"

"Yes and no." Forest shakes his head.

"Partly, from the moment I arrived in the city." I drag my hand over my chest, remembering. "Things were charged between us. At least I felt it. It was like I was seeing him for the first time through new eyes."

A tear falls from my eye as I remember the beginning, which wasn't that long ago. "And then one day, I was having a terrible day at work. I went to look for you and couldn't find you, but found Keegan instead, and without thinking, I kissed him."

I start laughing through my tears. "But he just stood there, frozen. He didn't kiss me back. Partly because he didn't want to take advantage of me. But probably mostly because of how much he loves you."

"Luna, I'm trying here. I am." Forest taps his chest.

Forest takes the exit, and now we're off the main highway as we continue to drive northeast. "When I spent the night at his place when he was so sick—"

"Something happened then?" Forest interrupts me, jerking his head in my direction.

I decide to leave out the part about Keegan coming into my room during our weekend in Montauk. Our first real kiss. I feel like that's just for the two of us—dare or not.

"No," I say immediately. "But it's when I realized he was probably the best friend I had. Until that moment, he was always my brother's best friend. But now he felt like mine too."

Forest doesn't speak for a while, as the plains around us turn into an expansive forest. The blacktop underneath our rental car is the only sound I hear.

"Are you in love with him?" Forest asks me, resting his elbow on the middle console.

I leave out the part that perhaps this all started for me eight years ago too. Through the emails we'd send each other, and the help he'd give me during my math-heavy classes. Keegan has always been an integral person in my life, even if I'm only realizing it more recently.

"What does that even mean?" I close my eyes and feel the sun on my face through the window. "Does this painful ache and emptiness in my chest mean I'm in love with him? Or the fact that life feels dull without him around. Or is it the self-hate I feel being part of the reason that he's sad?"

"This isn't going to make sense to you, Luna." Forest pinches the bridge of his nose again. "You and Keegan are the two closest people to me in the entire world. If this doesn't work out, what happens? And if it does work out, then what the hell is my role? But I know Keegan. He's a love-you-for-life kind of guy. Are you sure you're ready to be in that serious of a relationship? Cause you've never been in one before."

"I can't sit here and make promises that I'm not sure I can keep," I say. "But I also don't know if I can be with him if it means you two aren't in each other's lives." I once again close my eyes.

Forest glances at me and lets out a long breath as the first sign of Cherry comes into view.

Chapter Thirty-Three

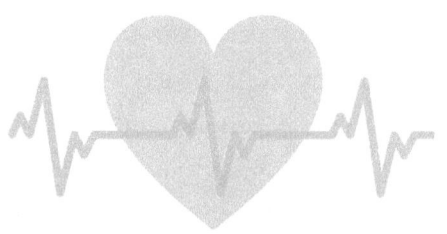

Forest and I don't bother to stop home. Instead, we drive out to Keegan's mom's land, where she's lived in a trailer right on the West Two Rivers. We step out of the car in silence, but two cars are parked out front, one of them being our mom's.

Forest and I enter the trailer, and the stale air hits me all at once. It's suffocating and musty, and the cramped space feels like it's closing in on me. Everywhere I look, there are piles of junk—old newspapers, empty bottles of alcohol, and worn furniture. A small orange kitten greets us.

We make our way through the maze of clutter, dodging discarded knick-knacks and tattered rugs. Finally, we reach the kitchen, where my mom and Keegan speak in hushed voices, leaning against the counter. Keegan's eyes land on Forest and me, and they seem to lock onto us like a heat-seeking missile. His gaze shifts between the two of us, and his mouth falls open in surprise.

The world around me fades away as Keegan steps closer, his features etched with exhaustion and sadness. His eyes are bloodshot, and his jaw is dusted with day two stubble. Keegan pushes off the counter and closes the distance between us. In a single, fluid motion, he wraps his arms around me, pulling me close to his chest. His hands grip my waist tightly, and I can feel the warmth of his skin through my clothes. My arms shoot up to wrap around his neck, and I bury my face into his shoulder.

Nothing Forest and I just discussed is even relevant anymore. Because I won't hurt this man again. I'm home.

Neither of us says anything, but we hold each other, and I move my hand to his chest and feel his heartbeat slow down, steadily. He then kisses the top of my head and pulls away.

With my thumb, I wipe away a tear from Keegan's cheek and then reach to my toes to kiss it. He doesn't take his eyes off of me and keeps his hand wrapped in mine. He needs me, and I don't care that my mom and Forest are here, or that I said we needed space because I need him more than I need anything else.

"I'm so sorry," I whisper into his ear. "We came as soon as we heard."

"Look at this." We turn to my mom when her voice rings out. "My three babies. All home. For the first time in, well, what feels like forever."

My mom wraps her arms around me and then moves on to Forest. And then, as if nothing happened, Forest walks to Keegan and embraces him.

"I'm so sorry, man," Forest says, and it feels like he's apologizing for more than the death of Keegan's mom.

My mom puts her hand on Forest's. "I need to pick up your dad, and then I should go to the funeral home. Forest, would you help me?"

"Umm." Forest looks at me, then Keegan. He hesitates. "See you back at the house?"

Keegan nods. "Yeah, I have a few things to wrap up here." And then he looks at me. "You don't have to stay."

"I want to." I lace my fingers in his. Keegan releases a breath in relief. "If that's okay?"

My mom and Forest navigate through the clutter, then walk out of the trailer.

"Thanks for coming." Keegan grips my hand as if I'm a life vest keeping him afloat. "This has been a lot."

Keegan leads me outside, and we sit on the front step of the trailer. The kitten follows us and nuzzles Keegan's leg. "I can't think in there. This is how she lived. This was her life." He shakes his head. "And apparently she had a cat."

I turn to Keegan, and our knees press up against each other's. "What do you know so far?"

"The sheriff called me this morning. And I was on the first flight out of Chicago. Your parents met me at the airport, but I had already rented a car, so your dad drove back alone and your mom with me."

Keegan reaches his arm out to me but then pulls back. "They found her in the river. Toxicology will take a few weeks, but I think she was higher than a kite."

I close my eyes and look up at the gray sky as thunder rumbles in the distance.

"I've been walking around this shithole of a trailer, and there's nothing salvageable. It's all garbage, and this is how she lived. I was in New York, making a decent living, and my mom was living in rodent-infested filth."

Keegan moves closer to me. The cat lets out a meow and tries to find a spot between us. "I was going to be here to visit tomorrow. I could have helped her. Brought her to New York with me. Got her into a treatment center. Something. But instead, she died completely alone in the fucking river."

"Keegan." My voice comes out strained due to fatigue, emotion, and the desire to take away all of this pain from him. "You tried so many times. You've been there for her, and she couldn't wait to see you. You've talked to her every day on the phone for the past month. She knew how much you loved her."

He puts his hand on my arm. "I need to get out of here. Let's head to your parents' house."

We get up, but the cat protests. Keegan secures it inside and promises to come back later with food. We then drive the short distance to town, where my parents still live in the four-bedroom, two-bath house that Forest and I were raised in. And Keegan too. We get inside, and there's pizza from our favorite parlor called Cherry's Pies.

"There you kids are." My dad wraps me in one of his hugs. And then puts his hand on Keegan's shoulder. "I hope everyone's hungry. There's enough pizza to go around."

"I think tonight calls for a toast to Rain." My dad reaches into a cabinet, brings out a bottle of whiskey, and pours five shots.

We hold our glasses out and simultaneously say, "To Rain."

"To Mom," Keegan says.

"The autopsy is tomorrow morning," Keegan says. "And then they'll release the body. I'm fine with an open house visitation, but then I'd like to do a private funeral and burial. Just us."

"Whatever you want, son," my dad says, gripping Keegan's shoulder.

My dad then turns to Forest and Keegan. "Grab a drink. I want to show you the progress I'm making on the car rebuild in the garage."

The three of them head outside, and my mom pours us a glass of wine. She leans against the kitchen island and studies me.

"How are you holding up, Luna?" She clenches the kitchen island. "You're pale. And thin."

I let the wine warm my stomach. "It's been a really hard week."

"Forest called me the day he found out." Her head bobs up and down, and in that one gesture, I know that she is aware of everything. "I then had a nice chat with Keegan. And you haven't answered my calls in several days."

"I'm sorry." I look down at my glass, tracing my fingers along the ridge. "I didn't know what to say."

"Oh, honey." My mom pushes off the counter and puts her hand on my face.

My eyes meet hers. "You're not mad at me? Disappointed?"

"Not only was I not disappointed." My mom takes my glass and puts it down. "But I wasn't surprised either."

"Really?" My eyebrows shoot to my forehead. How could she not be surprised? The entire relationship with Keegan caught me completely off guard.

"Luna." My mom reaches across the island and wraps my hand in hers. "T+hat boy has loved you for what feels like an eternity."

"But I wasn't sure if you were ever going to get there, and I certainly wasn't sure he'd ever admit it to you." My mom takes a long sip of wine. "But then I saw you look at him the night we were all having dinner at Forest's, and I suspected that maybe you were starting to feel something for him too."

My mom closes her eyes and shakes her head. "I knew that Forest was going to struggle with it. And not because you and Keegan don't make sense, but because Keegan was always his. From day one, Forest has felt this irrational protection over him. But Keegan didn't need protection. He's a very capable man."

My tears burn through the surface until they fall openly down my face. "You knew all of that? I wish you would have told me."

My mom puts her glass down and wraps me in a hug. "And most importantly, I recognized that the only person Keegan needed with him today was you. He relaxed the moment you arrived. It's the first time I saw him exhale a breath since he arrived here."

"I haven't been very good to him," I say. "I've been so concerned about not getting in the way of their friendship, that I detached from both of them. I should have fought."

She shakes her head. "Forest is an adult, and he will need to realize that while he's been out East becoming a doctor, you've been doing a lot of growing up yourself. He still sees you as his kid sister."

"Thanks, Mom." I wipe my face once again.

I don't need her blessing, but having it takes a weight off my chest all the same. I only hope Keegan will still want to try a relationship with me. I've been less than reliable. When things got remotely complicated, I tried to leave.

Every single time. If I was Keegan, I'd be the last person I'd want to invest in.

My mom excuses herself and makes her way to the bedrooms to get them ready. I take a step forward, my feet sinking into the plush carpeting that lines the floors of the hallway, and I work my way to my childhood bedroom, the one I moved into at twelve when Forest left home.

The sight that greets me is both comforting and disorienting. The walls are still painted in the same shade of yellow that I chose when I was a teenager, and the posters of my favorite bands and movies still hang above my bed. I take a step forward, my fingers trailing along the edges of the old posters as I take in the memories that flood back to me.

After putting on shorts and a tank top, I crawl under the covers, lie down, and stare at the ceiling. I can't quit thinking about Keegan directly under me, in the bedroom that my parents built when Forest and Keegan were teenagers. They called it their guest room, but as soon as the basement was finished, Keegan moved down there and out of Forest's room.

I don't recall when Keegan stopped sleeping at his mom's trailer, but in the years before he left Cherry to go to Harvard, he was a regular in our house. He was here for every holiday, special occasion, as well as the regular days.

Instead of trying to sleep, I quietly creep out of my room, and head down a floor. Keegan's door is shut, but a light glows through a gap near the floor. I knock once and then enter. Keegan glances up from the photo albums sprinkled across the bed and looks surprised to see me. He takes his glasses off and puts them on the nightstand.

"What are you still doing up?" Keegan asks as I walk to him. He sits up, shifting his legs off the bed.

"I couldn't sleep," I say.

"Yeah, me neither." Keegan's eyes focus on my legs before moving to my face. "I'm trying to put photo boards together for tomorrow's visitation."

I reach Keegan and stand between his legs. I go to sit, but then he wraps his arms around my waist and buries his head into my stomach. His shoulders start trembling, and even though no sound comes out of him, I know he's crying. I move my hands to his head and hold him. I run my fingers through his soft chestnut-colored hair, and his grip tightens on my back.

Keegan is always so stoic, but the dam breaks within him, and he outwardly expresses his grief. I stay still and let him hold me so tight, that I feel like a balloon on the verge of popping. Several minutes pass like this until he pulls away from me and wipes his eyes.

"Let me help you," I say, sitting opposite him on the bed. "I'm good at photo boards."

Keegan points to the dozen albums splayed out. "This pile is my mom's from the early years, and these over here are from your mom. She thought there could be photos of my mom and me in them, but I doubt it."

I open the pink and purple album with flowers adorned on the cover and start looking through it. It's from a trip we took to the boundary waters. I look to be about ten in the photos, which means Forest and Keegan would have been around sixteen.

"Look at this one," I say, leaning over to show Keegan the photo. He holds onto the corner of it and smiles.

In the picture, I sit between Forest and Keegan on a rock, with a lake and forest in the background. We're dripping wet in our swimsuits, and towels stretch out beneath us. My lips are bright red from the popsicle in my hand. My smile is big, and Forest and Keegan both have an arm draped around me. Keegan is tan compared to us. He always got so brown in the summer.

"I remember that day," Keegan says, continuing to study the picture. "It was warm, and we spent the day at our campground, swimming in the lake and hiking the trails."

"Wait," I say, remembering something. "Is that the night I forgot to put our food in the bear canister? And we woke up to realize a bear had visited our camp and eaten half our food?"

Keegan chuckles and hands the photo back to me. "And Forest was so mad at you and made you cry. I stepped in, lied, and said that it was me who'd left the food out."

"I'd forgotten that." I glance at Keegan for a beat too long. He looks so tall on this bed in his flannel pajama pants and shirt. He always had my back in so many ways. He still does.

We both lean against the headboard and look through albums together. I don't know why I ever thought Keegan was awkward and dorky. Because now when I look through the photos, all I see is a smaller and younger version of the person he became, and I feel this intense need to protect him from all the bad things in this world and to remove any pain he may feel.

I take a long blink, resting my eyes for a moment. The exhaustion of the past few days catches up with me. I lean back on a pillow, vowing to close my eyes only for a moment.

"Hey, Luna." I open my eyes to Keegan gently shaking my shoulder. I'm now lying down, as he leans over me. "You dozed off."

"I did?" I rub my eyes, and he comes into better focus. His eyes sparkle as he hovers over me. His hand squeezes my shoulder.

"You need sleep," he says quietly. "You should head upstairs and go to bed."

Keegan's dark tresses cascade over his forehead, casting a shadow over his face. I reach up and sweep the strands of hair out of the way so I can see him better.

"Luna," Keegan says, leaning into my touch, but then pulling away. "You don't have to."

"I don't have to do what?" I continue to lie back on the pillow, groggy, and stare up at him.

Keegan wrinkles his forehead and pushes away from me, but I grab his arm and pull him back.

"You don't have to make me feel better." Keegan glances at my fingers wrapped around his arm. "Not like this. I can't—"

"I'm not good enough for you." I move my hand to his face again, and this time, he doesn't flinch. "I've been all over the place. This is who I am. This is what I do. I find reasons to leave. But with you…" I let my voice trail off, suddenly shy.

He puts his hand over mine and removes it from his face. "But with me what?"

I go to cover my face, but he holds my hands, leaving me exposed. "You told me you'd wait for me to get to the same place as you. But the truth is—"

"Luna." Keegan's fingers trace the outline of my jaw. "It's okay if you're not."

"I love you. Actually, I've always loved you. Even before you took me to Chelsea Eats and ate tacos and funnel cakes with me. I've just never said those words to anyone. And it freaks me out. But I don't care about the fact that my longest relationship has only lasted a few months, or that Forest is going to take a while to come around. It's been exhausting pretending I don't love you, and I don't want to pretend anymore." I say the words quickly, and my face fills with heat the moment they are out.

"Sorry," I say, catching my breath. "I really need to start talking less."

"You love me." Keegan smiles and reaches his hand out for mine.

I pull Keegan's face to mine until our lips press together. His body is warm and heavy atop mine, and the sadness and anxiety I've felt in the past few days lighten. His hand cups my cheek, and I kiss his neck, and the smell and taste of him reminds me of everything good in the world—like the long gravel road we used to bike on at my parents' home. The lakes we used to swim in as kids. The camper we'd go on long road trips in. My mom's apple pie she'd bake for every holiday. He reminds me of my favorite ice cream, mint chocolate chip. Of the kid who patiently did science experiments with me in the garage. Of that boy who lied about leaving our food out so my brother wouldn't be mad at me.

"Have you ever had sex on this bed?" I whisper into Keegan's ear.

"No," Keegan laughs into our next kiss. "Why would you ask me that?"

"Because this was pretty much your room as a teenager." I reach my hands under Keegan's shirt and feel his warm skin. "I figured maybe you'd snuck a girl or two down here back in the day."

"Do I strike you as a guy who would have girls sneak into their bedroom as a teenager?" Keegan brushes my hair back.

"And I've already crossed every boundary with your family by being in love with you. I will not cross another boundary and have sex with you in their home."

"But, Keegan." I grab his face. "I'll be very quiet."

"Hard no, Luna." Keegan laughs as he sits and puts distance between us. "But I'd love it if you stayed with me tonight."

"Yeah, I can do that." I move closer to Keegan, grab his face between my hands, and kiss him.

We get to work going through photos. He picks the ones he wants, and I put them on the poster board. With each picture, he has a story to accompany it, and the more I learn about him, the more love I feel.

When we finish, we crawl into bed and face each other. We talk about everything. I tell him that I'm strongly considering applying to be at Jamaica Queens Hospital for years two and three. And then I'd return to Presby for years four and five, before applying for a trauma and critical care surgical fellowship. I'm not surprised when I'm met with nothing but support.

Keegan talks to me about his earlier conversation with Forest, and his thoughts on the dynamic that exists between the three of us that explains some of Forest's reactions. He methodically scrapes his fingers down my arm as he tells about the last eight years of his life, since the last time I saw him when I was a precocious eighteen-year-old at his medical school graduation. He shares the emails he'd get excited to receive from me. The Amsterdam trip with his roommates and fellow residents, when he got his tattoos, and how he always hoped life would somehow bring us together.

I don't know when we fall asleep, but we're awoken to a knock at the door. Keegan cuddles into my back and lifts his head. The door swings open, and Forest stands there, looking at us like he caught us in the act of something.

"Mom sent me down," Forest says. "You're due at the funeral home in an hour."

"Forest." Keegan rubs his eyes. "We were just sleeping."

Forest chuckles. "Yeah. I know."

"You look like you've seen a ghost," I say.

Forest leans against the doorframe. "I love you both. And if you guys are happy, I promise you, I will be too. I'm still processing. I know this isn't brand new for the two of you, but it is for me."

"That's fair," Keegan says.

"Alright." Forest taps the door. "One hour."

He closes the door, and Keegan and I look at each other.

"Maybe we need to ease the guy into it," he says.

"Agreed." I kiss Keegan's cheek and then get out of the bed. "See you upstairs soon."

Chapter Thirty-Four

We sit in the Funeral Home off Elm Street and stare at a picture my mom found of Mrs. Baldwin, Mr. Baldwin, and a young Keegan. Next to the photo, is a vase that will eventually hold her ashes and flowers from so many people in town. The poster boards we worked on all night are on display.

Keegan was adamant that the funeral be private. He allowed my mom to put a write-up in the local paper, and invite people to a visitation at the funeral home from one to three. And even though my mom insisted on having cookies and juice available, Keegan thought that was wholly unnecessary because he thought no one would show up.

A little before one, the door to the funeral home opens, and Keegan lets go of my hand, looks at me, and then the door. Forest also jumps to his feet and pats Keegan on his back.

"I love you, man," Forest says.

Keegan presses his lips into a thin line and then links his fingers in mine. "Stay close to me." And then he looks at Forest. "Both of you."

We stand near the vase and photos, and an older woman approaches us. She holds her hand out to Keegan.

"You must be Keegan." He nods his head. "I'm Delores. I own the flower shop in town, Cherry Blossoms. I was so sad to hear about the passing of your mom. She was a neat lady."

Keegan's body stiffens, but then he manages to curl his lips up. "Thank you for coming and paying your respects, Delores."

The woman wraps Keegan's hand in hers. "She used to come in every Friday and get a bouquet, and she'd bring it out to the cemetery and put it on your dad's grave. As the years went on, she came less and less. But then last week, she stopped again after not coming for years."

The line keeps forming and nearly reaches out the door. People stand around, nibbling on cookies and looking at the photos we tirelessly put together. I stay by Keegan's side as people come by to introduce themselves and share a nice story about Mrs. Baldwin. The shop owner who fixed her car all these years. A waitress at Cherry Pies who Mrs. Baldwin was always kind to.

"Keegan," an older gentleman approaches us. "I don't know if you remember me. I'm—"

Before the man can respond, Keegan interrupts with a smile. "Mr. Verny."

The teacher's lips turn up, and Keegan does something very out of character and wraps his arms around the gentleman, and they fully embrace.

"Luna," Keegan glances at me. "This is Mr. Verny. My ninth-grade biology teacher."

Mr. Verny smiles. "I believe I had your brother too." He then hugs Forest. "But then I retired a couple of years later."

He takes Keegan's hand and holds it. "And this here was my brightest student. By the time the year was over, he had devoured all of our textbooks, and the advanced anatomy and physiology books."

Mr. Verny puts his hand on Keegan's shoulder. "I don't get to town much anymore, but about a month ago, I was picking up something at the lumber yard, and I ran into your mom at the gas station."

He pauses to clear his throat. "She told me you're a cardiothoracic surgeon in New York City. She couldn't have been prouder. And I told your mom, 'Well, of course he is.' She was so proud of you Keegan. Her face lit up when she talked about you."

I glance at Keegan, and his Adam's apple bobs, and he tries to hold in emotion that is trying hard to escape.

"Thank you for making the effort to be here. And for your kind words."

Before I let Mr. Verny leave, I snap a photo of them. The line is constant and doesn't stop until well after three. The entire town showed up for Keegan, and every person who went through the line had something nice to say about Rain Baldwin. Her life was messy and chaotic, which brought pain to Keegan, yet every single person spoke easily about how she'd enhanced their lives.

It's hard for me to hold love for her, however. I keep thinking about an eleven or twelve-year-old Keegan, getting the shit beat out of him by her boyfriend, and Rain sitting back and doing nothing for far too long. But then I stare at our intertwined hands. He's hugged everyone today, tugging me along, because he hasn't let go of me. And I know that Rain couldn't have been all bad because she is part of what made Keegan. And well, he may be the closest damn thing to perfection that I've ever met. Of all the people he could love, he chose to love me.

There must have been good in Rain Baldwin too.

After everyone leaves, we sit in chairs, looking at the pictures.

"Thank you, guys," Keegan says to no one in particular. "I thought all of this was overkill. But my mom would have loved it."

My mom stands and starts gathering all of the pictures. Her back is turned to us, but I can hear the sniffle she tries to hide. She then turns to Keegan. "Until hearing all the stories today, I'd forgotten that there were some happy times too."

My mom's voice trails off, and she rubs her eyes. "She let us love and provide for you when she knew she couldn't. That's the most unselfish thing a person can do for someone else."

"I've never seen a parent as proud of her kid as she was of you." My dad stands and puts his arm around Keegan's shoulder. "I was reminded today of when she took out that full-page ad in the newspaper announcing that Keegan got into Harvard."

"She stopped everyone in town to let them know that you're a surgeon in New York," my mom says. "You were her pride and joy."

Keegan nods, and when I see thick, wet tears falling from his eyes, I reach over to him and rub them away with my thumb.

"We'd gone years without talking, or rarely talking." Keegan stares straight forward. "But for the past month, we got to the point where we'd talk daily and had really good conversations. I can't believe I missed her by only a day. I should have been here."

"The last time we spoke," Keegan continues. "I told her all about Luna." He looks at me and squeezes my hand.

"There's this peace I have, that in the end, we both said all the things we needed to say to each other."

"I hate when people tell a mourning person that everything happens for a reason," my mom chokes out. "And that's not what I'm telling you. But part of me thinks that the last gift you gave her was booking that plane ticket and the daily phone calls. But she was never going to be able to see your face as you witnessed how she was living."

Forest puts his arm around Keegan, and no one else says anything. It occurs to me how much better life is when we're willing to let go of things. Rain Baldwin was more than her mental illness, her struggles, and her choices.

Today isn't about holding onto the bad things. It's about wrapping Keegan in love and support while reminding him that there were also good parts of his mom that she shared with the community. Life is hard, for some more than others. At times, we bring on the difficulties, ourselves, but at other times, we get so lost in the billowing seas of grief to see straight.

Rain never recovered from losing her husband all of those years ago. And the shame and guilt that followed meant Keegan didn't get the best version of his mom that he deserved. When we don't face our demons head-on, we pass them on to the next generation.

Keegan clears his throat. "Well, that may have been my last gift to my mom, but I think her last gift to me was that adorable kitten who doesn't leave my side when I'm at the trailer."

"What?" My face jolts in his direction. "Are you thinking about taking that kitten home with you?"

Keegan slowly nods. "I think I am."

"A cat dad." Forest smiles. "I can see that. And you have the space."

"That's wonderful," my mom says. "They are so low maintenance. But now she needs a name."

"It's a he," Keegan corrects her.

"How about Purrcocet? Get it?" my mom suggests with a laugh.

"Or Prrmonary?" Forest offers.

Keegan thinks about this, and then I clap my hands together, thinking about the first case I scrubbed into with him. "Thoracotomy. We'll call him Thor."

"We will, will we?" Keegan gives me a sideways smile and grips my leg. "He does look like a Thor. I love it."

*****

Forest and I fly home together the next day. Keegan will spend a few days in Cherry, wrapping up some things. We share a ride from the airport, and I turn to Forest and finally ask the question that has been weighing on me.

"Are things good between you and Keegan now?"

"They will be." Forest nods. "We had the most real conversation of our lives while back home. I needed to hear a few things."

The car inches in the direction of my apartment, stuck in afternoon city traffic. "Are you still mad at him? At me?"

Forest inhales a sharp breath. "If I'm being honest, a little. Whether I have a right to be or not. I hate that you felt like you couldn't tell me. You two are so different. But now when I see you together, I'm kicking myself that I was so self-absorbed that I missed all the signs. I just wish you would have told me instead of having me find out the way I did."

"I take full responsibility for that," I say.

"I may be the asshole here," Forest says. "I've considered that. It's going to take me a moment, but I promise, I'll get there. I'm never going to lose either one of you."

Forest shakes his head but then continues. "Keegan is the best man I've ever met, Luna. He's the kind of guy who would come running, no questions asked, if I ever needed something. And if you hurt him, I won't be able to get over that."

"For—"

"But, Luna." Forest puts his hand up and cuts me off. "You are my sister. If Keegan hurts you, I'll have to kill him. I know none of this is about me, but I am in an unusual place of having no control over whether our relationships stay intact. And I hate not being in control."

"Look," I say, turning to face Forest and resting my elbow on the back of my seat. "I know my track record in relationships has sucked. But I've realized, it's not because

I'm bad at relationships. It's because I've never been with anyone I was willing to fight for. I feel so differently about Keegan."

"I know, I know," he says, waving me off. "But—"

"Hear me out," I say. "I can't guarantee what the future holds with Keegan. But I know when I picture my future, he's in it. And all I can promise you is that we'll never put you in the middle if things don't work out."

The car slows down as we approach my building. Forest lets out a laugh. "Who are Keegan and I going to talk to about our dating lives? We were each other's person. And as far as I'm concerned, he's taken a vow of celibacy for the rest of his life."

"I love you," I say, wrapping my arms around him. Peace spreads throughout me at the lighter mood. I breathe in my big brother. "Isn't there a little relief that the person you consider the best man in the world is the one I'm with?"

"I'll get there, Luna. I will." Forest gets out of the car and opens my door for me. "Be good enough for each other. Both of you."

"Let's grab dinner this week," I say, rolling my suitcase toward the door. "The two of us."

"You got it," Forest says through a smile. And I feel a lot of hope that everything is going to be okay.

Chapter Thirty-Five

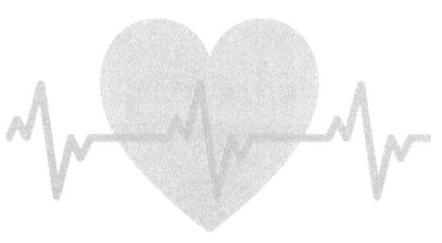

The next few days manage to both go by fast and drag as I anxiously await for Keegan to get back to the city. I throw myself into work and have a meeting with Dr. Parse about my desire to spend years two and three at Jamaica Queens. I also begin my new rotation in endocrine and robotics, where I'll be for the next four weeks of my residency.

"Are you ready?" I look up at Raven as she enters the changing room. "We have about two hours until Keegan lands, and we need to get your kitty a few things."

"Ready," I say, slamming my locker door shut. "The pet store is only a few blocks away, so we should have plenty of time."

Raven helps me pick up all of the supplies we'll need for Thor. I grab a litter box and a couple of cat castles, which will be such a contrast in Keegan's apartment. I hope he understands what he committed to. I pick up food, bowls, and a few toys. And as I'm in the checkout line, I see an adorable bowtie and decide to throw that into the cart as well.

"Are you kidding me?" Raven says when I open the door to Keegan's place. "This is where he lives?"

"Pretty nice, right?" I start to unpack the bags and get everything organized.

Raven looks around the place. "Maybe I should go into cardiothoracic surgery."

"Well," I say. "I have a feeling he gets a lot of his income from being faculty for industry partners."

"Damn," she says, looking into the bedroom and office. "This place is incredible. It makes our apartment look like a shack."

"Come help me figure out this litter box." I read the directions, and Raven comes to my rescue.

"I talked to Forest today," she says, kneeling beside me. "He asked if I was free Saturday night to go out to dinner with him, you, and Keegan. Some Italian restaurant near his house. Keegan's favorite. That's a good sign, right?"

"It's a start." I click the pieces of the litter box together and walk it to Keegan's laundry closet. "Keegan and I have talked about our strategy. There will be zero affection. And I want things to feel as normal as have always been when we all hang out."

"And Forest will have to not think about the fact that you're most likely going to come to this castle afterward and do his best friend."

"Raven." I throw a hand towel at her, and she laughs.

"Seriously though," she says. "I know I'm only starting to get to know Forest, but even in a week, he's gotten to a better place. He's going to be fine."

"I know," I say. "But in the meantime, I don't want anything thrown in his face."

When I hear a key in the door, I run to greet Keegan. He walks in with a bag slung on one shoulder, and a loud and scared kitten in a carrier in his other hand. He puts everything down just in time because I launch myself at him and wrap my legs around his waist. I nearly forgot that Raven is here. So much for being discreet.

"I missed you," I say, holding him tight, showering kisses all over his cleanly shaven face. I breathe in the intoxicating scent that is Keegan.

"Hi, Keegan." Raven steps out into the entryway, and he smiles when he sees her.

"Raven," he says. "Thanks for helping Luna get everything ready for Thor."

He walks in her direction and hugs her. I already know Keegan's heart. He's going to hold everyone dear that I do. It's who he is.

"Of course," Raven says. "And now I have piles of laundry to do and an early morning tomorrow, so I will leave you guys be."

"Thanks, Raven," I say, embracing her. "For everything."

She opens the door but then turns to me. "Love you, Luna."

When the door closes behind her, Keegan reaches for me and pulls me in for a kiss. "I missed you." He cups my face and stares into my eyes.

"How's our boy?" I bend over to look in the carrier and open it for Thor. "Everything is ready for our little Thoracotomy."

He meows as he walks around the place, sniffing it out.

"Hopefully that was Thor's first and last flight," Keegan says, shaking his head. "Everyone on that plane wanted to kick me off. But you are a sight for sore eyes."

Thor brushes up against Keegan's leg, and he lifts him. Thor cuddles into his chest, and I lean over to kiss our adorable orange kitten.

"Now that you're a cat mom, we'll have to figure out a parenting schedule," Keegan says as he puts down Thor. "I'm thinking you'll have to spend a lot more time over here."

"Hmm." I nod my head. "That's what I was thinking too."

Keegan bends over to grab his bag, and I follow him to the bedroom. Thor is only a foot behind us, as he refuses to let Keegan out of his sight. We reach the room, and Keegan turns to face me. He kisses me so tenderly that I sigh into his mouth.

"I'm thinking takeout, wine, and bed," Keegan says, holding my hand. "I feel like I need about thirty hours of sleep before starting back up at the hospital."

"That sounds like the perfect evening." I sit, and Thor jumps up on my lap. Keegan joins me, and we both fall back, laughing.

Keegan reaches over Thor to kiss me, but Thor gets between us, very protective over Keegan.

"I see how I rank now," I say.

Keegan pulls me toward him and buries his face in my neck. "You are forever my number one."

Epilogue

It's mid-May, and tonight, the attendings are hosting a celebratory party after all of the first years successfully passed the intern board exams and are officially moving on to our residencies. Forest offered up his rooftop for the party.

But first, it's work. I'm back in the Emergency Room after several months away doing other rotations. Spring means doing about fifty sutures a day. Scooter wipeouts, bike accidents, and tripping on uneven sidewalks. New York is officially out of hibernation as the weather warms up.

"Dr. Oliver, Dr. Craik, Dr. Worth." Chief Resident Parse looks at Myles, Raven, and me. "You'll all be with Dr. Lanson today."

I had such a nice break from Dr. Lanson, but now I'm back on his rotation of trauma surgery. But only for a short time, as I'm a month away from starting my two-year rotation at Jamaica Hospital in Queens. I find my way to Dr. Lanson who is in with a teenage patient.

He holds the film up for me. "What do you see, Dr. Oliver?"

"The entire side of his skull is fractured."

The trauma rotation has taught me a couple of things. One, I'll never get on a motorcycle. And two, I'll never ride a bike without a helmet.

Dr. Lanson looks at the patient. "Let's prep him for surgery."

We head to the operating room, while our patient is prepared.

"You're almost done being an intern. How do you feel?"

"Excited for what's next," I say, falling in step next to him. "It's been a long year."

"You'll be at the rooftop to celebrate tonight?"

"I wouldn't be anywhere else," I say.

He lifts an eyebrow in my direction. "And with your boyfriend, I assume?"

"Yes," I say. "With Keegan."

Dr. Lanson snickers and shakes his head, and I'm relieved when he goes into the operating room and I follow. Keegan and I are professional at work and haven't shared that we're a couple with anyone besides our close inner circle, but word travels fast at the hospital. Ever since we recovered from Forest finding out and me trying to walk away, we've been inseparable. We never bothered with the "what are we" conversation, because it felt redundant. Ever since I told him I loved him back, and we sat down and he told me that I'm it for him, I've felt confident in where this is heading.

Raven, Myles, Jules, and I have a drink at our apartment before we head to Forest's rooftop with the other interns and attendings. In one week, we'll officially be residents. One year done, four to go before I have to think about applying for a fellowship program in trauma and critical care. We'll also be on a month-to-month lease with our apartment and at a crossroads of what to do next in terms of living arrangements.

Myles and Jules have already found a one-bedroom apartment not far from the hospital. We are all traveling to their wedding in two weeks, and then after that, they come back to the city and move into their new place. Raven and I have been less sure what we want to do, especially with me moving to a hospital in a different borough.

"I wish I looked more New York like you guys," Jules says with her thick accent. "Why does my hair keep doing this?"

"Well." Raven attempts to flatten Jules' hair. "You'll be living here in no time."

"Once from Texas, always from Texas," Myles calls from the next room. "That's what I love about you, Jules."

We arrive at Forest's and head right up to the rooftop. When we step out into the sun, I gasp at how many people are there. The attendings went all out for us. There are so many familiar people from the hospital, and the first person to come up to me is Chief Resident Parse.

"Well, you made it." He sticks his hand out to shake mine, but instead, I pull him into a hug.

"Yes, and what, only four more years to go," I say with a laugh.

Dr. Parse steps back from me. "You'll make a great surgeon, Luna. Jamaica Hospital is going to be a great step to further your education."

A hand grazes the small of my back, and I turn to see Keegan.

"This is a party," he says. I look around at the lights, and the servers bringing around drinks and appetizers.

"You're here," I say. "I wasn't sure if you'd get out of your case in time."

Keegan's breath is warm against my ear when he speaks. "You made it through your first year, Luna. Congrats."

He leads me to the bar, and then we stand along the balcony. Keegan is eerily quiet, even for him. I bite my bottom lip and study him, as he looks out at the skyline. The light of the moon glistens off his eyes.

"What's up?" I finally ask him. "You're acting all weird and quiet."

Keegan releases a breath, pulls out a pamphlet from his back pocket, and hands it to me. "I want your thoughts on this."

I flip through the brochure. It's a beautiful and expansive condo for rent in a high-rise in the Forest Hills neighborhood in Queens. Three bedrooms, and three baths, with beautiful parquet floors, and a semi-open floor plan.

"It's beautiful, Keegan. But you have a place. And this condo is farther from the hospital."

"True," he says. "But you're going to be in Queens for the next two years, and this would be so close to your hospital."

I hand the brochure back to him, and he reluctantly takes it from me. He drags his hand down his face and takes a deep breath.

"What is it?" I put my hand on his arm. "What are you thinking?"

He glances at the brochure and then at me. "All you've been talking about for the past couple of months is where to live next."

"It's beautiful," I say. "But I don't need this much space, and it's so far from you. I love being able to walk to your place."

"Luna," he says, his big blue eyes staring at me, searching. He looks down at the brochure. "I was thinking we'd live there together."

"What?" I start laughing, realizing I missed all of the signs. We still have moments where Keegan thinks he is being clear with me, but I don't pick up on what he's saying. It's not lost on me that he wants to move somewhere that would make my life easier, instead of suggesting that I make sacrifices for him.

"You want to live together?"

"If this feels too fast, I understand. There's no pressure." Keegan leans back against the railing and looks suddenly shy.

"But then you'd have a longer commute," I say.

"It would be thirty minutes, which is nothing," Keegan says. "And I'd much rather be taking public transportation than you. Especially at night."

"You want to live together?" I put my hand over my mouth to cover my smile.

For the past few months, I've mostly stayed at his place anyway. He cleared out a couple of drawers for me, and I keep a lot of my bathroom stuff there. He's made me feel like his place is mine, but the saddest part of my days is when I leave his place to go back to mine.

"More than anything"—Keegan's lips turn up—"Thor wants more of his mama around too."

"But I'm a little messy," I say. "Are you sure you know what you're signing up for?"

"I don't mind that you're a little messy." Keegan reaches for my hand and runs his thumb along my palm. "You also keep the refrigerator stocked, bring me tea when I'm studying, and keep me warm at night. Your good qualities far outweigh your being a little messy."

"You're sure?" I say, not needing to give this any more thought. "Because I'd love to live with you. In Queens. But only if you're sure."

"Of course I'm sure." His eyes light up. "Because they are saving this place for me until noon tomorrow. We should go in the morning, and you could give it a final stamp of approval. But trust me, Luna, it's beautiful. Close to restaurants and shops, but it also feels residential. And you'll be so close to the hospital."

"I'll pay half the rent," I say.

Keegan starts laughing and reaches for my hand. "We'll sit down and talk through all of that."

I grab his shoulders. "We're really doing this. We're moving in together."

Keegan kisses my forehead and rubs a finger down my arm, somehow igniting all seven million nerve endings in my body. "We are."

"And you're moving to Queens," I say. "For me."

"At least for the next two years, yes," Keegan says. "See. I'm very romantic. Not even a little boring."

"But what happens after my two years there? Then I'll be back at Presby. I still have two years left of my residency, and then at least two years of a fellowship, and who knows where I'll end up for that?"

Keegan once again places a soft kiss on my lips, and I relax. "Yes, you still have many years of training in front of you, but that doesn't mean our lives can't move forward in the meantime. We spend every day saving lives, Luna. We're allowed to live the ones we got."

"You're right." I release a breath. "As long as we're together."

Keegan takes his pinky and intertwines it with mine. "Okay."

Keegan wraps me in his arms, and for the first time since arriving, I remember that we aren't alone, and there's music playing all around us and a party to enjoy.

"What's Forest going to think?" I scan the crowd for him.

"He already knows I was going to ask you." Keegan smiles. "He's very excited, although not the living-in-Queens part."

"Wow." I wrap my arms around his neck. "And he's good with this?"

"He's completely on board." Keegan takes my hand and leads me back to the group but turns to me and says. "Let's go look at the place in the morning before your shift starts."

Forest comes into view, and his face lights up as he makes his way towards us. He pulls me into a hug.

"Congrats, kiddo," he says. "It's all smooth sailing from here."

"Yeah." I hit him on the arm. "Says no one ever."

Forest laughs as he wraps an arm around Keegan and his other around me.

"How does Wednesday work for family dinner?" Forest glances at me. "There's a new Indian restaurant around the corner I want to try. Or we could go somewhere else. Whatever you want."

Keegan glances at me and smiles. "Let's go to that amazing sandwich shop near your house. Or Chelsea Eats starts next week. We could go there."

"Yeah, that could work," Forest says, smiling in my direction.

"I'm off at six that night," I say. "I'll be there."

The End

About the Author

When she isn't writing novels featuring strong female leads on a path to self-discovery, Leah Omar makes her career at a global medical device company. From Eyota, Minnesota, she holds bachelor's degrees in communications and English literature and a master's in business administration from Augsburg University in Minneapolis.

As a writer, Leah is devoted to giving her readers contemporary love stories that make us remember that we have more similarities than differences, and that love can conquer all. When Leah's not busy writing women's fiction and romance, she can be found watching a basketball game on TV, traveling somewhere far away, eating something spicy, or trying to shape the lives of her two amazing kids.

Leah now calls Minneapolis home, which she shares with her husband and two kids.

Check out more from Leah at: www.leahomarbooks.com

www.ingramcontent.com/pod-product-compliance
Lightning Source LLC
LaVergne TN
LVHW091659070526
838199LV00050B/2210